MW00817977

THE LOST LEGEND

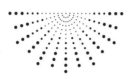

NELLIE KRAUSS

Jessica,
enjoy the adventure

Nellie Krauss

INTRODUCTION

The undying love of a Texas Woman for a Lakota man defied time and death. It made her a legend in her own time.

ALSO BY NELLIE KRAUSS

NEWSLETTER SIGNUP

If you would like to stay up to date on news and releases, please sign up for my email newsletter at http://www.nelliekrauss.com/

If you liked this book, please leave a review and check out these others:

Galveston Island Series

#1 The Moon Over Sea Wolf Bay

#2 Desperado Lucky

#3 Valentino's Fire

#4 (Zala and Ivan's story) coming winter of 2022

#5 (Chiffon and Sergei's story) 2023

For the Love of Misha (Short Story) Summer 2022

Winds and Tides Series

#1 Crossing Love Lines

#2 Sea Storms

#3 (Madison and Fedor's story) coming fall of 2022

Other full-length titles

East of Baghdad

The Lost Legend (Spring 2022)

Short Stories

Queen of the Black Roses Ball (Short Story)

2023 The DeAngeli Cousins Series begins.

PRAISE FOR NELLIE KRAUSS

And another awesome and satisfying story …

Ms. Nellie Krauss knows how to keep you on the edge of your seat…

Awesome book, never a dull moment…

Kept my interest from the first paragraph to the very last page.

FOREWORD

CHAPTER ONE

SILKI STARED through the bug splattered windshield at the dusty Texas highway taking her to the Ruins. Some things you don't forget; the way home is one of them. She was on her way to Aunt Mariah's house, a fortress, built to take on and take down a South Texas empire. It was the headquarters of the Rocking T Ranch.

Mariah, named after the wind that blew across Texas, had become Mariah Blue out of necessity. Her name would live forever in the Texas Hill Country. She had earned her place next to the outlaws, renegades, and rebels who refused to give up or surrender.

Texas legends traditionally rode off into the sunset and returned when they were needed most. Silki needed it to be true this time. She had run out of all other options, and Mariah was the only one left who could help her. But first she'd have to find her.

Mariah drove a black jacked-up, four-wheel-drive Jeep, rode wild horses and fast Harleys. Her only love was a handsome Lakota man straight off the northern plains of South Dakota. He was the only man alive strong enough to hold her when the cold winds blew.

Silki knew only too well what it was like to be around for the making of a legend. For years she watched Mariah build a reputation, and live a life that would have killed any other woman, or man for that matter. Not only had she survived, she had ruthlessly crushed her enemies. Like the land she lived on, she'd showed no mercy.

Mariah hadn't been seen since her mother's funeral. Now, that had been a scene only slightly better than her father's burial service. Mariah had walked up to the open grave and dumped a bag of bull manure on the old man's casket. She'd merely dropped a dead chicken on her mother's and walked away.

In recent months some people had started spreading the rumor that Mariah Blue was dead. If and when Silki saw the cold, lifeless body in the ground, she'd believe it and not one second sooner.

Sweat trickled down her back reminding her she was on her way back to the place where it had all begun. The place where Mariah had made her stand, taken on the Warfield empire, and brought it to its knees.

Nothing George Warfield, Mariah's father, and his cronies did forestalled the destruction. Mariah methodically dismantled their businesses one at a time. Relentless reckoning thwarted and crushed them until there was nothing left but ruined reputations, empty warehouses, a handful of soon to be foreclosed commercial buildings, and their personal fortunes bankrupted. That included Silki's father Harvey, Mariah's older brother.

Her darkest sunglasses did nothing to diminish the blinding afternoon glare and the heat waves shimmering above the Highway 46 asphalt. On either side of the battered pickup truck, cedar breaks and rocky hillsides stretched for miles. Her foot pressed down firmly on the accelerator, the heap rattled in response and gained enough speed to lumber over the next hill. The gardener had her mink coat and diamond watch. She had his rust-bucket truck. Hell of a deal, but it ran.

A few more miles and she'd be inside the stone walled fortress perched on the hills overlooking San Antonio. The doors would hold against the malicious gossip that followed her like a hungry wolf. She'd finally be able to shut out the world and enjoy a moment's peace.

A quick glance at the dashboard showed all the instrument needles had swung to the right again. Silki slapped the top of the dash and watched the faded orange needles move slowly back to the left. The hodgepodge of salvaged pieces and parts were put together good enough to make her excuse of a vehicle pass inspection. It did run, more or less, mostly less.

Her cheating ex-husband, Charles Hardcastle, had absconded with Silki's money and remarried. Her attorneys had not been able to get her premarital assets returned. Her life as she'd known it was over, and she wasn't sure where that left her except on the road to the Ruins.

The small pile of limestone gravel on the road ahead was no obstacle. Silki reasoned it should get the hell out of her way if it didn't want to be run over. The transmission howled, and the engine roared as the old Dodge Ram shot over the rise.

At the Highway 46 Tavern, Roy Meyers sat at the scarred table surrounded by the usual local ranchers. Good old boys who weren't boys anymore. They were all late middle-aged men struggling to hang on to what was left of their ranches and their way of life. Roy picked at the label on his beer bottle and stared into the brown glass like he was looking into a crystal ball.

"It was her. I saw her plain as day. I was out along the road fixing fence when I heard this awful screeching noise and looked up. This truck came flying over the hill with smoke pouring out from the fender wells and she was behind the wheel. Nobody has that color hair, nobody but Mariah Blue." Roy took his eyes off the bottle long enough to look at each man there and then took another long pull of the beer. Putting the empty bottle back on the table he said, "I'm telling you, she's back."

Junior asked, "What are we gonna do?"

A frightened voice whispered, "Make ourselves scarce. Stay out of her way and don't talk to Harvey if he calls. I've had nothing but trouble since I helped him load her cattle."

Old man Heimer shook his head. "I told you she'd be back. I warned you the ghost was guarding her place. I've known her since she moved out here and I'm telling you, she'll never rest until they pay for what they did."

All eyes turned on him. Even in the smoke-filled gloom they could see the resignation in his bleary eyes.

Roy glared at Heimer and said, "You know what happened to make her turn so mean. It's time you told us."

"Nobody knew I was putting supplies in the barn when Mariah's father drove up and they got into a shouting match. I ain't never heard the likes of it. It was awful what he did. But I ain't gonna repeat it. Some things ought to stay private. Mariah'd know I told and she'd never forgive me. I can't afford to lose my place. Don't go looking at me like that. Take my word for it. It was bad, terrible bad. I'm surprised she didn't kill him over it."

Memories and worries occupied Silki's mind all the way to the front gate. She locked it behind her and stared up the hill. The Ruins loomed forlorn and empty on the rocky ledge above the barns and hay fields. Dark windows devoid of life stared back at her.

The wind rustling through the leaves on the oak trees whispered the secrets hidden inside the thick walls. Built next to a medicine mound, spirits haunted the Ruins. Deer hunters camping in the hills claimed they'd seen Mariah's ghost riding through the cedar breaks on a tall, coal-black horse.

Silki climbed into the truck, pointed it up the hill and muttered to the stubborn vehicle. "Not much farther. We're almost there." Her words ground out slowly between clenched teeth as she bounced over the ruts scoring the caliche ranch road. "She survived and I will too."

She parked the truck in a shady spot and got out. Her boots crunched with each step she took on the dried grass and weeds as she made her way to the front door.

Silki shoved her key into the lock, prayed it would still work, and thanked all her lucky stars when it turned. She'd found shelter. The arched double doors were solid wood that weighed three-hundred pounds each and were carved with fanciful Mexican designs. The builders had known better than to hang flimsy doors. They'd also used enormous iron hinges, cut with a blow torch to secure the doors to the arched rock doorway that sat securely in the rammed earth walls.

Her shoulders slumped as she pushed at the heavy wooden doors. They didn't budge. Resting her forehead against the door she pleaded, "Please, Aunt Mariah, I need a roof over my head. I don't have anywhere else to go."

One side creaked open enough to let her squeeze through. Silki slipped inside, braced her back against the door and shoved it closed. In case the spirits were listening, she whispered, "Thanks, for a minute there I was afraid you'd deserted me the same as everyone else."

Dust sprinkled down over Silki's head and landed on the rose-colored tile floor at her feet.

Silki trudged across the garden room past the dead, shriveled plants and up two steps leading to the living room. Dropping her purse on the couch, she gave a small gasp of surprise as the sight before her registered in her exhausted mind. The place looked like a B-rated horror movie set.

"I guess you weren't planning on being gone long." Silki flicked the power switch to the ceiling fans and dragged herself to the nearest chair. She eyed it for scorpions, swiped some of the dust off the seat, and sank down gratefully onto the soft comfortable cushion. "What were you thinking? Where were you going?"

Mariah's accounts were automatically paid by her accountant. The electricity was on, the propane tanks should be full but Silki would check them to be sure. She'd have to cook some dinner on the gas stove. She'd have to be sure the water well was working. She needed a shower.

The ceiling fans turned slowly overhead, the refrigerator motor came on in the kitchen and the sound filtered through the dining room to the living room.

She was going to need more food than what was in the ice chest out in the truck. Her engagement and wedding rings were in a pawn shop in Fort Worth and the very bare necessities were all she could afford unless she found Mariah's emergency stash.

"First things first. I've got to get some money. It's got to be here somewhere. Then I have to figure out where she was headed." She glanced around the living room. "Where to begin?"

The Ruins didn't answer.

She had to think back. Mariah had come home from a vacation to the Black Hills with her new name. Someone very important had called her Blue. Finding that person would be a good place to start. Both she and Mariah were running out of time.

Sitting in the dust and cobwebs of the past wasn't getting her anywhere. If Mariah's old Harley was out in the garage, she'd be on the road in no time. The truck wasn't up to making the trip north.

CHAPTER TWO

THE SOUTH DAKOTA morning sun struck Jesse High Horse in the eyes. Moaning, he turned over trying to escape the searing pain stabbing his brain, or what was left of it. It had been another rough night down at the H&H bar. It was blessedly quiet in his tiny, dingy apartment. His dad wasn't there snoring like a bear in hibernation.

Jesse gave up trying to think past the idea of crawling into the bathroom and taking something to ease the pounding inside his head. He wasn't up to drinking all night long like his old man.

He'd learned the hard way that he and alcohol didn't mix well. It felt great while he was swallowing the stuff, but the morning after was hell on earth. He'd known better than to go downtown on a Friday night, but he hated sitting alone in the shabby apartment. He'd promised himself he'd take it easy, have a couple drinks, play some pool, nothing too crazy, and have a little fun for a while. Oh, yeah, he was having fun all right.

Jesse gagged, stumbled from the rumpled bed and headed for the bathroom. Bleary eyed, he rinsed his mouth and tried to focus on his reflection in the cracked bathroom mirror. Wavy, long black hair hung in wild disarray around his shoulders, bloodshot eyes winced in pain, he looked as rough as he felt. Living like this wasn't working for him.

He couldn't spend the rest of his life hanging out in reservation border towns waiting for something better to come along.

The only thing that had come for him was the prison bus. It didn't matter what else happened, he was never going back there. The thought of it made his skin crawl. He'd spent hours in the yard working out with weights, building muscle, and getting stronger to discourage anybody who might want to get too close. It had been the longest three years of his life.

As usual, there wasn't anything edible in the refrigerator and his stomach curled in protest at the thought of opening the last beer. If he was going to survive the day, he needed coffee and lots of it. If he was lucky, he'd be able to swallow a piece of toast to go with it. Then he'd start checking the local hangouts to see if any of the nearby farmers or ranchers needed temporary help. It was past their usual starting time, but he might pick up some work if someone came to town late for supplies. A few people had small herds of cattle or horses. Worming and vaccinating the animals needed two or three people. He could haul and stack hay. His strong back and arms were marketable for less than minimum wage.

After splashing some tepid water on his face and dragging a comb through his hair, Jesse pulled on his last pair of clean jeans, followed by an almost clean t-shirt and scruffy boots. He needed to do some wash, but he couldn't worry about that at the moment. He forced himself out the door. Quickly stabbing a pair of cheap sunglasses over his eyes, he ambled slowly down the street toward the diner. His long, lean legs easily ate up the distance.

Ten minutes later he slid onto a stool at the counter. Jesse fished in his front pocket and pulled out a few one-dollar bills and some loose change. Separating a dollar from the mess in his hand, he pushed it out in front of him on the counter.

With his reputation, he had to show he could pay before the waitresses would so much as set an empty cup down in front of him. He guessed they'd been shafted enough by customers leaving without paying that there was an unwritten rule about seeing the money first.

The cup hit the worn counter with a dull *thump*. Ginny asked, "Do you want anything to go with that?"

"Not now." He'd see how the coffee went down before ordering anything else. He didn't have money to waste on food he couldn't eat if his stomach remained uncooperative.

She snorted softly. "I'm surprised you have any money left after last night." She snickered, "You must not have been in the mood for anything special."

Jesse glared at the waitress's back as she casually walked away. Life went on, people went about their business, and nobody cared what happened to anybody else. But they sure liked the gossip. Wasn't that a hell of a way to start the day?

He'd been so drunk he'd been in the back seat of an old rez-ride before he figured out it was going to cost more than a few drinks for the pleasure of Dahlia's company.

He stared at the black liquid in his cup. He wasn't supposed to have ended up like this. A long time ago, his dad had been a strong man with a good job. Zach had met a pretty, young woman from Texas and they were going to get married.

Wow, that memory hadn't crossed his mind in years. He must be in worse shape than he figured. He really needed to get the alcohol out of his system before he dredged up any more crappy memories. There was no ranch in Texas and there wasn't any redheaded, white woman to take them away from living in cockroach infested, isolated poverty. He'd been born here but that didn't mean he had to die here.

Zach was somewhere sleeping off his drunken stupor if he wasn't already dead. Jesse finished his coffee, paid the tab, and stepped back out into the hot dusty streets of Martin, South Dakota.

The tiny town sat squarely between the Pine Ridge and Rosebud Reservations. It was a map dot at the crossroads of two highways. You could follow one along the southern edge of South Dakota, or you could go north into the Badlands or south into Nebraska on the other. Eighteen-wheelers rolled along the routes twenty-four hours a day. The wind blew constantly and the dust never settled except when it rained or snowed.

Jesse stared into the alley next to the diner. How many times had he scrounged in their dumpster looking for enough food to get him through to the next day. Stray dogs lived better than he did most of the

9

time. Cats still had their claws and could hunt. There was no shortage of rats and mice for dinner.

He died a little more every day. If he ever found the woman who had promised them a future and then disappeared, he'd find a way to even the score. The only thing stopping him from hunting her down was his father. He couldn't leave Zach to fend for himself.

Jesse searched the shadows and bushes as he walked. His father was down to skin and bones. He could curl up and disappear without any effort at all. His clothes were the color of dirt most of the time, and it was all Jesse could do to wrestle them off Zach when he was passed out.

They'd been handed a dream, a chance to be part of something, and then had it drive away and never looked back. No explanation, gone, never to be seen or heard from again. He should have known it was a lie, even if Zach had been blinded by love or whatever spell the woman had put on him.

Jesse checked for any oncoming cars and crossed the street. This wasn't his idea of any kind of life; this was the ragged edge of nowhere and it had his name written all over it.

Jesse spotted a familiar looking lump under some bushes across the street from the park. It was cool and shady under the trees and Zach was still sound asleep. For once his father appeared relaxed, the pained expression that usually pulled his mouth into a grimace was gone. As the dappled sunlight wavered over Zach's gaunt features it almost looked like he was smiling.

Now, that was a first. Zach hadn't smiled since before the big blizzard almost four years ago. The time seemed a little hazy in Jesse's memory, but four years seemed about right. They had survived another freezing winter and spring had rapidly blended into summer.

"Hey, Dad, wake up. It's time to get out of here before someone sees you and calls the cops." Jesse crouched down ready to help Zach sit up. When nothing happened, he reached out and jostled Zach's shoulder. "Come on, we gotta get you outta here."

A low groan escaped followed by a dry cough. Zach's body lurched and jerked with each cough as he struggled to suck air into his lungs. "Stay here where she can find me," he croaked.

Jesse rolled his eyes. Not again, he didn't want to listen to this.

"She can't find you under these bushes. It'll be easier if you're home. She knows where you live. Remember?"

"It's been a long time."

"Yes, it has. But she has the address. The place still looks the same. Come on, let's go." Jesse reached for Zach's arm. "We don't want her to see you like this. It would break her heart." Not that Jesse cared if her rotten heart got broken.

That got Zach's attention. He rolled to his hands and knees preparing to crawl out from under his temporary shelter. Even after all the years and all the pain, Zach would still do whatever he could to keep her from being disappointed. She didn't give a damn, and never had. Jesse hated Mariah Blue. When he caught up to her, she was going to pay for this.

Standing up he reached down to help Zach as he stumbled to his feet.

"Lean on me and we'll get home. A little sleep and a shower will have you feeling better, you'll see. We'll get you all cleaned up so she'll recognize you."

"She'll know me," Zach's sandpaper rough voice rasped.

"Sure, she will."

She should, she'd made him into the sorry excuse of a man who hung on Jesse's arm. The stumbling drunk was a creation of her lies. Jesse grabbed Zach as he tripped over his own feet. Both men grunted as Jesse worked to keep them upright. It had been close, they'd come within an inch of rolling into the gutter together. Jesse sucked in a breath of hot air and swore under his breath. Someday, he'd hunt her to the ends of the earth and make her pay for this.

CHAPTER THREE

THE WIND BLEW hot and dry, same as it had for the last thirteen-hundred miles. Silki rolled her shoulders trying to ease some of the tension that had been building since leaving Valentine, Nebraska. Her short rest stop at the local burger joint to check the map, and get out of the sun for a few minutes had done nothing to relieve the impending sense of doom that hung over her head like a vulture waiting for something to die. Well, it wasn't going to be her.

So why was she so tense? The answer to that should have been simple, but it kept getting interrupted with little nagging side issues like food and money. Once she was in the one-horse town where Mariah Blue had last used her credit card there was no telling what she'd find. It could be the answer to her prayers, or it could be the beginning of a longer road. There was a third possibility, but she didn't want to think about that. Legends never died, never, there were rules about that. She was almost sure there were rules.

What would Zachary High Horse be like? He was still alive. The county clerk's office and the tribal membership rolls listed him as living. What would he look like? Would he still be the hunk her aunt had described in the yellowed, dog-eared journals Silki had found in the strongbox? What would he say? What would he think of her? Not that she really gave a rat's ass what he thought, but he'd been important to Mariah, so his status was up there along with hers, at least temporarily.

All the questions seemed to tumble through her mind like pebbles down a rattlesnake hole. Their destination could have deadly results.

Silki kept telling herself she had to face the facts. Mariah hadn't been heard from in four years. If this guy had killed her, he would not be happy to see anyone coming around snooping and asking questions. What she knew about Native Americans would fit in a thimble. She wasn't in Texas anymore, and she was definitely out of her element.

A couple hours later, the Heritage growled through the left-hand turn at Highway 20 and roared past a drive-in grocery. The road to Martin was long with sweeping turns and dips as it wound its way through the rolling prairie. Green meadows, tan fields, and distant grey outcroppings of barren rock stood in contrast to each other reminding her of the harsh contrasts to be found in this place.

Silki swayed and flowed with the road, the Harley's big engine roared on never missing a stroke. She had reserved a room at the Crossroads Inn. Aptly named, it stood at a crossroads in her life as well as at the intersection of two highways in Martin, South Dakota. When her stay was over, nothing would ever be the same. Decisions would be made that would alter not only her future, but her family's future as well.

Too much responsibility waited for her in Martin. But this wasn't the time to let down the only person who had ever cared about her. Failure wasn't an option. She'd be there in time for dinner.

After checking in and unloading the bike, Silki found the town's best diner, the one recommended by the motel desk clerk. She wanted a real meal with homestyle food. She didn't care if the locals stared or not. She was too tired and too strung out from the road to sweat the small stuff. Her money spent like anybody else's. Pulling the black half-helmet off, she plodded toward the glass door. Her legs were stiff and her back ached. She hadn't ridden a motorcycle in years and she'd pushed herself through the unrelenting summer heat and thunderstorms to get to this ink dot on the map.

Her steel-toed engineers boots clomped across the floor to the nearest empty table. Pulling out the old-fashioned chrome tubing and vinyl chair, she sank down in relief. Her damp doo rag remained plastered to her head. Silki rubbed the dust from her face with the bandanna hanging around her neck. It was the best she was going to do. Nothing short of a long, hot shower was going to melt the road grime from her body.

She read the short menu and wondered when the waitress might get around to bringing her a glass of water. She didn't have time to waste on the looks she was getting from the old men surreptitiously glancing her way from across the room. What did catch her eye was a group of teenage boys who were stopped on the sidewalk eyeballing her Harley. The metallic cobalt blue paint sparkled and the flame chrome exhaust pipes added a custom finishing touch. Damn, she didn't want any trouble. She was still watching them when the waitress finally stopped next to her.

"What can I get you?"

Silki turned at the sound of the woman's weary voice and answered, "I'd like the steak medium-rare and mashed potatoes with a large iced tea." She closed the menu and put it back in its holder.

"Green beans or corn?"

"Beans." Another decision had been made. "Green beans will be fine."

This was what her life had come to. Green beans or corn in a small-town diner. A glass of water was a luxury and iced tea was at a premium. This was Friday night, and the most exciting thing she was going to do was sleep. Saturday she'd begin the hunt for Zachary High Horse.

Across the room at a small table in the back corner by the slot machines, Jesse watched the biker babe order her dinner. He couldn't stop staring at her. Dark tendrils of hair curled out from under the rag that fit like skull cap over her head and framed her face, while a long braid hung down her back. Even from across the room he caught a flash of annoyance and a serious frown when she caught some kids admiring her Harley a little too closely. When she turned her face toward old Irene, the waitress, Jesse forgot to breathe. She was beautiful, a babe, a centerfold, a ten plus.

He smiled his best I'm-interested smile. It was Friday night and he was on the prowl, babe in sight. If she could afford to ride a Harley, she could afford to buy him a drink.

Nothing happened, she didn't return his smile. She didn't see him, that was it. He was sitting too far away. Getting up, he sauntered past her table on his way to the men's room. A few minutes later on his way back to his table, he flashed her his sexiest come-on grin, an open invitation to look his way.

She barely glanced up from her plate and continued wolfing down her steak. Something was not right. No living, breathing woman had ever resisted his best come-and-get-me look. No woman except her. Maybe there was something wrong with her.

He slumped down in his chair, sipped his coffee, and pouted. She kept eating. Guess he couldn't compete with one of Georgina's steaks. Since when had that happened? He'd turned thirty-two last week, but that didn't mean he was old. He could still get it up, and give her a ride that would get job done and put a smile on her lips. So, what was the problem? Everyone knew biker babes liked to ride and ride hard.

Before he could come up with a plan to meet her over dessert, she was already up and on her way to the cash register. This babe didn't waste time. He was going to have to act fast where she was concerned if he got another chance to introduce himself.

The Harley wasn't bad either. Older, but in great shape, one of the classics. Ride the babe, ride the bike, life was looking up. Bikers liked to drink. He'd check the bars later.

Jesse watched the babe swing her shapely leg over the bike and settle onto the seat. The way her legs wrapped around the engine, cradling it like they would a lover was enough to make him gasp for breath, when he did, he darn near choked on is coffee. It didn't take much to imagine those thighs wrapped around his hips. *Oh, baby, have I got something for you.*

After watching her roar off down the dusty main street, Jesse paid his check and stepped out into the twilight. No telling where Zach was. Probably in one of the bars or behind one of the bars. As long as Zach and the biker babe weren't in the same bar, he'd be okay. It was hard to hustle and keep an eye on his old man at the same time.

Several hours later, Jesse still hadn't found the babe. He had found his dad, head bowed over his bottle and muttering some crap about seeing Blue. Jesse couldn't make any more sense out of it than usual, and that was no sense at all.

Zach's voice was rusty and raw from too much booze. "She's come for me. Can't let her see me this way."

"What way is that?" Jesse grumbled into the hazy darkness. "The way she's made you? She ought to see what she's done with all her lies."

Anymore Jesse could have picked his dad up and shook him like a rag doll. Zach was so emaciated, there was nothing left of the big strapping man who used to be his father. He was a shrunken, stumbling skeleton with a little leathery skin stretched over the bones to keep them from scattering all over the ground.

"I should have looked. Maybe she was in trouble." His head swung slowly from side to side.

"The only trouble she was in was us. She needed to get rid of us, pretend we never existed. It was all lies. When will you get that through your head?" He swallowed a shot of whiskey and ordered another.

"She never lied, always kept her word. I never looked."

The shaking bottle made its way to Zach's mouth and his throat made a hesitant attempt to swallow the liquid forgetfulness.

There was no use trying to talk sense to Zach. He'd go to his grave thinking she was coming back someday. Jesse's hand tightened around his glass. He didn't want a drink; he needed a drink. He raised the glass of cheap whiskey and swallowed.

His eyes watched the door, but it didn't open. Instead, he caught the subtle movement in the corner booth. Mary Claire was getting up and walking his way. She was all tits and legs. What more could a man want? The image of the biker babe flashed across his still flickering brain cells. Yeah, well until he could get his hands on her, Mary Claire would do. He put his glass down as she approached.

"Hey, Jesse. What's going on?"

Her sultry voice held an invitation he recognized.

"Not much. Wanna sit down and talk about it?"

"Sure." She pulled a chair over by his and slid onto it. Leaning over she pretended to whisper in his ear. But what she did was give him a clear shot down the front of her low-cut blouse as she said, "I'd love to talk. I haven't seen you in a while."

"I've been busy."

Jesse leaned back when he should have been leaning forward drooling over her breasts. What was wrong with him? Mary Claire had great tits. Big and soft with fat dusky nipples, the kind he liked. He had big hands; it took a lot to fill them.

She wiggled closer. "My car's outside. I have a bottle under the seat. We could go for a ride."

"Sounds good." Jesse turned toward Zach whose head rested on his folded arms on the table. "I'll be back in a little while to take you home. Don't go wandering off."

Zach didn't move and there was no way to know if he'd heard. It didn't matter anyway; he'd wouldn't remember a word of it two minutes later. Jesse got up and walked out behind Mary Claire. Great legs, not much ass, definitely not as fine as the biker babe. It didn't matter, he could do this.

Silki muttered, "They should have named the place, The Swinging Door."

From across the street, she watched people wander in and out. They either staggered out to cars and drove off, or they drove in, got out of their cars, and staggered inside. The place looked like it hadn't been painted in years, but it didn't matter because it was the same color as the dirt and dust swirling around it. A dingy little hole to crawl into and hide. Time to go see what the local trolls were up to, get a feel for the place. The thought made her shudder. She squared her shoulders, took a deep breath, and walked across the road.

She surveyed the dimly lit room and made her way to the bar. After her relaxing shower she was wide awake, and as nervous as a cat in a dog kennel. After a nightcap she'd be able to unwind and sleep through an atomic blast which was comparable to the sound of the eighteen-wheelers screeching to a stop at the intersection outside her motel window. The "No Jake Brake" sign was apparently not written in the appropriate "trucker speak".

It wasn't first class, but then she hadn't seen anything first class in a long time. It was like a thousand other local bars in rural areas. It had a little air-conditioning to take the heat out of a summer's day. In the winter, it was a shelter from the wind and cold. It was better than sitting at home alone if you were lonely.

She wasn't that lonely yet. She wasn't sure if there was a rating system for small town taverns, but it definitely wasn't the River Oaks Country Club in Houston, Billy Bob's in Fort Worth, or the Midnight Rodeo in San Antonio, that was for sure.

After ordering a drink from the burly bartender, who probably doubled for the bouncer, she took a longer look around the room. Shabby was in these days making the place right in style. Right down to the passed out drunk in the back. Every self-respecting dive had to have one. She turned back to the bar at the same time her drink landed in front of her with a *clunk*. Hell, it didn't even come with a napkin. They must be into saving trees or something.

The melancholy song on the juke box wasn't helping the dreary atmosphere, and her drink had two sips left. She was running on empty. Silki took one last look around the room. The locals were keeping their distance. She wasn't going to find what she was looking for in there.

The poor old drunk in the back had finally lifted his head showing vague signs of life. In the dark it was hard to tell, but it looked like his face morphed into an expression of sheer terror, or was it horror? Either way it didn't matter.

Silki wrote it off as shock. That was it. He'd come around and realized he was awake and not comatose. She turned back to the bar and from the corner of her eye she caught sight of the old man as he lurched out of his chair and stumbled across the room on rubber legs. She slid off the worn-smooth wooden bar stool, and headed for the front door. Old Jack Number Seven was on top of things. The knots in her back were unwinding. She'd be able to sleep.

She moved toward the door as he staggered toward the bar. The last thing she needed was for him to pick her for a soft spot to land. She wasn't buying some old lush another drink. At the last minute, he tripped over his worn-out boots and hit the cracked linoleum floor arms outstretched, and unconscious.

Heaving a sigh of disgust, the bartender slapped his towel on the bar, glared at the prone derelict and grumbled, "We'd better get him out of here before he pisses all over himself and the floor." He looked at the men sitting closest to him. "How about one of you helping me haul him out the back door?"

Silki stepped out the front and quickly closed the door saving herself from seeing any more human kindness in action. So, that's how drunks ended up in back alleys. Nobody felt sorry for them. People were willing to take their money and never give them another thought.

The poor bastard could have used a cup of coffee and something to eat. He was going to be sicker than a dog in the morning, and that was if he lasted till morning. There were always stories about boozers and homeless people being robbed and beaten by thugs or dying from exposure. What were his chances of survival?

It wasn't her problem.

The lights from the all-night Texaco on the corner caught her eye. She walked over and bought a large Styrofoam cup of coffee and a slightly wilted roast beef sandwich. It wasn't much and it wasn't great, but it was food and the bread might soak up the alcohol. She'd heard that somewhere, but didn't know if it was true. And it didn't matter. The old man was a pitiful mess. And no, she wouldn't buy him another drink, but she'd feed a homeless dog or cat, so she'd do the same for him.

Picking her way slowly along the pitch-black alley she cussed herself all the way back to Texas. Nobody in their right mind went looking for an old drunk in a seedy back alley. It was suicide, not to mention nasty smelling. She wrinkled her nose and tried not to breathe one extra breath of the putrid air. Why did garbage collectors always drop some of their load? Was it some kind of rule or what?

Silki slipped on something unidentifiable. That did it. If she didn't find him in the next sixty seconds, she was out of there.

A few seconds later it occurred to her that God must have heard her and decided to be merciful. The clouds moved away from the moon and its light briefly illuminated the darkness. There, slumped against the wall sitting on the filthy ground, was the old man. Silki approached cautiously and squatted down facing him. If he grabbed for her, she'd be up and running in a heartbeat.

"Hey, old man. Wake up. I've got some coffee and food for you."

Nothing.

"Hey, open your eyes." She put down the coffee and poked him on the shoulder. "Look what I brought you."

He grunted and his head jerked, but his eyes didn't open. She was running out of patience, and she was more than a little nervous. The alley was making her skin crawl. She poked him again. She didn't dare grab on to him in case he had lice or something equally nasty.

"Old man, open your eyes. I haven't got all night to fuss with you. Look, I brought you some coffee." She dropped the sandwich in his lap.

She was about to give up when he moaned, picked his head up and rested it back against the wall. His eyes cracked open and grew wide as a look of wild terror filled them.

He rasped, "You've come for me."

"No. I brought you some coffee and a sandwich. You need to eat."

Silki stood up and took a step back while cautiously eyeing him.

"You want me to eat?" He stared at her, then at the wrapped sandwich, and then back up at her. "Now?"

"Yes, I want you to eat, and drink the coffee. I've got better things to do than spend my nights in an alley with a drunk. Now, promise me you'll eat it."

"Will you stay with me this time?"

He still hadn't touched the food. She looked toward the mouth of the alley eyeing her only escape route. There wasn't much traffic, and there weren't any voices on the night air so she was safe enough for the time being. He was frail and Aunt Mariah had sent her to the best martial arts school in San Antonio. If she couldn't fight off a semi-conscious old man, she was really in bad shape.

"Okay, but you have to start eating, or I'm leaving."

His frail fingers fumbled with the wrapping.

Silki lost patience. She squatted down, took the sandwich, and said, "Here, let me help you." She unwrapped it and handed it back.

She stayed there with him until he'd finished the sandwich and drank the coffee. That was all she could do for him. She sure as hell couldn't put him up for the night. It wasn't cold or likely to rain, but her conscience bothered her. She had the distinct feeling she wasn't supposed to leave him there alone.

Hearing voices and car doors opening and closing signaled her that it was getting busy out in front. Checking the lighted dial of her watch, she saw it wasn't near closing time for the local hot spots. The night was just getting started.

She asked, "Don't you have somewhere you can go? You can't stay here all night. It's not safe."

A glance toward the mouth of the alley did nothing to reassure her. She had the feeling it was time for her to get out of there. The place was getting creepier by the nanosecond. She stood up and shook off the slight cramping in her legs. Squatting wasn't her thing apparently. She tried to stomp the circulation back into her tingling feet.

"My son will come for me. He always does." The old man's head dropped onto his chest. He was out again.

That's it, feed a lush and he passes out. Only this time he's full of food and coffee. Silki planted her hands on her hips. No more Miss Nice Girl. "Fine, you just sleep there and let's hope the rats don't bite you."

She turned on her heel and marched down the alley toward cleaner air. Some alleys smelled worse than others, and some fools never learned. She might be one of those fools.

CHAPTER FOUR

JESSE SLAMMED Mary Claire's car door shut. It was another one of the indistinct rez-rides that littered the landscape. Four doors of faded silver-gray oxidized metallic paint and threadbare upholstery. He was glad to be out of the miserable thing. It stank of stale beer and cigarettes. A lot like the woman driving it. The back seat had seen better days and nights. He turned and walked away. Nothing came to mind, not even to say goodbye. It didn't matter.

She seethed, "You didn't even drink that much. You're the same as your old man. Do you need a white bitch to get it up for you? Don't think people have forgotten."

The car shuddered into reverse and barreled out of the parking lot into the street. Then it lurched forward, the tires spinning on the blacktop before it found traction and sped off leaving a choking trail of dust and burnt rubber in its wake.

Standing in the dimly lit parking lot on the deserted main street, Jesse watched the red taillights disappear into the dark. He didn't care. He'd been there and done her before. There hadn't been anything much worth getting, and he'd probably been saved from an STD of some sort. The condom he'd tucked in his wallet was still there.

Maybe the biker babe would be around tomorrow. Now that was a piece of ass. He'd get hard for her no problem. Hell, she was probably passing through and he'd never see her again. That was as good as his luck was running. Something he could see but never have a snowball's chance in Hell of having.

He stood in the dismal spot, stared at the deserted street and tried to decide where to go next. The bars were open and the apartment was empty. There was no telling where Zach was. He'd been told to stay put but that didn't mean Zach hadn't wandered off.

Jesse caught movement from the corner of his eye. He turned, blinked and stared at the stealthy figure who materialized out of the black mouth of the alley behind the bar.

Faded butt-hugging jeans, white tank top and long dark hair. It was her. The babe. His mouth was in motion before his brain engaged.

"Hey, what were you doing back there?" Oh brilliant. He wanted to kick himself.

"None of your business," she snapped back.

Jesse watched her walk briskly across the parking lot leaving plenty of space between them. If he made a grab for her, he'd miss. She looked light on her feet and ready to run. She could reach the Texaco before he'd be able to get to her. And she was right; it was none of his business what she'd been doing back there. If she was selling drugs, he didn't want to know about it. He didn't want any part of that shit.

He noticed she'd picked up her pace, she was afraid of him. There wasn't anything to be afraid of. He wasn't into forcing himself on women. They sure loved to ride him, but they didn't want to keep him around. That was fine with him. This one didn't look like she'd bother to spit on him if he was on fire.

"It could be dangerous to be back there alone. You could get hurt or something."

A few more steps and she'd be out of the parking lot and on the road. He didn't see headlights coming from either direction, a good sign. At least she wouldn't end up road-kill. That would be a terrible waste of a gorgeous babe. Even if he started running now, she'd be across the road and halfway to the motel on the corner before he could catch up with her.

Silki shouted, "Mind your own business and leave me alone. I don't need anything from you."

"I've got something I'd like to give you." He chuckled and watched her quicken her pace.

"Stay away from me."

"Hey, what room are you in? I could stop by later." He didn't mind being her backdoor man.

"Screw you!", she yelled, before breaking into a jog.

Jesse shouted, "Oh yeah, screw me, please."

He watched her disappear into the motel. He doubted that she'd heard him. No one seemed to hear him anymore. He talked, but nobody listened. What a lousy night it was turning out to be.

He kicked at some loose gravel as he walked toward the corner. The motel room windows were dark, except for the one that blinked on that very second. Great room, right in front over the office. Damn the bad luck. He wasn't going to get anywhere near her without waking up the manager, who'd wake up the cops, who'd throw him in jail, again. Then he wouldn't be able to take care of Zach.

Feeling too restless to go home and stare at the blank walls of the apartment, Jesse opted for searching the gutters and alleys for Zach. If he found him now, he wouldn't have to get up early in the morning to go looking for him. He could sleep in and mercifully escape the nightmare he was living in for a few hours.

Silki leaned against the locked door and exhaled. She was in, safe and sound, at least for the time being. She had tried to help out an old man and look at the thanks it had gotten her; harassed by some two-bit would-be playboy, stud type. Did he think he was so irresistible that all the girls would line up for a chance to get some of what he had in his pants? Not likely, not even in this out-of-the-way town. Whatever he had, he could keep it, germs and all.

All the dead bolts and security locks were fastened and checked. She checked the window lock as well. Being on the second floor would stop most people. But a determined person could find a way. They'd have to break the glass and that would wake her up.

Flopping down on the bed she let out a slow breath. It had been a long time since she'd had to deal with anyone more dangerous than the parking lot attendants at the country club. They could be vicious if they didn't like the tip she gave them.

This was the level of lower-than-low she'd sunk to. Not too long ago, she hadn't been afraid to take on the world. But here she was in a one-horse-town, scared of the dark, an old drunk who couldn't stand up and a two-bit gigolo.

The streets and highways looked deserted. There were a few lights burning here and there, but not many. It was a quiet little town by the looks of things. Yeah, that veneer didn't fool her, she was well aware that appearances could be deceiving. The man in the parking lot had disappeared. No telling where he'd gone off to. Probably lurking in the shadows somewhere. As long as he wasn't in her motel, she didn't care where he went or what he did when he got there.

Hopefully, he wouldn't go snooping in the alley, but if he did, there wasn't anything she could do about it. She mumbled a quick prayer that the old man would be okay, that a guardian angel would watch over him.

Silki dug in her backpack, pulled out the next to last of Mariah's aged journals, pulled off her boots, and stacked two pillows at the head of the bed. She was way too wound up to sleep thanks to the tall, dark, and lean prairie Casanova outside the bar. Reading for a few minutes would help her relax.

She was trying to do the right thing, but she wasn't exactly having much luck with it. She had found Martin, South Dakota. At least there was a map for that. But how was she going to find Zachary High Horse?

From what she'd read so far, he was a heavy boozer. He probably had a liver the size of Milwaukee. If she did find him, and if he was coherent, what was she supposed to do? Walk up and say, "What the hell have you done with Mariah Blue? Where is she? Tell me, or I'll cut your heart out and feed it to the coyotes." That certainly sounded ladylike and was extremely likely to get a positive response. No, she needed a better plan.

She didn't know the first thing about being a detective, regardless of all the police shows on TV. This was real life and people were more than likely going to tell her to get lost. Now, there was a subject for discussion, only she didn't have anyone to discuss it with. She was lost in so many ways. Mariah would know what to do, and how to recover from this growing turd-pile of chaos her life had turned into.

Early in the morning, she'd start with the tribal offices. First, she'd try the Rosebud Reservation, and if he wasn't listed there she'd try Pine Ridge. Monday, she'd check with Shannon County for a death certificate. She'd already tried the old stuff, like the phone books, no listing for any High Horse. It wasn't like she'd expected this to be easy, but why did it have to be so hard?

With a sigh, she opened the journal and took up reading where she'd left off. She was deep in the darkest days of Mariah's turbulent years of fighting with George. Silki never would have guessed that it had all boiled down to a fight over the man Mariah wanted to marry.

From the looks of things, some of the rumors weren't just rumors. Silki wasn't sure where that left her, but one thing was certain, she had to finish reading the journals. There had to be clues buried in there somewhere. The whole truth might never be known, but what truth there was needed to come out in the open.

One thing was already certain. Mariah Blue loved Zachary High Horse more than she loved herself or anyone else on this planet. What she'd done about it was frightening. It also fascinated Silki. What would it take for her to become that fearless and invincible?

The light in the motel second-floor window glowed a dim yellow around the curtains until after midnight and the bars closed. Jesse knew because he watched. He'd watched and waited. She didn't come out or open the curtain to check the street a second time. He guessed once had been enough. There wasn't much to see. There never had been.

He'd checked the bushes at the park, and side streets between the bar and the park. He'd even tried behind the diner in case Zach was looking for food. But no luck. There was no telling where his old man had wandered off to.

The one place he hadn't checked was the alley behind the bar. It was nasty. He'd been flung out the back door once or twice himself, and he remembered the nauseating stench clearly.

The booze he'd swilled down earlier had worn off. Zach had been drinking in the back of the bar. The biker babe had come slinking out of the alley. The puzzle pieces were coming together. She'd probably followed Zach out into the alley and stolen his stuff. Not that he had much. But there was his medicine bag.

As much as he hated the idea, Jesse made his way to the mouth of the alley. Oh man, it reeked. He turned his head away to catch his breath and keep from vomiting.

"Hey, Zach, you back here?" He listened for any sound at all that a human might make.

"Zach, answer me if you're back here."

He was going to hurl in another minute if he didn't get some decent air. Zach was probably out cold. He got drunk to get numb and it worked. If he stayed back there the rats would find him. Their sharp teeth could take chunks out of him and he wouldn't feel it. Rat bites tended to get infected, that's if you didn't die from rat bite fever first.

Jesse took a couple of deep breaths and turned toward the alley. He had to make sure Zach wasn't passed out next to the garbage. Muttering under his breath to keep his mind off the stink he started walking.

The dumpster loomed up ahead on his left. Sure enough, there was Zach slumped against the wall, half-hidden in the shadow of the dumpster. His eyes were open and his lips were moving, but no sound was coming out of him.

"Hey Dad, didn't you hear me calling?" Jesse waited for a signal that his question had registered. Nothing. But Zach's lips kept moving.

"What are you doing?" Jesse waited again. Still nothing. His patience was at an end and his stomach was turning. He had to get Zach up and get out of there. He bent down, took his father by the arm and hauled him to his feet. Zach didn't weigh anything. He had been close to two-hundred pounds once. Now there was nothing left of him. Jesse had to swallow to keep from vomiting. This is what fantasies and white-woman dreams got you. Retching drunk in a rat-infested alley.

"Come on, quit talking to yourself and let's get out of here." He hauled on his dad's arm and started guiding him toward the parking lot.

Zach followed, stumbling and muttering. "She's here. She's come for me. I have to pray."

"Shit! It's too late for prayers. Don't you get it? She left you. She didn't want you, or me. We were nothing to her; it was some twisted game she was playing. She's not coming for you. Not now, not ever." Jesse had listened to enough for one night. "You've waited all these years for nothing. She doesn't care if you live or die."

Zach groaned an agonizing sound. "She came back for me. She's young again. I saw her. She talked to me." He slipped, gripped Jesse's arm tighter to break his fall. "She brought me food and coffee. She wants me to get strong so I can go with her."

Zach was getting worse. Jesse had been around alcoholics long enough to know that when the hallucinations got this bad their days were numbered. Maybe he ought to take him to the hospital. Then again, maybe not. Zach might not survive the DTs again. He was fifty-four years old and all but dead.

You had to live fast on the Rez because you were going to die young, if you were lucky. Only the unlucky ones lived to get old and be tormented by all the wasted years of their lives. They had nowhere to go because nobody knew the way out of Rez life and those that did try to find a way, found themselves shuffled to the fringes of their families.

Jesse refused to abandon Zach. He didn't know why but he couldn't bring himself to do it. He'd told himself a million times at least, that he'd be better off without the old man. He'd even walked away a few times. But he always came back in the end. If Zach died, he'd have no one. He was empty enough; he didn't want to lose the only relative he had.

"If somebody gave you coffee, it wasn't the ghost of your lost love. She drove away years ago. We're the ones who got stuck here, not her." Jesse gulped the clean air at the mouth of the alley and continued guiding Zach across the parking lot.

"Let's go home and get some sleep." In case it would get Zach to stay put for the night, Jesse threw in, "Sleep will make you strong."

The putrid smell of the alley followed them down the street. It clung to Zach's clothes like a bloated tick on a dog.

Taking a shower and putting on some clean clothes wouldn't hurt either. One step at a time. He'd start by getting Zach to their apartment, do his best to give him a shower, and finally put him in his bed. All that was a big enough challenge. Getting Zach into clean clothes could wait until morning.

CHAPTER FIVE

SILKI WOKE UP STARVING. This was day six after five days on the road and it was catching up with her. The body needed fuel same as the bike. She had to feed it or it wasn't going to take her much farther. The diner was her best bet.

The waitresses might even know if there were any High Horses living in town. Waitresses knew a lot more than people gave them credit for. She waited until her breakfast came and coffee cup was refilled before asking the question of the day.

"Do you know if Zachary High Horse still lives around here?"

Stoney silence and an icy glare were the first clues that this was not a good day to ask questions, or maybe it wasn't the right question to be asking. Either way it looked bad from the stern look aimed her way.

She added, "I'm not here to cause trouble. He was a friend of my aunt. I promised I'd look him up is all." Nobody wanted to bring trouble on other people. Maybe if she explained herself she might get some cooperation.

Dark eyes narrowed and the mouth shrunk to a pencil thin line before any sound came out of it. "He's not here." Then she was gone, along with the coffee pot, never to return.

Well, okay. Since there was no hope of getting anymore coffee or any information, Silki finished her breakfast quickly and headed out for the Rosebud Reservation.

Zachary High Horse was an enrolled member of the tribe. That was the sum total of any and all information she could get out of anybody. She'd have to ride into Rapid City to check the DMV for a driver's license and address. If it was current, and if it was accurate, she might have something. Then again, people moved around a lot.

It was already after noon. She was hot and sweaty. The dust caked on her skin felt like it was starting to crack. She needed to shower and put on some clean clothes. The hundred-eighty-mile trip to Rapid City would have to wait. Maybe the local police department in Martin would know if Zachary still lived in the area. She could save herself a long ride if they'd help her.

Silki pulled into a parking space in front of the police station, a nondescript beige building that looked like a standard government mass-produced shoe box. The interior was cool thanks to the air-conditioning.

She approached the information desk quietly, walking carefully to keep her boots from clomping. The female officer sitting there was an attractive brunette who filled out her uniform like a recruiting poster model. She looked slightly uncomfortable as Silki drew closer. That reaction was fairly common. No one knew what to expect from her. Most people were mentally preparing for the worst. Bikers weren't known for good manners.

"Hi, I was hoping I could find out if someone is still living in this area?" Silki smiled and felt the dust crinkle on her skin

The officer's eyes darted around the room. There were some other officers over in the far corner looking intently at something on the desk in front of them.

"I'm trying to find an old friend of my aunt's. There wasn't any listing in the phone book. I only want to see how he's doing, give him her regards. That's all."

"We're not exactly the lost and found, you know." The officer's mouth pinched up a little and it made her look older.

Until then, Silki had guessed the woman's age to be a couple years younger than herself, probably in her middle to late twenties. With makeup it was hard to tell anymore.

She set her smile in concrete. "I'm only trying to do my aunt a favor. She's getting old and can't get around too good. She doesn't have many friends left. They keep dying." The hairs on the back of her neck tickled; she waited for lightening to come down and strike her dead. Aunt Mariah was not old, and she'd have beaten the daylights out of anyone stupid enough to insinuate that she was feeble.

Silki reasoned she must have sounded as distressed as she felt because something made the officer's face relax and a sigh escaped her lips.

"I guess I could check. Sort of off the record."

The silver name tag said the officer's name was Suzanne. She didn't look like a Suzanne but so what? People liked to hear their names. Schmooze was the word of the day. Make like this is the biggest client in Dallas. Silki's mind raced to remember anything that might help get her what she wanted.

Leaning a little closer and dropping her voice to just above a whisper, she said, "I'd really appreciate it, Suzanne. My aunt means the world to me and I'd hate to disappoint her. She has so little to look forward to these days."

"Yeah, I know. It's hard when they get older. My grandma is like that. I try to get her to go to the community center to get her out of the house, but most of the time she won't go. She can't see to drive anymore and her arthritis is so bad she can't crochet to keep herself busy like she used to. I try to get by to see her as often as I can but it's hard." Suzanne's face fell into a bottomless pit of sadness.

For a minute it looked like the woman was going to cry. She hated preying on other people's weaknesses. It was the lowest of the low. She'd thought Charley the Weasel was disgusting with his line of business bullshit and here she was doing the same rotten thing. She was going to have a hard time looking at herself in the mirror over this.

"You know, anything we can do for them, no matter how small it seems, means so much to them." She had to get to the point. "Like finding this old friend. I guess she met him on her summer vacation when she graduated from college. It was a big deal back then." Silki shrugged. "Those graduation trips were major landmarks to that generation. I guess some of her friends got to go to Europe. Poor Aunt Mariah got a trip to the Black Hills and Yellowstone Park."

Suzanne blinked. "It's not quite the same thing, is it?"

"No, not really. But she still talks about it like it was the best time in her life. The guy worked for the park service. She really liked him. They kept in touch for a few years, then she lost track of him. I'd like to be able to tell her something good."

Suzanne's fingers tapped at the computer keyboard. "What's his name?"

Hallelujah, at last. "Zachary High Horse."

Suzanne's face fell even lower, if that was possible. Silki cringed inwardly. The news wasn't going to be good.

"I'm sorry to have to tell you this. I mean, there's no telling how people will turn out. He's here in Martin. Lives over on Third Avenue. He's been arrested several times for public intoxication."

"That doesn't sound good. Things happen along the way in life and good people end up in bad ways. If I could get the address, I'd stop in and check on him one morning. Maybe catch him while he's still sober. He might feel better knowing someone still remembers him in a good way."

It wasn't exactly a lie. Personally, Silki didn't care if he felt better or not. She did want to catch him while he was sober enough to answer a few questions. If his life was a screwed-up mess it was nobody's fault but his own. He hadn't had the courage to fight for what he wanted, so if he ended up empty handed that's what he deserved. She wrote his address on a paper napkin she'd pulled out of her vest pocket.

Not forgetting her manners, she returned Suzanne's pen and said, "Thanks, I really appreciate this. It'll mean so much to my aunt." At least that much was true.

Silki was out the door and down the street in a matter of minutes. Third Avenue couldn't be that hard to find. The whole town consisted of not more than two-dozen streets. She knew Third Avenue wasn't between Main Street and the highway. She'd already seen those streets. She'd located the laundromat and was going to stop in there later. At the moment, she wanted to find Third Avenue.

It was too much to hope for that Zachary would be home or that he would be sober that late in the day. But knowing where he lived would bring her one step closer to finding Mariah.

She was probably kidding herself thinking he'd be home, but she found the address, parked in front of the run down fourplex and gathered her courage. The original two-tone tan and brown paint was weathered and peeling, the yard or what might have passed for a yard at one time was dead, dried up, and mostly blown away.

Something that used to be bushes next to the front steps had withered into a pile of dried sticks and twigs sticking out in all directions. Skeletal fingers reaching desperately for the sun, only needing a drink of water to survive. They hadn't made it, and five to one the inhabitants of the dilapidated building weren't in any better shape.

Silki stomped up the concrete stairs without touching the rusty iron railing. It looked like one measly little tap would send it toppling over. She didn't need a hand rail. She needed to get her hands on Zachary High Horse.

She pushed the door bell, but nothing happened. There was no sound, no buzz, no nothing. Well, what had she expected? The place was a wreck. The doorbell probably hadn't worked in years. There was no knocker either. Knocking would only skin her knuckles and the man was likely well on his way to being too drunk to hear a simple knock.

She raised her fist and pounded on the door. Going for broke, she yelled, "Zachary High Horse, you answer this door right now!"

Nothing happened. The door didn't open. She couldn't hear any sound coming from inside. The door wasn't that sturdy judging by the way it gave under her fist. Hollow core and not top of the line. Maybe he was passed out. Silki pounded on the door again.

"High Horse, you can't hide from me. I'll follow you straight into Hell and drag you back out, you gutless wonder."

She tried to swallow and found her throat was as dry as the dust blowing across the dead grass. She was hoarse, and he wasn't home, or so out of it that it didn't matter.

Giving up she stomped back to the bike, swung her leg over the seat and settled in. The engine revved as she shifted out of neutral. With one last glance over her shoulder at the seedy apartment she put the Harley in motion. She could feel her braid whipping in the wind against her back as she roared down the dreary street. He wasn't going to get away. She'd be back and she would get answers if she had to wring them out of him.

∾

Jesse came around the corner in time to see the biker babe disappear down his street. What was she doing there? There was nothing a tourist would want on Third Avenue. It was and always had been the low rent district. There were more cockroaches than people living in the rundown apartments and houses.

For all that it sounded fancy, Third Avenue didn't have a sidewalk. There was the cracked black top that occasionally turned to dirt where chunks of it had broken out over the years. The city wasn't in any hurry to maintain the back streets. It didn't matter anyway, even if they patched a part of it, the snow and ice would break it up someplace else next winter.

He stopped in front of the apartment he shared with Zach. The bike had been there. He could see the tire tracks in the soft soil. She'd been at his place and he'd missed her. Damn! He frowned at the deserted street. Even if she wasn't there to see him, he could have gotten an eye full of her. He would have helped her with whatever it was she wanted. All he needed was a chance to get her to spend some time with him.

He plodded up the stairs and dug around in his front pocket for the key. He needed to lie down. It had been a long, sleepless night watching over Zach and a longer day. After a little rest and a shower, he'd feel like going out and having some fun.

Zach had been restless all night, calling out for Blue. Why couldn't he get it through his thick head that the woman didn't want him, didn't want anything to do with him. If she did, she'd have come back from Rapid City and taken them to Texas with her. But no, she'd driven off saying she had to take care of some important business in Rapid City and be back in a few hours. That was the last they'd seen of her.

Zach wasn't any better that morning when the sun came up. He'd continued to mumble about getting strong so he could go with her. It got bad enough that it frightened Jesse into thinking his father might do something stupid. He'd called around and found them a ride to the hospital in Pine Ridge. It had taken hours in the Emergency Room to get seen and then to convince the Indian Health Service doctor that Zach was losing his grip on reality. For the time being, his dad was safely tucked up in a locked ward with DTs and hallucinations.

Jesse could still hear Zach shouting, "No, you can't keep me here. She won't know where to find me. I have to go with her this time."

The memory of it made his skin crawl.

He could still see the attendants hustling Zach off down the sterile corridor toward the metal doors that had more locks than Fort Knox. Zach wasn't getting out of there anytime soon.

Jesse had turned to the doctor to ask how long they would need to keep Zach, but the guy must have read his mind and answered before he could ask.

"He'll need to stay about a week to get him through the worst of it. After that you can put him in a day treatment program."

Jesse had mumbled, "Sure, a day treatment. I'll look into that."

He hadn't bothered telling the fresh-faced fool that there was only a handful of programs around and Zach would die of old age before his name would make it to the top of any list.

But he had a week of not having to search the gutters and alleys every night. A week to wash their clothes and change the sheets, and not have the place smell like beer and unwashed bodies. It was almost too good to be true.

He could open the windows and air the place out. The odor of stale cigarette smoke might actually fade for a few days. He couldn't do anything about the smoke discolored walls. Zach had stopped smoking years ago, needing the money for whiskey and beer.

Jesse flopped onto the sagging mattress that served as his bed and closed his eyes. The biker babe was still in town. After a little rest, he'd get cleaned up and go check the diner at dinner time and the bars after dark.

CHAPTER SIX

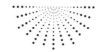

THE DINER WAS NOTICEABLY QUIET. Silki studied the evening sun sinking slowly behind the buildings across the street. Dying rays cast a soft warm glow over the ordinary white walls opposite the windows. The waitress on duty was different from Miss Congeniality on the early shift. This one looked forty-something and tired to the bone. Everything about her drooped. It would be pointless to ask her any questions, the strain of trying to think up an answer might kill her and then who would serve dinner?

Silki opted to relax and eat her dinner in peace. Zachary would eventually show up at one of the bars or at the apartment. Either way, she'd find him. There wasn't any reason to hurry her meal. It was going to be a long night waiting and watching for that cockroach of a man to crawl out of his hiding place.

A glance out the window reassured her the street was deserted except for a few parked cars. She guessed most people ate their evening meal at home. They could find out what the kids had been up to all day and what gossip the wife had gathered from the neighbors. The breakfast crowd was the time the old boys got together to do their gossiping under cover of the latest farm reports.

Another quick survey of the room reinforced her suspicions. This was a hanging-on-by-the-skin-of-their-teeth farm town. Well-worn jeans, boots and cotton short-sleeved shirts of various faded colors were the fashion highlight of the night. But even the smallest farm town had its dark side, its dirty little secrets.

She'd bet her best doo rag that these guys knew whose wife was lonely, whose kid was a little too wild, whose sister wore her jeans too tight. It was a sure bet they knew which of the local natives was sleeping with a white woman. She just needed an opening and they'd spill their guts.

Once in a while one of the gambling machines in the back corner made an electronically garbled noise distracting her from her thoughts. The die-hard gambler perched on the stool in front of it kept desperately pushing the buttons, no doubt hopeful his luck would change. The other machines winked and blinked their lights trying to attract someone else to part with a dollar. Hope for the hopeless. She didn't gamble, and she was all through wishing things would turn out all right. They would turn out one way or another, good or bad, she'd see to it. She owed it to Mariah Blue, and she owed it to herself.

All in all, it was totally depressing. Silki wished for better days, at least a little better. Not that she wanted to be back at the country club with its deceptive glitter and endless chatter, but something not quite so dismal as her current situation would be nice.

When her dinner arrived, she occupied herself with unrolling the stainless-steel utensils from the paper napkin and placing them in their correct positions. It was better than flinging them across the room. They were beat up enough from years of uncaring use and abuse. Her mind screamed she shouldn't be there as her hands went about their tasks. She didn't belong there. But frustrated or not, there she was and there she would stay until she got the answers she needed.

As she settled the napkin in her lap, the bell over the door jingled. She glanced up along with everyone else in the room. Silki's eyes narrowed and her jaw clamped tight. She recognized the roadside Romeo. Her hands fisted in her lap and her legs tensed as she prepared to meet any unwanted advances.

She watched in dismayed fascination as he calmly took a seat at the table directly in front of her. Every time she looked up from her plate, she'd be face-to-face with him. He was doing this on purpose, she knew it as sure as the sun would come up in the morning.

She snarled silently at him. The right side of her upper lip twitched in a half-sneer. He smiled smugly at her.

He reminded her of all the reasons men were no damn good. Their smugness when they thought they were being charming, that look that said, Here-I-am-babe. Yeah, well, there he was, and she wasn't as naïve as she used to be. She knew the game and she wasn't playing. He could sit there till closing time preening like a peacock and she wasn't buying whatever worn out charms he was trying to sell.

No doubt anything female on two legs in this town had already tried him on for size. He was used merchandise at best. Judging by his smile he thought he was still a real hot catch. He did have straight white teeth and smooth skin. Under different circumstances she might have looked twice. But not now. Now, she knew the smile was a lure, and the white teeth would chew her heart to ribbons in a New York minute.

Nope, she wasn't interested in any part of him. But that wavy black hair was a terrible temptation. She could almost imagine how soft it would feel running through her fingers. Giving herself a mental shake, she picked up her knife and fork and went to work on cutting her steak.

Jesse sat quietly watching the babe. He had to have that woman. Her face gave her thoughts away. She could have been listening to KILI radio, or watching a movie on a wide screen TV for all the attention he wasn't getting. She wouldn't bother to spit on him, didn't need him, and from the way she stabbed at her steak she was perfectly capable of cutting his guts out with a dull knife. She reminded him of someone else.

It came to him so fast, the memory slammed into his brain with stunning clarity. He blinked and consciously closed his mouth which had dropped slightly open. His old man wasn't crazy. She was back. Blue was living, breathing, and eating dinner in Georgina's diner. He could wrap his fingers around her throat and end her life now, before she could get away.

He started to get up, but stopped as quickly as he'd started. He had to get a grip on his temper and his racing heart. This woman was too young to be the bitch who'd deserted Zach. She was no way the same woman. This one looked to be in her late twenties, the real Blue would have been pushing fifty, closer to Zach's age.

He grabbed the glass of water that had materialized on the table along with a menu and took a gulp. The condensation on the outside of the glass oozed around his fingers and cooled his anger. The cold water trickled down his throat and eased the constricted band around his heart and slowly cleared his mind.

He had to think. Think back on everything he could remember about Blue. What she looked like, where she lived in Texas. Did she have children? He wasn't sure. He'd concentrated so long on hating her, he'd forgotten the details.

Damn, he was more like his dad than he wanted to admit. Everything people said about them was true. He was panting after a woman who couldn't even be bothered to look at him. He drank too much, slept with any willing female he could, and didn't work more than he had to. He was no good, same as Zach. He'd only been good for one thing, and like Zach he was losing that too. Well, almost. At the moment something was definitely stirring between his legs.

Fine time for that to make an appearance. Last night he couldn't get a rise out of it. It was definitely the babe. She could give a dead man a hard on. The challenge in her eyes was enough to make him hard. His balls tightened at the thought of having her under him. He was in worse shape than he'd figured. There had to be a way to get that woman. His mental ramblings were interrupted by the waitress.

"What can I get you, High Horse?"

The babe over there would be fine. Oh, she'd be so fine.

He turned his face toward the waitress. He recognized her voice. "Burger, fries and coffee," came out of his mouth automatically. He knew how much that would cost and he had the money to cover it.

"I'll be at the Acres later if you want to come by for a drink." She smiled invitingly at him.

"Yeah, sure." He laid his later-babe smile on her. He'd been there and done that.

There might have been a little more energy in her step as she walked away to turn in his order. It was hard to tell, but maybe. His lips formed an obligatory grin as his head turned back to his target of the evening.

The next instant he was nose to nose with the babe. His eyes met her icy stare. That alone would have made a weaker man pee his pants. His hard-on got harder. His blood got hotter and his breaths came faster. The devil had blue eyes and a steak knife in her fist.

The man reflected in those blue eyes looked tired and worn out. For a moment Jesse didn't recognize himself. What the hell had happened to him?

Her lips moved. "She called you High Horse. I'm looking for Zachary High Horse. Do you know him?"

Jesse sucked in a deep breath. He needed air. His eyes darted around the room in front of him and he caught the curious looks of the other patrons staring in his direction and knew not one person there would lift a finger to help him. She could cut him up like a Thanksgiving turkey and nobody would say a word. They'd throw what was left of him in the dumpster and shut the lid. He hated every last one of them, too. That made them even.

"I'm Jesse." The less said the better.

"You're his son."

It wasn't a question. It was a fact and she knew it. He could tell by the tone of her voice that she knew more than that. He was one piece of a bigger picture. The knife remained pointed in his direction. It didn't waiver. She wasn't scared. Her hand didn't shake. She'd cut him without hesitation. He knew it as well as he knew his own name.

"Yeah, that's me. What do you want?"

"I'm Silki Warfield, Mariah Blue's niece and I've come for Zachary. Where is he?" She leaned closer and inhaled. Like a hunter she could smelled the fear, hate, anger, a combination of all three that rolled off of him and he couldn't stop it. He'd tell her what she wanted to know. Fear was good. Hate was mutual and anger was a given.

Jesse shrugged. "He's not here."

The knife point pressed against the hollow of this throat.

"Wrong answer," she hissed. "Now, try again."

The steak knife was old and dull, but deadly in her hands. She wasn't afraid to use it.

"I put him in the hospital at Pine Ridge this morning. He's locked up with the DTs."

"Get up." She pulled the knife back out of his reach.

He knew the drill. She wasn't taking any chances on him grabbing it as he stood up. He was a tall man with arms that could easily reach across the table.

He asked, "Where are we going?"

"You're going to have a seat at my table. We're going to eat dinner, and then we're going to my motel room. I'm going to give you what you've been after. You're going to be my guest till morning. Then we're going to go see Zachary."

"Okay." Jesse got up slowly. He stepped toward her table as she stepped back. He was going to spend the night with her. Not exactly the ideal circumstance he'd hoped for but it could work. He pulled out the chair opposite hers and lowered himself onto the seat. She picked up her fork and went back to eating. Her food looked cold but that didn't stop her from shoveling it in.

"Why do you want to find Zach? He's an old man. He hasn't done anything but drink and tell stories. He can't hurt anyone."

Silki moved so fast Jesse never saw her coming. He felt her hands grab the front of his shirt, felt her fingers graze his chest. He'd been wanting to get close to her but this wasn't exactly how he'd pictured it.

Her arm muscles flexed as she held him firmly in place. He reasoned she had to be strong to handle the bike she rode. There was no getting away from her unless he dragged her across the table. Even then, she wouldn't let go and when her feet hit the floor, she'd take him down. He'd be going where she said, when she said. And sure, if he got the chance, he could try to fight it out with her, but there was something in the way she moved that warned him that wasn't a good idea. She'd had training, some combination of martial arts. He had brute force. It could get ugly but he had a better idea.

He'd never in his adult life been so close to a white woman, espe-

42

cially not a beautiful one. He couldn't help but inhale her scent. It would stick in his brain for a hundred years. It was different from anything he'd ever smelled. She was hot, sweet, and something enticing. It made his brain beg his mouth to taste her. He could feel his heart pounding in his throat. His nostrils flared, his breaths quickened supplying oxygen to every male molecule in him, and there wasn't a damn thing he could do about it. He watched her lips move, and his ears barely registered the sounds.

"You don't know the first thing about hurt." Each word ground out slowly, distinctly. "But I'm going to teach him and you all about pain. Years and years of it."

He choked out, "I don't know what you're talking about."

"I've read her journals, and I've had thirteen-hundred miles to feel the pain Zachary caused my aunt. It's a part of me now."

Silki let go, settled back down onto her chair, and Jesse settled back against his. He didn't scare easy but there was something in her words that struck a chord deep down inside. They could run but she'd find them. She would be relentless. Nobody had that kind of commitment to anything anymore.

The waitress slid his plate onto the table in front of him and plunked his coffee down sloshing it over the rim before clomping off.

He watched the emotions play across Silki's face, and instinctively knew he was not going to change her mind. He ate his hamburger and contemplated the possibility he might be the sickest bastard on the face of the planet, but she turned him on like nobody ever had. She could cut him, beat him, hurt him, and he'd still be hard for her.

She didn't know it, but she didn't need a weapon to make him go with her. He'd go anywhere she wanted if it meant he could be near her a little longer. With enough time he'd change her mind. He'd get her into bed and everything would work out fine. He'd have the babe all to himself. He exhaled a silent breath. Everyone was right. He was the same as his father. He wanted what he couldn't have.

CHAPTER SEVEN

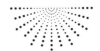

OUTSIDE, the evening brought a chill wind to the prairie and the nearly deserted streets of Martin. Silki rubbed her arms and wished she had her jacket with her. It wasn't far to the motel, and she'd ridden in worse weather. This wouldn't kill her. High Horse riding behind her was another story, but he was her ticket to finding Zachary.

She'd studied him carefully over her cold steak. Men weren't supposed to be beautiful. But that was the only way to describe him. No wonder every female in this half-dead town wanted him for a bed partner. Everyone but her. She didn't want any part of him.

Unfortunately, she needed him, at least temporarily. However long it took to get to Zachary. After that, Jesse could fall off the face of the earth and it wouldn't bother her.

Grabbing the hand grip of the old Harley, she swung her leg over the seat and settled down for the ride. She looked over at Jesse. He was checking out the street in both directions. It probably wouldn't do any good but she warned him anyway.

"If you're thinking of running, forget it. This bike can last longer than you can. I'll run you till you drop, and then I'll cut your balls off. Are we clear?"

He grumbled, "Right. Got it."

Silki pulled her fringed, black leather gloves out of her back pocket, slid them on, adjusted the fit and started the bike. She pulled it out onto the street, stopped, looked at Jesse and said, "Get on."

～

Two simple words that caused a riot in his head. This was what he'd been waiting for, praying for. Hell yes, he'd get on. Get on the bike, get on her, ride them both as far as they'd take him. If a man had to be taken hostage, this was the way to go.

He wasn't interested in running. He'd checked out the street to see who was watching. Who would be spreading the news that he'd left the diner with the biker babe? He spotted a couple of teens wandering the street checking out the store windows. They didn't bother to look his way. The people inside the diner would be flapping their dentures telling anyone who would listen about what they'd seen and heard.

By the time breakfast was over tomorrow morning, he'd be the subject of every filthy speculation and dirty joke they could come up with. He'd been there before.

"You sure you want me behind you? No telling what I might do." He grinned. "I might put my hands on you. You might even like it."

～

Silki knew the game he was playing. This was where she was supposed to deny it all. Too bad, she wasn't playing. She had two choices. She could tie him behind the bike and drag his worthless ass to the motel, or she could play along for as long as it took to get him in her room and hog tie him with a gag in his smart mouth. Smart, sexy as sin, made to be kissed mouth. Her jaw clamped tight. Her teeth were going to crack if she didn't back off. There was no way she could relax with Jesse looking at her like he would eat her alive if he had the chance.

The man was a menace to every woman, young or old, living or dead. Any kind of humane feelings she might have been thinking fled instantly. Talk about a menace, Zachary was responsible for years of misery and pain. She would not feel sympathy for him or his son.

Standing before her was her ticket to connecting with Zachary and finding out what had happened to Mariah. She wasn't going to let Jesse distract her with his phony lines of bullshit. Assault, torture, and kidnapping weren't beyond her. They would have been one month ago but not anymore. Grandpa Warfield, her dad, and Charley the Weasel had fixed that. She was the new, improved, daring Silki Warfield, Mariah's niece, and she would have answers.

There was nothing left to say except, "Get on and hang on. You're going to like it fine, but don't plan on getting used to it. It'll be over before you know it, and I promise not to hurt you too much." She grinned at Jesse the way a wolf might grin at its supper, feral and lethal.

It worked. She watched his eyes widen and his throat work as he swallowed hard. The game was getting interesting. Who would have thought little Silki could make a big, bad High Horse shake in his worn-out boots? For added emphasis she revved the engine then let it go back to its rhythmic pulsing four-stroke beat.

Silki watched the man's emotions play out across his face. He could never play poker or run a bluff successfully. He'd be useless in a cut-throat business. He'd never be able to convincingly shake hands and smile warmly at his intended victims right before stabbing them in the back and taking their money the way Charley had. No, this guy would glare, snarl, and make blunt statements. He'd never make a businessman.

Stepping off the curb, Jesse sauntered toward Silki. His long easy strides reached her quickly. He stopped within inches of her. So close, she could smell him, feel the heat radiating from his body. He was hot. Way too hot for someone like her to handle. She had absolutely no experience with a man like Jesse High Horse. But he didn't know that.

She braced herself as he rested one hand on her shoulder and swung his leg over the bike. She waited for him to settle behind her. She'd have bet her last dollar he was dawdling on purpose. She all but jumped over the tank when he clamped his hands on her waist.

There was a riot going on inside of her. She wasn't sure where it came from or what it meant, but it started with Jesse touching her. Nobody had the right to have hands that big or that strong. He could break her neck using only one of them. And she'd thought she was in control. Yeah, sure. Not in this century. Well, too late now. She'd called the shots and she'd have to live with the results. If he strangled her, the bike would go down taking them with it. Unless he had a death wish, she was safe for the time being.

$\sim$

Now, he wanted to run. He could hate himself later for going with her, or he could hate himself now for not getting on the bike, but sooner or later he'd hate himself. He wasn't man enough for her, and he was too much of a man not to try to get her. Get her any way he could, whatever he had to do or say to make it happen.

What came out of his mouth was, "I'm all yours, babe. Ride me as far as I can take you." He pulled her back, fitting her tightly between his thighs. "I can take it. Try me." He was hard and getting harder. He couldn't remember a time when his jeans had felt this uncomfortable. He wanted to wriggle into a more comfortable position, if there was one, but right then the Harley rumbled under him and she moved between his legs as she set them in motion. "I'm strong. I can give it to you really good."

"I can hardly wait," Silki grumbled under her breath.

In the few short minutes it took to get to the motel, Jesse felt his body go through any number of changes. He was hard and aching. His heart raced, and his mind scrambled through the possible outcomes when they got to the motel. Not in his wildest dreams had he imagined being taken by the biker babe. It was supposed to be on his terms not hers.

Silki was related to Zach's Mariah Blue and that made her dangerous and way out of his league. If he didn't want to end up like Zach, he needed to get away from her. The sooner better. He still owed Mariah Blue a world of hurt, but he didn't plan on sacrificing himself to do it. No, he was going to come out on top for a change, and the Warfields were going to lose. He had to think about this, make sure he was the one calling the shots.

The bike rumbled into the motel parking lot bouncing him over the driveway and rubbing his very aroused cock against her behind. He thought he just might die if he didn't get away from her in the next five minutes. The hell of it was, he thought he might die if he didn't throw her down and bury himself deep inside of her. Now wouldn't be soon enough.

Silki cut the engine and put the kickstand down. Studying her hands as she pulled off her gloves, she growled, "Get off."

"You only have to tell me where and when. I'll get off on you any way you say, babe." Jesse smiled and got off the bike.

How many times had he said those words? How many times had they been noise to fill up the emptiness? The one time he meant them, they didn't count. They would never count with her.

His lines were old, over worked and hardly worth bothering with. Straight out of some very low budget skin flick, they were laughable. Did he really think it was a turn on? It didn't matter to her one way or the other. As long as he went along peacefully, he could practice his pathetic come-ons all he wanted.

"Let's get one thing straight. This is for one night and one night only. Tomorrow you're getting me in to see Zachary and then we're done."

"Yeah, no problem. I've got all night to make it the best you've ever had." He wore the same smug smile she'd seen on him at the diner and in the parking lot. He had that smirk down pat.

She was out of breath and not from her speech. The man made her short of breath simply by being alive. Maybe it was some sort of Native American pheromone. The same thing had happened to Mariah when Zachary had touched her. It made Silki angry thinking about it. Mariah might have fallen for that nonsense, but she knew better. She knew a trap when she saw one, and Jesse High Horse was the worst kind of trap a girl could fall into.

Silki unclenched her jaw and studied her shaking hands. "I heard my ex-husband whispering those same sorts of sorry lines to his pathetic secretary on his cell phone. Keep your lousy pick-up lines to yourself. Charley the Weasel is history and I'm not interested in your prairie dog version."

She grabbed the hand grips to keep from grabbing Jesse's neck and squeezing the lying, cheating breath out of him. Getting off the bike that had been Mariah's, Silki turned to face Jesse.

His grin faltered. "We don't have to talk. I can still give it to ya real good. The best you've ever had."

She huffed, "That's it!" She slapped her gloves against her palm and snarled, "I've listened to your sorry lines of bull-crap long enough. Get this through your thick skull. I am not interested in what's in your pants. I'm sure the ladies here love it, but I know what you are. You're wasted, used up, worn out, good for nothing but catching a case of the clap. I don't want it, or you."

His smile was a little off, not quite so cocky. She'd hit him below the belt. Even if she wasn't sorry, she should apologize. A few short months ago she would have, but that was then. She wasn't that timid, placating person anymore and never would be again. She'd lost that part of herself somewhere in Kansas and it wasn't coming back. Miss Civilized Manners was gone for good, scattered in broken pieces along the road from Texas.

She tipped her head toward the building and she said, "The back door is down there."

"No problem. I've been in and out of that door plenty. I'm a real good back-door-man. The housekeepers really like to relax on their breaks." A lazy grin spread slowly across his lips. "Know what I mean?"

"Yeah, you're a real hot date."

They walked silently side by side toward the back entrance. His steps slowed and faltered. As she opened the door he came to a dead stop, turned and ran.

Silki made a grab for him and only caught a handful of air. He was all but gone, and she'd never catch him on foot. She eyed the bike but it was too far away to do her any good. By the time she got to it, got it started and turned around he'd be half-way to Rapid City or at least lost down some slimy alley with the rest of the rats. Damn!

She shouted, "I'll hunt you down. See if I don't!"

Jesse disappeared around the corner of the motel.

What would Mariah do? That was anybody's guess, but Silki was pretty sure she wouldn't be standing at the back door of a modest motel watching her captive get away. Silki trudged up the back stairs contemplating her mistakes. She'd underestimated Jesse. Mariah would have cut his balls off back at the diner and cooked them on the grill for dinner. There wouldn't have been any running away. The thought sent a shiver down her spine.

She couldn't help but think that it was probably for the best that Jesse had bolted. She locked her door and took a hard look around. The room was too small for him and her. Even with him tied up, she wouldn't have been safe. He had something, male hormone scent or secret aphrodisiac cologne that sent her heart racing and her insides fluttering. Not good, not good at all. He was a bad man who had inherited defective DNA from a detestable man. Zachary was the worst kind of man. He was a coward. She'd read about that the night before. Each journal entry added another layer to the saddest story ever written.

Silki sat down on the edge of her bed and studied the worn gold carpet. How many feet had walked on it? How many people had sat there and wondered what to do with the rest of their lives? Who else had wondered what they were doing here at the crossroads of their lives and wondering where they should go next? She had to find Zachary. She had to find Mariah. She had to get a life. She had to forget she'd ever seen Jesse.

She flopped onto her back and checked out the ceiling. Standard commercial white with only one crack in it. That wasn't so bad. There was at least one crack in everybody's plan. Jesse was the crack in hers. She would have to work around him. Cracks in plans, cracks in lives, cracks in doors. Yeah, that was it. She needed to get her foot in the door at the hospital.

How to get in to see a patient with DT's became the main focus of her thoughts. There had to be a way. They weren't prisoners, there had to be a visitor's policy or something. Being a government hospital, they probably had rules out the wazoo, but there was always a way. She only had to find it and use it. She'd get in and then what? She couldn't kill Zachary in front of witnesses. She couldn't beat the whereabouts of Mariah out of him with doctors and nurses watching. Twisting his arms off would probably get attention she'd rather not have. And there was no way to get a weapon inside, so she couldn't slice and dice him if he refused to talk. No, this situation called for finesse.

Silki lifted her leg and wiggled her foot. The steel-toed boots she wore to protect her from the highway were going to come in handy. A girl had to make good use of all her resources. Her foot hit the floor with a *thunk*. Yep, safety first.

He hadn't meant to run but damn, the woman scared the hell out of him. Confident she wouldn't find him in this back-street bar, Jesse gulped down his glass of cheap whiskey, rolled his shoulders and tried to relax. Beer wasn't strong enough to clear the scent of her out of his head. It was definitely a hard booze kind of night. He waved at the bartender to bring him a refill. He had money sitting in front of him on the bar, and as long as it lasted the whiskey would keep coming.

He glanced at his wrist to check the time, but his watch and the beaded band were gone. It was a habit he'd have to get over. He was drinking his watch. He stared at his reflection in the hazy mirror hanging behind the bar. His face was hard, his eyes dark and lifeless. What kind of man had he become? What would he do to survive? Deep inside something protested at the thought of what he might sell next to buy another night of forgetfulness. He needed to forget her, forget the empty promises of Mariah Blue, forget his dad, and forget who and what he'd become over the years.

How much would it cost to forget he'd been to prison, forget that he'd gotten a degree from Black Hills State University and couldn't get a job in his field? Did they make that much whiskey? Could he sell his soul for enough money to buy it? But that brought up the subject of a soul that he didn't have, and didn't want. Souls were for white people; he had the spirits and his were missing in action at the moment. They were still around someplace but he didn't know where they'd gone off to. But they damn sure weren't sitting there with him.

He glared at the golden-tan liquid filling the whiskey tumbler the bartender placed in front of him. It held empty promises, unfulfilled dreams, pain relief, and temporary oblivion. It was within reach. His head would ache tomorrow, his stomach would wretch, and his eyes would burn, but tonight he would be free.

His hand wrapped around the glass; it would have to be his lover for the night. The one he wanted wouldn't have him on his best day or her worst, so this would have to do. He lifted the glass and took a sip. He meant to savor the flavor, let it slowly slide down his throat but it stuck and it was all he could do not to choke.

"Hey Jesse, I haven't seen you in a while. How've you been?"

He turned toward the familiar sound. His eyes met the voice's owner. She was looking at him with hungry eyes. The kind that told him he could do anything he wanted to her and she'd like it. They were deep brown pools set in an oval face that hadn't seen too many hard years yet. She still had a pretty smile and all her front teeth. The red lipstick was an invitation and he sure wasn't going to get a better one any time soon.

"Hey, yourself. How've you been?"

She licked her lower lip and bit it gently. "I've been okay." She sidled closer. "You looking for some company tonight?"

He raised his glass and took a leisurely swallow. This time the liquor went down easy. "No, I'm good."

He was tired of being used.

CHAPTER EIGHT

SILKI RESTED her arms on the worn countertop. The nurses were busy, all two of them. The place was a mad house, literally and figuratively. The phones were ringing, call lights were buzzing, and there wasn't a clerk anywhere in sight. She waited impatiently until one of the nurses made eye contact with her.

At last, she had somebody's attention however fleeting it might be. While waiting for the woman to get off the phone she took in the sights. Sad pale-green paint and old worn-out tile covered the walls in the old style, paint on the top half and tile on the bottom. There were only a few windows and a set of grey metal doors next to the nurse's station that Attila the Hun couldn't get through. Maybe it was a prison after all.

Her thoughts were interrupted by a strained voice asking, "Can I help you?"

The sound made her jump. Her mind had been wandering down the corridors. She focused her attention on the nurse in front of her, temporarily blocking out the noises around her. Hopeless noises she wasn't prepared to dwell on or identify.

"I'd like to see my stepfather, Zachary High Horse."

The nurse wasn't good at hiding her feelings. Surprise was replaced by suspicion. There was no mistaking the doubt that was written clearly in the lines on her face and the stubborn set of her jaw. Too many years of patients trying to manipulate her into giving them what they wanted and weren't supposed to have. Too many years of working in the system.

"Zachary High Horse is your stepfather?" The note of inquiry was punctuated with a certain amount of disbelief. "The record only shows he has a son to contact."

"Jesse is Zachary's son, but I'm his stepdaughter. He was married to my mom for a couple of years, but things didn't work out." It could have almost been near to the truth, sort of. "He's the only dad I've ever had." That was a little closer to the truth if you considered the Grand Canyon a tiny ditch. "You can ask him if he wants to see me. My name is Mariah."

Silki could almost see the wheels turning in the nurse's head. Nothing got past nurse Ratchet or Hatchet, whatever her name was. Her name badge was upside down making in unreadable. They were past busy and time was the one thing they didn't have enough of. With a little luck there wasn't time to run down the hall to ask Zachary if he wanted to see her.

She had come a long way to see him. It took all she had to sound sincere and sympathetic at the same time. Convincing the woman to press the door release was going to be the real trick. If she pulled it off, maybe she'd go to Hollywood and try her luck in the movies.

"I've been so worried about him. He hasn't been eating right, and his drinking has gotten worse. He really tried to do right by me and Mom. I hate to think of him being here and thinking I don't care because I didn't come when he needed me." Silki gave a little sigh. "Life has been so hard for him."

"Well, the chart doesn't say he can't have visitors, so I guess it's okay as long as you don't upset him." With a tilt of her head toward the grey doors, she added, "Go over there and I'll buzz you in. He's down the hall in Ward C."

"Thank you." Silki moved toward the cold metal doors. "I know he'll feel better knowing somebody still cares about him."

The buzzer sounded and she pushed on the door. It opened smoothly and with less effort than she'd expected. She was in. Now, to find Zach and get back out.

The third door on the right was Ward C. Six beds were lined up along the sickly green walls with pathetically drooping privacy curtains in a slightly darker shade of depressing green hanging from a water-stained ceiling. It was exactly what depressed people needed. Whoever had invented this nightmare should have had to spend the night there. It wasn't too late to turn around and run, but Zachary was in there, so no running away was going to happen.

Not behind curtain number one, that bed was empty. Not behind curtain number two, that man was maybe thirty years old, too young. Not behind curtain number three, he was missing both legs from the knees down. Number four was empty, but number five was a good bet from the looks of him.

There was something familiar about the guy. "Zachary? Zachary, wake up. I need to talk to you."

The man moaned and his eyes fluttered open and were instantly filled with trepidation.

Hallelujah! She'd found him. "We have to talk." Silki stepped closer after pulling the curtain closed. "Don't be afraid. I won't hurt you."

He was pathetic, no human being should look so shrunken, so defeated. Road kill had more life in it than Zachary High Horse.

She whispered, "What happened to you?"

"You did. You happened to me." A voice paper thin and dry as the desert wind whispered back. "I've been waiting. I knew you'd come back someday. You promised."

Oh, whoa, something was really wrong with this picture. She hadn't promised him anything. She'd barely found him. But that voice, she'd heard it before, and the words were familiar.

Have mercy, it was the man from the alley. She'd had him in her hands and not known it. That didn't change anything, she had him now, alcohol-soaked brain and all.

She asked, "Do you recognize me?" He'd been so drunk it didn't make sense that he'd recognize anyone or anything, but then who could tell what a drunk would remember.

"I'd know you anywhere. My heart knows yours, that never changes. You look like you did the day we met. It was so long ago, high in the mountains, you were so beautiful standing in the sunshine."

His eyes lost focus and Silki knew he was visiting some faraway place in the mountains of his past. She needed him in the here and now.

Closing the short distance between them, she slipped her hip onto the side of his bed. She leaned in close and whispered, "Tell me what you remember. How do you know me?" Her eyes darted over his features looking for some kind of reaction.

"So beautiful, so strong, you ran ahead of me. I had to follow you, had to catch you. You said you'd always be mine. You gave me your heart. I still have it. I keep it in my medicine bag. It's safe there." Zach patted his front pocket. "I never let you go, like I promised."

Great. What could she say to that? What would Mariah say? His eyes were so sad. He'd hung on till all hope was gone, and then kept hanging on because he had promised. Hopelessness was all he had and she was there to make him relive it. It was going to hurt but he might have a clue where to look for Mariah.

"Zachary, you've got to hang on to the memories. We can still make it. First, we've got to get you out of here. You've got to be strong to do that. Will you get strong for me?"

She took Zachary's hand in both of hers. It was large and boney. The once firm skin was darker than hers, wrinkled and weathered. He was more human than she'd imagined. He wasn't the monster she'd come for. He was a desperately broken man.

Zach studied the face above him while his hand touched living flesh. Everything was going to be all right. The waiting was over. She wasn't a ghost. His eyes widened as he sucked in a breath. His heart pounded in his chest trying to get out. His mouth opened but there was too much to say and he closed it again and swallowed hard. He looked from where their hands met to her eyes. It was then he knew she was real, and it was time to go.

He could start living again, his heart could feel something besides emptiness, pain and sorrow. This time he would be the kind of man he'd always meant to be and never had the strength to be. Yes, he would be strong this time.

The alternative was death, because he couldn't go on the way he was. His love for Mariah would finally surrender to the constant regrets, and leave him empty and alone. The blue heart in his medicine bag would turn into a cold stone and he'd have nothing left to hold on to.

Silki said, "I'll come back every day to see you and make sure you're getting better. Don't leave without me." She gripped his hand and gave it a small reassuring shake. "I'm going to take you with me when you're ready." She stood up and walked away.

A cold chill passed through Zach and he knew death was waiting for him. He lost track of time and the next few days passed in a blur of eating, sleeping, choking down the medicine that would keep the delirium and tremors at bay, and waiting. Waiting for Mariah to come back and take him away from the hospital, away from loneliness. Nothing could take away the knowledge that he'd never been the man she needed him to be. And yet she kept coming back to him. No matter how many times he'd let her down, she'd still loved him.

This was his last chance; he could feel it. He'd go wherever she wanted to take him, no more stalling, no more waiting for the right time.

Jesse wasn't a little boy anymore. He was a man, an irresponsible clown most of the time but he could take care of himself. Zachary stared at the water stain on the ceiling above his bed and wondered where the rain was. Wondered why it didn't come and wash away his sadness? It cleansed the earth, why couldn't it take away the ache in his heart, the darkness that filled his days, the anguish that held him prisoner at night?

Every day he listened for her footsteps coming down the hall. And every day she'd come, silently appearing at his bedside. Was he crazy to listen for a ghost, and yet not a ghost exactly? He had touched her. Her hand had been warm and she had smelled like the outdoors, the scent of prairie grass carried on the wind. It was the smell of freedom. He rolled to his side, closed his eyes, and waited.

CHAPTER NINE

Silki rolled down the two-lane highway toward the Pine Ridge Reservation. Today was the day she was going to take Zachary out of the ancient brick building they called a hospital. She'd seen the new one being built close by. Something modern was bound to look better and might not be so depressing.

Five days was all they would keep Zachary and the time was up. The alcohol was physically out of his system and he was over the worst of it. Maybe as far as they were concerned, but from where she sat on Mariah's Harley the worst was yet to come. Zachary didn't know it, but she was fixing to take him on the ride of his life. He might want a drink but he wasn't going to get one where they were going.

Mariah was out there somewhere and they were going to find her.

She revved on the throttle and sent the Harley Heritage Classic streaking down the grey ribbon of road a million miles from nowhere. She and Zachary had a long overdue date.

The undulating hills and empty pastures echoed the solitary nature of existence on the northern plains. Survival was for those who could make it on their own. She'd make it. She had to. Not only was she not going to quit, she'd go down fighting if it came to that. She wasn't going to roll over and play dead for anybody ever again.

The outskirts of Pine Ridge Village came into view. Low, dusty, run down, even the store signs were covered with a layer of summer dust that could choke a horse. Didn't it ever rain?

A few minutes later she was facing the same tired nurse she'd faced every day for the last week. "Hi! The doctor said I could take Zachary home today."

~

Jesse's smile disappeared. His eyes narrowed to slits and he glared at the cantankerous woman in a nurse's uniform. Everything about her dared him to challenge her. As far as he was concerned, she was out of her mind! "What do you mean, he's gone? Where the hell would he go?"

He watched her plant her hands on her hips as she puffed up to answer him. He'd challenged her and she was getting ready to put him in his place. Fine, she could go ahead and try.

"Your stepsister came and got him this morning. See." She stabbed a finger at the chart sitting on the counter, pointing to a signature. "Right there. She signed him out. If you'd bothered to come visit him you might have run into her, or he might have told you she was here checking on him." She snatched the chart back and held it against her ample bosom like it was a precious treasure.

Jesse eyed the chart and the soft flesh it was mashed against. A man could suffocate. Raising his eyes, he inhaled a deep breath and was thankful for the air.

"I don't have a stepsister." Let her figure that one out.

For a flash of a second her eyes widened then narrowed suspiciously. He had her attention, but it wasn't in a good way. Once again nobody believed him. He was the liar, the bad guy.

"It doesn't really matter," she smiled triumphantly. "Any adult can sign him out when his commitment is up. And it's up today. He wanted to go with her."

Jesse wanted to wipe the self-satisfied, superior look off her face but she had him. He hadn't been to visit Zach. He didn't have a ride, and he'd seen his old man in every condition a human being could be in and still be breathing. He'd enjoyed the rest from worrying about where Zach was and what was happening to him. Detoxing wasn't a pretty sight. Compared to Silki, neither was the nurse in front of him. If he never laid eyes on her or this place again it would be too soon.

He rubbed the back of his neck and grumbled, "I don't suppose you have any idea where they were going?"

Wherever it was, it wasn't good, but nobody cared. Even he didn't care as much as he should. It wasn't like Silki was going to kill Zach. At least not until she got what she wanted from him, and probably not even then.

"No," she paused, then added, "he said he'd take her as far as she wanted to go. I thought that was strange since he didn't have a car."

Jesse felt like he'd been poleaxed. His mind went fuzzy and he couldn't quite focus on the nurse in front of him. How long had it been since he'd heard those exact same words said to a woman who'd gone off and deserted him and Zach? He was reliving a nightmare without end. If he wasn't careful, they'd be sticking him in one of their padded cells. Then he'd be seeing the grumpy, well-endowed nurse every day. He shuddered at the thought. He'd rather be dead.

He didn't remember leaving the hospital or the walk to White Clay, but the bar stool under his butt felt right. At last, he was grounded to something familiar. The cold beer in his hand helped stop the trembling in his gut. There could be some mistake. Zach might have been confused and running off at the mouth.

The cool, dark interior of the bar soothed him with its comfortable familiarity. He needed the darkness to hide from the memories; the quiet to sort out the details that had grown jumbled and dim over the years.

Lost in his thoughts, he barely acknowledged the man who ambled up and perched on the next stool. He looked vaguely familiar.

The low voice reached his ears. "Hey Jesse, it's been a while. I wasn't sure it was you. The light in here gets worse every time another light bulb burns out."

"Yeah, it does. I'd forgotten how dark this place is." He still couldn't place the face or put a name to it.

"I think the sun was playing a trick on me. I thought I saw Zach on the back of a Harley holding on to a broad with a great set of tits. Man,

how'd he get so lucky? He always did have a thing for white women."
The sly chuckle that followed was a universal male noise, part envy,
part ridicule.

Jesse commented, "If you liked the front, you should see her from
the back. It doesn't matter what color it comes in. That's one fine
piece." Jesse took a long swallow letting the cold beer flow over his
overheated innards. "Didn't see which way they were going, did you?"

"Yeah, highway towards Martin. Hey, man, you ready for another
round?"

"Yeah." Jesse fished a few crumpled bills out of his pocket and
threw them on the bar.

She'd found Zach. Not only found him, but had gotten him out of
the hospital and onto her motorcycle. His old man must still be out of
it. There was no telling what she'd told him, or what he might believe.
Zach had been seeing ghosts a few days earlier. Now he was headed
down the highway with the biker babe of Jesse's dreams.

He lost himself in the next round of whiskey with a beer chaser.

A few hours later Jesse climbed out of a rez-ride on the side of the
highway in Martin. He'd caught a ride to town, but that was as far as
they were taking him. Getting to the apartment was his problem. He'd
have to walk the rest of the way, no small feat in his condition. It
wasn't a case of one too many beers. It was way too many beers.

He stumbled on Third Avenue's uneven ground and fell on his
hands and knees in the road ditch. The words, "just like your father,"
echoed around in his head. He groaned, pushed to his feet and stumbled a little closer to the apartment that was his destination, his shelter
from the night. It wasn't his home. He'd never had a home and wasn't
likely to ever have one.

Mariah had promised him and Zach a good home and then she'd
vanished without a trace. Now it looked like some version of her was
back and he wasn't falling for that lie again. The toe of his boot caught
on a gnarled tree root and sent him sprawling face down in the dust.

Grown men never cried, so the water running down his face
making tiny wet spots in the dirt, had to be rain drops, so many rain
drops on a dry soulless night. Jesse couldn't bring himself to stand up.
After struggling to his knees, he sat back on his heels and let the

anguish of his wasted life force its way out of his heart, up through his throat and escape into the night. He knelt there in the dark letting the hurt pour out. Letting mother earth absorb his pain, frustration, and the ugliness that had been his life. He sent a prayer into the night sky.

"Please, help me be a better man, let me find the strength to make something of my life." And finally, he whispered, "Don't let me die this way."

CHAPTER TEN

SILKI TOOK Zachary where they wouldn't be disturbed. It was a long ride to the Badlands. They set up a primitive camp and settled in under a clear northern sky. The stars twinkled brightly, almost merrily in the heavens. Their fire crackled softly sending a few wayward sparks dancing on the lazy evening breeze. Silki watched them spiral up and wink out. Across from her, Zachary sat cross-legged, staring into the glowing coals. It was a good night for healing. It was a good night for praying.

Softly spoken words drifted on the night. He said, "I knew you weren't her when I touched you. But I wanted to believe. I wanted her to come for me. She promised."

It was then that Silki knew she was hearing the sound of a heart breaking. She wasn't ready for this. She'd never been heartbroken, not like Zachary.

She'd been angry, disappointed, frustrated, cheated on, and lied to, but nothing had ever come close to the kind of pain she saw in Zachary. How could Mariah have done this to him? There wasn't much left of him, but over the past few days she'd seen glimpses of the man Mariah had described in her journals. They were only thin shadows now, but once he'd really been something. Now, she had to look hard to find it, but the remnants were there, the tattered remains of a love too strong to die.

"You named her Mariah Blue-eyes. I read all about how you two met in the Black Hills, how you fell in love. All she ever wanted was to be with you. She closed up the Ruins and went to get you after grandpa and grandma died. She never came back. You have to help me." Silki took a deep breath, leaned toward the fire wrapping her arms around her drawn up knees. "Tell me what happened?"

She had to give Zachary's mind time to drift back through the fog of time and misery.

He said, "I want to help. I'd like to find my beautiful Blue and ask her why she deserted me when we were finally going to be together. I want to understand what I did wrong."

Silki shifted her weight, her heels digging small ruts in the sandy soil. He was an old man. Maybe not so much in years but in experience and despair. The night was still young, and out in the Badlands the ghosts wandered freely. They would come and somehow Zachary would remember. She had to wait.

His voice came gently at first. She had to strain to hear it over a distant wail carried on the breeze.

"I was sitting at the bar drinking."

His eyes took on a lost look, empty, they reminded Silki of the windows in the Ruins. No light to guide a wandering spirit, no sign of life, only darkness. His soul, his spirit was lost. This might be his last chance to come home. It was hers. She'd figured that out on the road.

"I looked up and Blue was standing there in front of me. I thought she was a dream. I used to dream about her. She said, 'It's time to go. I've done this to you, but I'm going to fix it. We're never going to be apart again.' She held her hand out to me and I took it. I had a hard time getting on my feet. I had to use her strength to pull myself up. She stood there until I was standing. Then she put her arms around me and held me like she'd never let me go." He looked across the fire at Silki. "I knew she'd come back. We were going to make it out of here together this time."

Silki waited for Zachary to go on. When he didn't speak, she gave in and asked, "So, you left the bar with her. Did you go to your place, or did she take you to a motel?"

Zach looked past Silki off into the distance. "She's out there. She's waiting for me to come to her." He buried his head in his hands and doubled over. Rocking back and forth he sobbed, "I should have gone out looking for her. She wouldn't have gone off and left me. I knew it, but I didn't want to look like a bigger fool than I already was."

He kept rocking and Silki watched his body shake, wracked with the sorrow of losing his love and his hope. It was all catching up to him and there wasn't a drop of booze within a hundred miles to dull the hurt. He was going to have to cry it out. *Patience old girl, some things take time.*

Silkie checked behind her. She could have sworn she'd heard Mariah whispering in her ear.

When his shoulders quit shaking and his breathing got a little easier, she nudged him along. She needed the rest of the story, some-place to start looking.

"Zachary, where was she going the last time you saw her?"

The breeze had been steadily increasing. It was strong enough to kick up the dust around their campsite. Not a lot, but enough to make little dust devils from time to time. Silki watched them twirl at the edge of the light. The spirits were restless.

"She went to Rapid City. She said she wanted to surprise me. We'd have a celebration when she got back. We were going to leave for Texas. She wanted me to see the home she'd built for us. She told me everything was there, the horses, the cattle, exactly like we'd planned."

A chill ran up Silki's spine and made the hairs on the back of her neck stand up. It was all for him. Everything Mariah Blue had done was for this man. She'd built him a future, a fortress, a life they were going to share. Where was she now? Something wasn't right. Actually, something was really wrong.

"Zachary, listen to me. Mariah never said anything she didn't mean. Do you have any idea what she was going to do in Rapid City? Was she going to see someone? What road would she have taken?"

Out of the corner of her eye, Silki watched a dust devil dance behind Zachary's right shoulder. It whirled and skipped, coming closer, going right, then left. Fascinated by the sight, she couldn't take her eyes off of it. It seemed to be hovering, waiting for him to answer, the same as she was.

"This road. The same one we're on to get here. It goes through the Badlands and runs into Interstate 90 up by Wall. It's the fastest way to get from Martin to Rapid. She would have been out here in the storm alone that night."

It was all Silki could do not to launch across the fire, grab Zachary by the neck, and shake him till his teeth rattled. But the dust devil had grown bigger and was whirling like a mad dervish behind his back. She kept her seat and did her best not to yell when she asked, "What storm are you talking about? It was late in the fall when she left Texas."

"Winter here comes in late October or early November. The snow starts and the roads get icy. The roads are always bad on the Rez. But the sun was out that morning and she wanted to go to Rapid. She had it stuck in her mind that we'd be home at the ranch by Christmas." Zach shook his head. "It was my fault. It took me a long time to get straight." He gazed across the smoke plume at Silki. His arms rested on his knees, his hands dangling helplessly in midair a few inches above the barren ground. "If I'd been stronger, we'd have been gone before the storm came."

Silki nodded. "She would have taken you to Texas whether or not you were strong, drunk, or fixing to die. She'd have packed you there on her back if it was the only way to get you there. So, try again. Think back. What happened?"

Mariah Blue would have dragged Zachary home to the ranch and healed him when she got him there. She wouldn't have cared what condition he was in, as long as he was home with her. It was in the journals, and Silki had read it for herself.

Something wasn't right with his story. "Come on Zachary, you know all she wanted was to get you home. She'd have fixed everything after that. She wanted you with her more than anything else on the face of this earth. She spent her whole life proving it. So, what was the hold up?"

His head dropped, hanging in defeat between his shoulders. He'd always been defeated. Silki didn't want to say it out loud in case the spirits were in a bad mood. She wasn't up to running for her life in the Badlands, but as far as she was concerned, he was a loser with a capital L. He was not the man in Mariah's journals. This was a very poor shadow of the man he used to be.

Bullying him wasn't going to work, not without destroying what little was left of him, but she needed answers, clues, something to work with. In her best charitable donation coaxing voice, she said, "Zachary, please tell me what you remember."

He didn't look up, didn't move, didn't even look like he was breathing. He could have been dead. But Silki gritted her teeth and waited, hoping he was gathering his thoughts, and that could take a while if he could even find them. He was technically dried out but that didn't necessarily clear the cobwebs or rejuvenate dead brain cells.

The breeze died down and the dust devils disappeared. Silence settled over the Badlands. It was as if the cliffs were waiting for his answer and had commanded everything beneath them to silence.

His words came slowly, each one a drop of blood from a wounded heart. "I wanted it to be perfect. I wanted her to be proud of me. Be able to hold her head up and look people in the eye when she told them I was her husband. I didn't want her to be ashamed she'd married me. I wanted it to be like when we first met. I was tall and strong then. She was mine."

Either Silki's ears were ringing or a cougar was screaming. Her skin crawled and the hairs on the back of her neck stood straight up. "Married," Silki whispered to herself. He'd said they were married, Zachary was Mariah's husband. Holy Hell, this was going to make for one gigantic dust-up back in Texas.

"Zachary, when did you marry Mariah?"

Zachary jerked to attention. Silki watched as he turned his head to the right and then to the left like he was listening for something. Then he faced her. She sucked in a breath. She caught a glimpse of him when he was young and handsome, and for a moment she could have sworn she saw fire in his eyes and the burning hunger for victory on his sharp features. No wonder Mariah had fallen for him.

Even his voice came out strong and sure. It echoed across the canyon and back to where they were camped. "We married the summer we met in the way of the people. We married again in the white way when she came back. She wouldn't wait for us to get to Texas. She got the Justice of the Peace to marry us at the courthouse in Martin."

Good God in heaven! Mariah was married to Zachary. "Do you have the Marriage License?" That would tell the tale for sure. The first marriage could be litigated for years and maybe not be recognized by the State of Texas. The one signed by a Justice of the Peace was good in any state.

"No, she took it with her to Rapid City. She said she needed it so she could get things put in order. She wanted to make things right. I told her we were together and that was all we needed, but she wanted to make up for all the time we'd lost."

Silki nodded. "She hated every day she spent apart from you. She made them pay for it. She hurt them where they could feel it most. Nobody knows how she knew, but she always found a way to ruin the most important business deals for Grandpa Warfield. She blamed grandma and my dad for not trying to protect her, for never supporting her relationship with you."

"I hated being separated from her." Zach cleared his throat. "I did stupid things. Drank too much, didn't work, didn't raise Jesse like I should have. I didn't want any other woman, but I'd get so lonely and I'd drink too much and do things I'd regret. Then I'd drink to forget what I'd done. I didn't want to feel anything."

Man, oh man, what a train wreck. "We can't fix the past, can't change it, but we can do something with the here and now. We can finish what she started. We have to find Mariah and carry out her plan. Will you help me?"

"Yes, but I don't know what I can do. I never did much to help her back then. Her father said he'd have me thrown in prison if I didn't stay away from her. You don't know how it was around here. One white man talked to another, they put an excuse on the paper and it was done. She didn't want me in jail. I had Jesse to look out for, so we stayed away from each other, but it was hard.

"Grandpa Warfield was a mean old bastard that's for sure. He always got his way. It didn't matter how. Mariah was the only one who ever stood up to him. She didn't need his money. I never understood how she got away with it till I read her journals. I guess my dad was too embarrassed to admit he was too chicken to stand up to their father. But I know it made him mad that she could do what he couldn't. It must be tough not having any balls."

Zachary grinned at that. "No balls, huh, what a shame."

He looked off into the distance and then back at Silki. His eyes twinkled in the dim firelight. Maybe it was the moonlight she saw reflected there or maybe he was smiling for the first time in a very long time.

He said, "I used to wonder what happened to mine. If I'd had any of my own, I would have taken Mariah and Jesse, and made a life for us somewhere else. But we were young and didn't know how to fight a man like Warfield. She said everything would be okay, we just had to wait."

Silki sighed and did what Zachary had done earlier. She looked out over the Badlands hoping to find the answers to her questions. Should she tell Zachary about the journals, should she keep Mariah's words to herself? He'd been through so much but didn't he have a right to know what had really been going on? How could she look him in the eyes and lie? Well, hell, she wasn't a good liar and this didn't seem like the time to start pretending she was.

She sucked in a deep breath. "I had no place to go." Not that Zachary would care but she had to start her story somewhere. "Mariah always said I could stay with her if I found myself all alone in the world stuck between a rock and a hard spot. When my marriage fell apart, I called home but I wasn't welcome there. That's when it hit me, what she'd been trying to tell me all those years. I wasn't somebody's daughter or granddaughter. I was a business asset. And if I didn't get the right results, I was out. Out of luck, and out on the street. Mariah had been gone for years and the Ruins was empty. I was desperate, so I drove out there. I've been staying in the Ruins trying to get myself together. I was cleaning and scavenging when I found Mariah's journals. Everything I never wanted to know is in them."

Silki collected her thoughts and tried to size up Zachary's reaction to what she'd said so far. But it was like looking at a statue. Nothing moved. She raked her hands through her hair, as if finger combing it away from her face would help her see better. What she saw was herself sifting through the lonely years of another person's life and knowing she didn't want to end up that way herself.

"I know it's not nice to look through other people's things, but I had to find out what to do, how to keep my dad from taking the ranch and selling it. If he can have Mariah declared dead, that will leave him as her nearest living relative, and without a will he'd get the ranch. Then he can sell it to a developer and laugh all the way to the bank. Mariah would hate that. So, I admit it, I went through her things."

Silki leaned back, planted her hands on the hard ground behind her and stretched her legs out in front of her a little off to the side of the fire. "I found her journals, her jewelry, her stash of cash, and the name of her attorney and bookkeeper. There were a couple pictures of you and Jesse when he was little. I'd never seen her look that happy, not even when we were on the road. We used to load up the Harleys and go riding in the summer. Route 66 and all that."

She shifted her weight from one hip to the other and wiggled her feet side to side. She had to go way back down memory lane. "I always believed that Grandpa had forced her to move out to the ranch, that he'd given it to her. But that wasn't it at all. That old place belonged to my great-Grandma Drew. Daddy and Grandpa hated her. She was an old-timer who had made it through the tough years, the depression, the drought, all that. She didn't take anything off of anybody, and apparently, she didn't have any use for George Warfield, called him a fast-talking, good-for-nothing. But he managed to marry Grandma. He couldn't wait for the old lady to die and leave him all her land by way of Grandma. But Granny Drew fooled him and left it to Mariah. It was never his. He didn't force her to go out there. She went out there, slammed the gate shut in his sorry face, and declared war on him."

She had to rest before finishing. "Great Grandma Drew told Mariah, 'If you want a roof over your head, be sure you own the roof.'"

Silki studied the toes of her boots. They were scuffed and worn. "She left the ranch to Mariah, and the executor was an attorney who Grandpa Warfield couldn't buy off. The will was set up so that Mariah couldn't sell the ranch until she was thirty. That way Grandpa couldn't bully her into selling it and giving him the money when she was too young to know better. By the time her birthday rolled around, she was making money and working like a dog to build the place up. She wanted the best for you and Jesse. He would have had money for college and you would have been raising the finest cattle and horses in Texas. Life was going to be good for all of you."

But somehow it hadn't turned out that way. Zachary nodded, and she watched his eyes tear up and his shoulders droop. It had all gone wrong. Mariah had systematically beaten the Warfield empire to dust, but she'd failed to bring Zachary home. Neither one of them had a life worth living. Somehow that didn't seem right.

Silki shook her head slowly, and to think she could have ended up the same way with Charley the Weasel. Her life with him hadn't been worth living. The farther down the road she went, the clearer the picture in her rearview mirror got. And the trail of misery led straight to Grandpa Warfield who was hopefully roasting in Hell. Yep, the Devil surely had his hands full trying to hang on to his throne.

"Zachary, you and Mariah lost a lot of years. She was trying to protect you, you were trying to protect Jesse, and in the end, nobody was happy. There should have been a better way. You deserved better."

"If I'd been a better man, yeah, things might have been better, but I wasn't. I let her go, let her fight for us, but I didn't fight. I gave up. Now Jesse is doing the same thing. He drinks to get numb. He goes looking for company and doesn't like what he finds, so he drinks to kill the loneliness. He's strong, he could get a job, but he says he has to keep an eye on me." Zach snorted. "He's my son, he shouldn't have to worry about me. He shouldn't have to look in bars and alleys to find me. I know better, but I keep letting him down. I was supposed to get us out of here."

Silki crossed her ankles and studied her boots again. They'd seen better days but they could still kick the shit out of anything that got in her way. "Okay, so how do we all get out of here this time?"

Zach looked over at her and asked, "Where would we go?"

"Home, Zachary, we'd go home."

CHAPTER ELEVEN

JESSE TOSSED AND MOANED, fighting off the worst nightmare of his life. Mariah Blue was standing over him pointing a skeletal finger to a place in the distance. The Grim Reaper had nothing on her. He looked where she pointed, but all he could see were the white cliffs of the Badlands under a cloudless, pale blue sky. The brightness hurt his eyes.

He turned away searching the empty street outside the diner for Little Red. His biker babe had the face of an angel. He needed to talk to her.

His throat had a lump the size of a boulder caught in it. He couldn't speak, only stand there reaching for her. She was too far away. But she beckoned to him. Instinctively, he knew he'd be whole if he could get to her, make her his. She was meant for him.

Fear overwhelmed him when she started to turn away. No! She couldn't leave him. He belonged with her. They belonged together. She was his, but she was walking away. He wanted to scream at her to come back, to wait for him. His feet refused to move. He was left standing there alone.

The breeze lifted his hair blowing it around his face temporarily blinding him. He reached up and brushed it out of his eyes. He was standing in the middle of the highway running through town looking down the road. He could see a black spot on the horizon. It grew in size as it came closer, closing the distance between them. It was the Jeep, the big black four-wheel drive monster that Mariah Blue drove. It was headed straight for him. The windows were down and he could see her behind the wheel. Dust billowed out from under the oversized tires creating a dull gray cloud in her wake. She was going to run him down. This was it. His life was going to end smashed into the South Dakota asphalt.

He turned his head and saw Little Red standing on the side of the road. She was waiting for him.

~

Silki looked down at the sprawled hunk of male animal. Why did he have to be so fine? It would be so much easier if he were an ugly little troll, but no, he was built like a panther. All sleek muscle, shiny black hair, pearly white teeth, long tapered fingers, all the better to rip her heart out with. Jesse groaned in his sleep.

"Jesse." Nothing. She softly called, "Jesse."

"Help me, Little Red."

The words hit Silki like a body blow, knocking the wind out of her. She sucked in a breath. Her hands trembled and her heart pounded hard and fast. It felt like the first time she'd put her Harley in gear and released the clutch. She was moving. Where she'd end up was another matter.

His hands twitched; his fingers curled. He was trying to grip something. She didn't know what made her do it, but she reached down and took his hand in both of hers. Warm, smooth skin with a few rough spots, and heavy, a man's hand. Definitely not the cold, clammy paw of Charley the Weasel. What was she thinking? She must be out of her ever-lovin' mind to touch him.

"Jesse, wake up. We've got to go."

~

He gasped for air at the same time his eyes flew open. It was her. She'd found him. She was there holding his hand. He remembered reaching

74

for her and touching something warm. His heart was caught in his throat. He needed to say something; he couldn't get the words out. Focus, he needed to focus, but his heart was racing too fast, his sight still too blurry from sleep, and he needed something to drink.

If he didn't get to the bathroom soon, he was going to piss on himself. Now, that would really impress her.

He snatched his hand free of hers and swung his legs over the edge of the bed as he sat up. His bare feet hit the floor, he came off the bed in one fluid motion, but stumbled all the way to the bathroom. With the door closed, he gripped the edge of the sink to keep from falling to his knees. He felt sick. Sicker than he looked, if the reflection in the dingy mirror was accurate.

Silki stood back and watched him stagger across the room. How could someone so beautiful be such a disgusting mess? Well, tough, she needed him and he'd have to straighten up. Maybe the coffee in the front room would help. She'd stopped with Zachary on their way back to town and picked up coffee along with breakfast-to-go plates from the diner. She'd sure gotten the looks from the customers and waitresses. Even the cook had popped her head over the tall kitchen-line-counter to get a look at her. They could have been looking at Zachary, but if she had to bet, it was most likely the combination of seeing them together. Well, that was tough, too. She needed Zachary and he needed her. They were going to be together from now on until the mystery of Mariah's disappearance was solved. The fine people of this wide spot in the road better get used to it.

As for Jesse, as soon as he got through barfing up his guts, he'd have to make peace with her or suffer the consequences. She didn't care which way it went, so long as she got what she needed. And she needed him awake and moving. She would use a cattle prod on his ass if she had to, but he would move.

Zachary looked up as she ambled toward him. He'd sent her into the bedroom to wake Jesse. "I'm sorry you had to see him like that. It's what I taught him, what I showed him. It's hard to face what I've done to my son." Hanging his head, Zachary asked, "Is he okay?"

"Yeah, he'll be better as soon as he gets his stomach empty of whatever rot-gut whiskey he drank last night. Once he eats something, he'll be fine."

Silki sank to the floor, and pulled her breakfast container across the scarred coffee table and popped the lid open. The apartment was hopeless, a real pit. People shouldn't have to live like this, not when scum lived in mansions. Charley the Weasel didn't know it yet, but his high-rolling days were numbered. Once she got this situation straightened out, she was going to straighten him out. Spread eagle, naked on an ant hill sounded about right. His pasty white skin would blister under the Texas noon-day sun.

She picked up one of the plastic forks that came with their order. The aroma wafted toward her. It was heaven, real food, and she was really hungry for the first time in months. Screw manners, she shoveled the scrambled eggs and country sausage into her mouth and chewed. She washed it down with her creamy coffee. Ah, yes, a little bit of heaven.

Zachary laughed. "Slow down, girl. It's not going anywhere."

Jesse leaned against the doorjamb with one shoulder holding him up. "Well, this is like old times." He pushed upright, sauntered across the room, and sank onto the lumpy couch next to Zachary. "So, what's for breakfast, Little Red?"

Zachary's eyes went wide and he coughed to clear his throat. Before he could get his food swallowed, Silki stabbed her fork across the table at Jesse who leaned back moving out of reach.

"You drunken pig. I'm going to spit you and barbeque your worthless hide." She pulled her fork back. Glaring at the son-of-a-bitch she growled, "Eat your breakfast. We've got work to do and you're going to help."

"Help do what?"

Zachary spoke up first. "We're going looking for Blue. Like we should have done a long time ago." He looked down at his food. "It's not right that she's lost out there. I've got to find her."

"Sure, okay, but we all won't fit on the Harley."

Jesse looked at Zach and then at the angry angel sitting on their filthy floor. He didn't want to think about it too hard, but the mental image of her with Zach's arms wrapped around her while flying down the road didn't sit well. He wanted his arms around her. Man, he was in big trouble, white woman kind of trouble. The kind that could get a man killed or jailed.

Silki went back to eating, answering around a mouthful of hash browns. "I'm going to rent a car. We need to check the roads between here and Rapid City. She's got to be out there. Since the cops never looked for her, we've got miles to cover. There's a clue somewhere. That Jeep of hers will be hard to hide. We find it, we find where she went."

Jesse sat back. He didn't have to look at Zach to know what he was thinking. Zach had all but begged him to go look for the Jeep when Mariah hadn't come back that snowy night. But he'd been so sure she'd driven away and left them, gone without looking back, that he'd brushed it off. Nobody wanted them. All these years he'd figured she'd gone back to Texas glad to be free of them. Today it didn't look that way anymore.

"I need a drink," was the first thing out of his mouth. Realizing too late that it was the worst possible thing he could have said as Silki swiped her plastic knife through the air between them.

"Just try it and I'll cut your throat. The booze will never reach your stomach." She glared at Jesse while holding the plastic fork in her other hand. She was ready to butcher him with plastic utensils.

She snarled, "I paid good money for this food and you're going to eat it. Then you're going to get showered and put on some clothes you haven't slept in. Your days of lying around here feeling sorry for yourself are on hold, but they'll be right here waiting for you when I'm done with you."

Jesse felt like he'd been punched in the stomach. She was going to use them and throw them away.

He snapped back, "You don't get to use us like Blue did. No way.

I'm not going to bust my hump for you so you can ride away and leave us here to rot. Thanks, but no thanks, honey."

"I'm nobody's honey, you two-bit gigolo. And for your information, you're already rotting from the inside out. You're just too dumb to know it."

Zach groaned. "That's enough. I can't sit here watching you two carving each other to bloody pieces like this. We have to work together."

Silence fell over the room. Zach took a breath and said, "Jesse, eat your breakfast. We've gotta get moving." His eyes met Silki's. "Please, give him a chance. Do it for me."

Silki nodded stiffly, the muscles along her jaw working to keep her mouth closed.

Jesse could sense it was killing her to agree but she'd done it for Zach. He was the man's only child and he was a failure, pure and simple. Jesse didn't know how he was going to get through the next few days but he'd figure it out. He had to get a grip on his mouth and stop pushing Little Red into fight mode. It didn't take much to push that button and he seemed to have a knack for it without even trying.

Jesse reached for the food container with trembling fingers. He had the shakes. He needed to stop drinking, stop shaking, stop throwing himself away on women who didn't care if he lived or died. He needed to start living a better way. He'd start today after he ate breakfast and took a shower.

A few minutes later, his belly was full, and the water running over him washed away the cigarette smoke that clung to his skin and hair. He rested his hands against the shower wall and hung his head under the running water. Her words hurt him. "You're already rotting," echoed in his head. It was true. He was rotting on the inside. How did she know? He'd hidden the truth so well behind laughter, smiles, flirting and fucking anything and everything that would hold still long enough for him to undo his zipper.

He'd been pretending to be a carefree, happy-go-lucky kind of guy for so long that he didn't know where the act ended and he began. This was possibly his last chance to be himself, to be Jesse High Horse. He had a college education, thanks to a full-scholarship that had fallen on him like a miracle at the end of high school.

He could get out of Martin, get a job and make something of himself. For the first time, there was hope that Zach could stay sober and be able to take care of himself for a change. Jesse didn't want to get his hopes up too high. It hurt too much when it didn't happen and he ended up disappointed. The water cooled, pretty soon it would be cold. He turned off the taps and stepped out of the shower, toweled off, and rubbed the water from his hair.

It was time to let the old Jesse go in peace and start a new life.

While Jesse showered, Silki took out the trash and returned to the apartment. She stood in the so-called living room with her hands planted on her hips staring at Zachary. "You don't belong here."

"You sound like Blue. She said the same thing many times."

"Well, she was right. We have to take you where you belong. You have a fine home in Texas. You should live in it. You're wasted here." She'd misjudged the man. It was time to do better.

He flat out stated, "I can't leave without my girl. We go together or I don't go."

"We're going to find her." Silki blinked, inhaled a shaky breath and did her best to hide the tears threatening to make an appearance. "I hate to say this, but you owe it to her to keep the ranch out of my father's hands. She worked too hard to have it end up lost to the likes of him. It was always meant to be yours."

For a moment Zachary looked lost. Silki knew the feeling. He was being torn apart. If she could have made it easier for him she would have.

Zachary sighed. "We'll get the papers from the courthouse and you can use them to keep him out. I can't go without her."

Was their love strong enough to withstand another beating?

Silki noticed the water had stopped running. Jesse would be strutting through the door any minute. His arrogant self would be refreshed and in fine form. Why her?

She said, "I'm sorry about Jesse. He has a way of making me so angry. It's like he doesn't care about anyone or anything. I want to beat him so he'll feel something."

"Since he was a little boy, he's felt too much. I couldn't protect him from the stares and the hurtful things people said about us. He knew he was different; he didn't understand why people treated him the way they did. He didn't understand why his mother didn't want him." Zachary turned his face away. "She had him and left him in the hospital. They called me to come get my son." He cleared his throat. "She didn't want to explain us to her family and friends. I was a summer fling to her. We never heard from her again."

Silki staggered back and caught herself on the kitchen counter. Her mouth opened and closed several times before she could get a single coherent thought formed. "Did Mariah know? Not that it makes a difference now, but hell, in our family that kind of thing was unthinkable. No wonder Grandpa Warfield went ballistic. He wouldn't have let a bastard kid in the family for any reason." Horrified at her own words she slapped a hand over her mouth, at the same instant Jesse stepped into the room.

Jesse stopped dead in his tracks. "Bastard kid, that's me."

Zachary gasped and looked like he'd been sucker punched. He choked out, "Yeah, Blue knew what we were, and she loved us anyway. We were so young and Jesse was turning three that summer. We didn't think it would be any big deal if we got married. She said Jesse was going to be her son, she'd adopt him. He was hers, same as I was. For a few weeks we were a family. Then Warfield showed up with some cowboys and took her away from us. They beat me unconscious. When I came around, Jesse was sitting in the corner of our cabin crying and Blue was gone."

Jesse watched Silki sink slowly to the floor. Her eyes were wide and unfocused right before they rolled back in her head.

"Quick, get some water, a cold rag." A couple long strides brought him to her. "She's fainting on us." He knelt down on one knee and scooped her up. He had to give it all he had to get back on his feet. It was the whiskey that made him weak. He reminded himself this was why he needed to get his strength back. He had to take care of his dad and now the added burden of Little Red.

A few feet away was the couch, the safest place to put her. "That's it. She's out," he grunted as he placed her on the couch, straightened her legs, and tucked her arms against her sides.

He grabbed a loose back-cushion and stuffed it under her legs, at the same time Zach put a wet towel on her forehead. That was all they could do for now. Jesse didn't doubt that she'd come around and probably be more obnoxious than ever.

Zach patted her hand. "How long till she wakes up? Is she going to be okay? Blue never fainted."

"Yeah, she'll come around in a couple of minutes. Guess we scared her. It must be a hell of a shock to find out you're related to the likes of me." Jesse shrugged his shoulders. "Who knows with these people. They're all crazy."

Zach watched Silki and muttered, "You don't know the half of it. Love is more than a little crazy."

"I wouldn't know about that. Never been there. You're not falling for her, are you? She looks like Blue but she's not the same. She's not tough enough or mean enough." Jesse took her hand in his and fingered the small bones. He could crush her. He wouldn't even break a sweat and she'd be a small pile of broken bones.

Zach watched Jesse gently caressing Silki's hand. "Blue wasn't always mean. She got that way after Warfield took her home and she couldn't come back to us. She had to get tough to beat him. This little one hasn't had to fight for survival like Blue did. She hasn't had to destroy her enemies to save the people she loves. Her heart hasn't been broken so bad it can't be mended."

Jesse didn't believe his ears. "What about you, and me? We have feelings, too." He spared his father a glance and quickly went back to watching Silki. She was so pretty and so small up close. An avenging angel on a Harley. Her skin was smooth, creamy, soft as silk, and when her eyes flashed fire at him, he felt it all the way to his toes. He was glad for the few minutes her eyes were closed and she couldn't see what a fool he was.

Zach sniffled and swiped at his nose. "I cheated on Blue. I slept around and Warfield made sure she knew. It was all he had and he used it to hurt her. She should have forgotten me, gone on with her life, and married someone else." He looked across the room and blinked.

"The last time she was here I asked her why she'd waited for me. She told me she couldn't stand the thought of anyone but me touching her. I was the only man she wanted. The other women didn't count since my heart hadn't cheated on her."

Jesse grumbled, "Shit! What did she expect? You had to get sex from someone. What were you supposed to do, become a monk?"

Heaving a heavy sigh Zach said, "You don't get it. I was supposed to love her as much as she loved me."

Silki moaned and sighed. "Where the hell am I?" She opened her eyes and stared up at Jesse. "Oh, yeah, now I remember. I've landed in Hell and you're the Devil."

Jesse stared back. Her eyes were stormy sky-blue. He smiled. "Welcome back, Little Red. Think you can get your butt moving so we can go look for a real Texas woman? Mariah Blue is out there waiting for us to ride to her rescue."

She pushed her way off the couch. "Get out of my way, High Horse. Let's go, Zachary."

Well, at least she hadn't called him a bastard, again. Things were improving. At this rate he might make it to human status in a couple hundred years. He grabbed his wallet on the way out the door and stuffed it into his back pocket. It was as empty as his life, but it had his driver's license and tribal membership card in it.

There wasn't a car rental agency for over a hundred miles in any direction, but for a substantial fee the local garage had an old rez-ride they could use. It was amazing what some people would pass off as a car. The old Buick had seen much better days about fifteen years ago, but it ran and they could all fit. That had to be worth something. Its worn-out paint had been a medium shade of blue, but now it was gunmetal grey and dull white. The air-conditioning had died about ten years ago and the headliner was loose in places, hanging like a torn curtain over their heads.

Yeah, she'd sunk lower than a snake's belly. But sometimes a girl had to do what a girl had to do. And today she needed the Regal to take her to the Badlands. Then there was the disreputable company she was keeping. Well, it came with the territory. They weren't called the Badlands for nothing. She almost smiled. At least she hadn't completely lost her sense of humor. Right. Then she did smile, what the heck, it couldn't hurt. At least she didn't have to go alone.

Silki glanced at Zachary from the corner of her eye. He sat in the passenger seat with is arm resting on the window ledge. He stared straight ahead knowing there was no turning back. The look on his face said he was resigned to this expedition. At long last he would have an answer. He'd know why Mariah hadn't come back for him, why she hadn't kept her promise.

Jesse lounged in the backseat with his legs stretched out across the seat. He was riding in style. He was sitting behind Zach and had a clear line of vision allowing him to watch every move Silki made. Every expression that crossed her face was visible to him from the side, and could she make faces.

Yeah, Little Red was definitely at the wheel as they sped out of Martin. Jesse hadn't enjoyed a back seat this much in his whole life, and that was saying something since he'd been in more than his fair share of them. Now, if he could get Little Red to join him, it would be perfect. But that would be the last thing to happen on earth, right after Hell froze over.

She wasn't a back-seat kind of girl, but that didn't stop him from wanting her. He shifted restlessly and stared out the window. He needed to get his mind off of her and on to something else or his semi-erection was going to expand and bust his zipper.

CHAPTER TWELVE

THIS WAS the fourth day they'd done this and Jesse was tired of it. Mariah was gone, disappeared, never to be seen or heard from again. Today, they were trudging along a stretch of BIA road near Wanblee that would take a person to Rapid City. He had the west side of the road headed south. Some places dropped off pretty steep, but nothing too drastic. You could slide off the road but it probably wouldn't kill you. You'd have to hit something head on to do that.

He walked on, his mind on other things, more pleasant things. Things like Silki waking him up in the mornings. She'd been coming into his room, standing over him and daring him to wake up every day for the last three mornings. He'd hear her coming and burrow deeper into his pillow to irritate her. He got a hard-on just thinking about her coming for him. It sure made his mornings hell, but he loved it, wanted it, was going to miss it when she left.

The other good thing was that she always brought breakfast and that made it worth getting up. She'd resurrected their old coffee machine and bought a can of ground coffee. Zach looked more like a man than a skeleton with skin draped over it. It felt good to see his father putting on weight and staying sober. When Silki left all that would change, go back to being the way it was, and he didn't want that. Didn't want the bars and the beer, the smoke and hangovers. For once he wanted to stay strong. He liked feeling strong, healthy; he could take a deep breath without coughing for ten minutes afterward.

His legs had their strength back. All this walking was boring, but it had been good for him at the same time. It had given him time to think. Think about where he was, where he'd been, and where he was going. It had also given him peace. For a few days he'd finally found peace of mind, peace of heart, peace of spirit. He wasn't angry, wasn't afraid. Zach was okay and Little Red was with him.

Little Red, sometimes he wanted to wrap himself around her like a tune from an old-fashioned love song. He imagined holding her tightly to his body and feeling her shiver with anticipation of his loving her. He shook his head to clear the image and pulled on the pant leg of his jeans to stop the crotch from cutting him in half. Damn, the girl made him hard, and he was wide awake. In his sleep she made him come. She needed to go away. She needed to stay.

He took three more steps before he stopped. It had taken that long for his brain to process what his eyes had seen. It was black and red and it didn't belong there in the white rocks. Oh, please, no. He didn't want to be the one to find her. His heart skipped a beat. Not him. Not now. Maybe it was nothing, but he'd never know if he didn't go back and look.

Zach and Silki were on the other side of the road. Her eyes searched the far crevices with high-powered binoculars while Zach looked over the edge of the road. They weren't watching him. He could keep walking. They'd never have to know. But he'd know. He really didn't want to know, not ever. He'd been angry and lazy, and he'd refused to go looking when it might have made a difference and now it was too late. He backed up and peered over the side of the short precipice.

He hated himself.

He hated what he was about to do.

He shouted, "Hey, over here. There's something down there in the rocks."

～

Silki and Zachary hurried across the road. She needed it to be something. After all their hours of searching she'd started to run low on hope. She'd watched Zachary slowly sink into a dark well of despair. Finding Mariah could pull him out and change their lives forever. Not finding her would leave them with their questions unanswered and unable to close the circle. The looming shadow of change made them hesitate when they reached Jesse. Neither one wanted to be the first to look over the ledge.

Silki was the first to speak. Call her cowardly, but right then she didn't care. She grasped Zachary's hand. "I don't want to do this alone." She was scared and she'd never admit that with Jesse standing there listening.

"It's okay, we'll go down together. You hang on to me and we'll be fine." Zachary gripped her hand a little tighter in reassurance. "Come on girl, you didn't come all this way to give up now. We'll get through this and a whole lot more."

"Yeah, well, promise you won't let go." Her hand turned into a dead weight in his. She wanted to squeeze him back but nothing seemed to want to work. The moment she'd been dreading had arrived. It was a fine time to ask, but she needed to know, "What will we do if it's her?"

Anger, hot and burning, surged through Jesse. She was supposed to turn to him, hold on to him. He hadn't done much to deserve it but he was there, walking for miles and trying to make up for all the things he'd done wrong. Zach had his chance with Blue. Heat crawled up his neck and over his face. He wanted to snatch her away from Zach. There they stood clinging to each other like their lives depended on it. What about his life? But then he was the bastard nobody wanted. Even his mother hadn't wanted him.

Cold and unfeeling he growled, "If she's in there, she's dead. We'll bury her, move on and forget about her."

Zach's jaw dropped, his eyes flew to Jesse's with a dazed and incredulous look Jesse had never seen before. He realized a second too late that he'd stepped over a line, but something had broken loose inside his heart and the anger mixed with years of defeat erupted. Before he could begin to think it through, Silki pulled free of Zach's grip and launched herself at him.

A hundred and twenty pounds of shrieking banshee hit Jesse around his middle, knocking the air out of his lungs when her shoulder slammed into his diaphragm. He couldn't breathe and the stars were sure out early. He went over backwards with Silki biting his arm and tearing at his shirt. They rolled down the embankment over rocks and brush with obscenities thrown in every chance they got.

She kicked, she bit, she pulled, she clawed, she hit, she swore she'd kill him if it was the last thing she ever did. And she didn't have any problem screaming, "I'll kill you, you lousy bastard," as she sat on his chest with a rock in her fist. She only had to bring it crashing down on his head and he'd be dead. Chest heaving, sucking in air for the final blow, she raised the rock as high as her arm would reach and began the downward arc. Her eyes met his just before they drifted shut and he lost consciousness.

∽

The rock slammed down hard buried in the dry dirt beside his head. She couldn't kill him. She couldn't even hate him. He was Jesse. Mariah had thought he was worth saving.

She straddled his chest catching her breath. His broad chest moved under her taking in air. Thank her lucky stars he was alive. She hadn't killed him. She leaned closer, her nose mere inches from his.

She asked, "Jesse, are you okay?" Nothing. "Jesse, open your eyes. I'm sorry. It's not supposed to be like this."

Silki didn't get any further with her plea for Jesse to wake up.

Zachary called out. "Silki, get off Jesse and come look at this. We found her."

∽

During the rolling brawl that had landed her on top of Jesse at the bottom of a dry gulch, Zach had scrambled down the hill and made his way to the black SUV partially hidden in the shadows of the rocks. It was a Jeep 4x4 resting at a crazy angle. The driver's side was up and the front end was down. It was tilted at about forty-five degrees. It was wedged between two huge boulders on the side of the gulch and shaded by a few small trees.

He had crawled over the boulders and peered in the dusty windows. It was a sight he'd hoped never to see and one he'd been seeing in his nightmares for years. It was what was left of his Mariah Blue. It was red hair and bones with denim clothes clinging to a skeleton. His hopes, his dreams, were over, turned to dust.

Everything he'd lived for was gone. Everything except Jesse. He was still alive. A little beat up, but still alive. It was good he'd found a woman he couldn't push around, couldn't feed bullshit to, and one that didn't spend every second of the day drooling over him. Zach had leaned against the boulder next to the Jeep and watched Silki miss crushing Jesse's skull by a couple inches. It had been close, but in the end, she couldn't kill him.

The girl was falling in love with his boy, even if neither one of them knew it yet.

Zach waved at Silki, motioning her to come to him. When she got within a few feet where they could talk without shouting, he said, "Look there…" he pointed to the driver's door, "and there…" he pointed to the area below the door handle. "We need to call the cops. Somebody shot her."

Silki's cell phone was in the Buick and thankfully not smashed to electronic smithereens in her back pocket. Zachary went to make the call to the tribal police figuring it would sound better coming from him than a crazy white woman.

In the meantime, Silki had the Jeep and everything in it to herself. Jesse was still out cold in the sun. Served him right for disrespecting the dead. She shrugged at the thought and dug in her front pocket for the spare key to the Jeep. Never leave home without a spare set of keys to everything. Good motto and one that Mariah had preached at nauseam. Of course, it had kept them from being stranded or locked out more than once. Experience was the best teacher.

She muttered under her breath, "Not to worry, Aunt Mariah, I've got the extra spare key right here. I'll have you out of there in no time." She chuckled a small strangled sound. "Why did you have to go and get yourself killed? You're a legend. You're supposed to ride off into the sunset with Zachary, not get shot behind the wheel of a Jeep."

She twisted the key in the passenger door lock and heard it click. The door unlocked. The cops would come and snatch up everything for evidence if she didn't reach in there and nab it first. "Can't let Warfield win now, can we? Nope. Sorry about this, but I gotta play by your rules this time. It's us first." Her hand gripped the door handle as her thumb pressed on the release. The door opened.

"What the hell are you doing?" Jesse demanded.

Silki jumped and turned to see Jesse staring daggers at her. "What's it to ya?" She tightened her grip on the handle.

"It's a crime scene. It's evidence. Hell, it's a coffin. You can't go poking around in it. The cops will have a fit." He made it sound like he was talking to an idiot.

"Yeah, it's a crime scene, and cops who couldn't care less will snatch up everything in here, lose half of it, and not give a rat's ass about the rest of it. So, the way I see it, I got here first, it's mine." With that Silki yanked the door open, grabbed the doorjamb and climbed in. She knelt on the passenger seat and started pawing through the scattered papers gathering them into a pile she could shove back into the legal-size file folder laying mixed in the clutter.

Jesse was still standing there watching her. She could feel the heat from his body behind her.

She glanced up into the empty sockets that had once held the bluest eyes in all of South Texas. The side of the skull rested against the steering wheel with the lower jaw gapping open. What could she say to the dead?

"I'm so sorry, Aunt Mariah. I did some pretty stupid things, but I'm smarter now. I'm going to make this right." Well, that wasn't exactly true, she couldn't bring Mariah back to life. So, she amended it to, "I'll make it as right as I can."

She could have sworn she heard someone whisper, "Take him home," but nobody was there except herself and Jesse, and he hadn't said anything.

Then came the tricky part. Silki stretched as far as she could reach and still she came an inch short of reaching Mariah's purse strap. It was on the floor behind the driver's seat. She leaned over the seat with her butt in the air stretching herself until she was in danger of falling into the space on her head.

Jesse's hands grabbed her hips and pulled her back. She screeched, and he swore. He wrapped his arms around her waist securing her back to his front. "Let me get it. You're going to hurt yourself."

"No. I'll do it. I almost had it."

"I can reach it easier than you."

She elbowed him in the ribs. "No. I don't want you touching anything of hers."

He grunted and grabbed his bruised ribs.

She scrambled into the middle of the Jeep, pulled the door shut, and slapped the lock into place.

Jesse was still holding his side when Zach made his way back down the hill. "Where's Silki?"

Jesse nodded toward the Jeep.

Silki smiled and waved at him.

Zach turned to Jesse. "What's she doing in there?"

Jesse grunted. "Robbing the dead." He glared at the Jeep and its occupants, living and dead.

Zachary walked over to the window and raised his voice. "What are you doing?"

Silki stopped rummaging long enough to answer, "It's okay. I'm getting Aunt Mariah's things together before the cops get here. We'll never get her stuff back if they get their hands on it." She shook her head. "We need it more than they do."

She crawled over the seat and cracked open the door. Shoving the envelope and purse out into Zach's hands, she said, "Here, put that in the trunk. We can look through it later." Then she tugged the door shut and locked it again, all the while glaring at Jesse over Zachary's shoulder.

Nothing either man could say or do got her to come out of the Jeep. She was still sitting in there with the skeleton when the tribal police arrived followed closely by the Rapid City news vans.

~

Jesse saw the cameras first. "What the hell is that? How'd they find out so fast?"

"I called them first, then the cops," Zach said quietly so only Jesse would hear. "I don't want this getting hushed up or swept under the carpet. Somebody murdered Mariah Blue and they're gonna pay. It's been a long time coming."

"But Silki's in the Jeep. The cops are gonna be madder than hell."

"Yeah, but they'll have to listen to her if they want to get her out of there. Think of the headlines. Girl locks herself in Jeep with dead aunt to get justice. How would it look if they locked up the poor grief-stricken niece of the victim who was so devastated that she shut herself inside the car with the corpse?" Zach smile slyly. "Yeah, they're going to have to do something about this. It won't look good to let it go as another unsolved crime on the Rez."

Silki was all over the inside of the Jeep but mostly sitting next to the skeleton and wailing her eyes out. Kneeling in the luggage area with her hands pressed up against the rear window made the most pitiful picture of a distraught family member. The press loved it. The cops hated it.

They finally got her to unlock the doors when the FBI arrived. She had everyone's attention. And Mariah Blue's murder would not be ignored.

Jesse heard an audible sigh of relief from the tribal police officer when the Feds took over. He smirked silently to himself. He'd been sitting on a rock a fair distance away watching the show. And what a show it was. Little Red really had them jumping through hoops and Zach wasn't any better egging her on from the sidelines.

Zach struggled up the embankment and shuffled across the road to the Buick. Jesse had already moved to a better vantage point and sat on the hood of the old rez-ride.

Getting her out of the Jeep was only the beginning. Jesse and Zach watched helplessly as the FBI dragged her past the cameras, put her in the back seat of their car and hauled her off to their office in Rapid City to answer a few questions. The special investigations unit arrived to collect the skeleton and the Jeep.

Jesse and Zach followed her. She'd need a ride home eventually. Mariah was beyond harm, but Silki was still alive.

"Come on, get in. We're going to Rapid. Whoever killed Blue is still out there, and now they're going to know she's been found. They're going to know Silki found her. This isn't over yet." Zach slid into the passenger seat.

Jesse got behind the wheel and fastened his seatbelt while asking, "Will this never end?"

They followed the road to the Interstate, stopped at Wall Drug to use the restroom, eat and get a few snacks for Silki. If the FBI let her go before morning it would be too late to get her a real meal.

Rapid City was a couple hours up ahead, and the day was ending, turning into evening. Zach muttered, "We'll be lucky to get her back tonight."

Jesse's ribs still hurt, and he was covered with dirt from his tumble down the hill. He grumbled back, "We'll be lucky if we don't get her back tonight."

"Yeah, keep telling yourself that and maybe you'll believe it in a couple of years."

"Look what she did to me. I'm supposed to miss being bitten, kicked, and having my hair ripped out by the roots? I don't think so."

"Yeah, you'll miss that and more. You'll miss hearing her call your name. You'll miss the touch of her hands, and the way she smells. You'll miss hearing her footsteps in the hall. So, while you still have a chance, put your pride aside and take a look at what you have to win and what you have to lose."

Jesse groused, "She bit me."

"Yeah, she almost brained you with a rock. Got that? Almost, but she didn't."

"Bad aim."

"Not really."

Jesse rubbed his hand across his mouth. He was sweating. "She's violent, a menace, doesn't know her place."

"You've been in your share of fights, and it seems to me you've never known your place either." Zach glanced at Jesse. "She's desperate, she's lost everything and she's trying to fight her way back. She's a Texan; they fight to the bitter end, no matter what. You, on the other hand, have quit fighting. You don't care anymore and you're not listening. You don't leave the girl much choice. She has to reach you anyway she can."

Zach shut up and looked straight ahead for the rest of the ride leaving Jesse to fight the internal battle raging inside his mind and heart alone. He had a quiet ride all the way to Rapid to face his feelings. This was something he had to work out for himself. His father couldn't help him this time.

Jesse didn't feel like talking anymore anyway. He sat silently staring at the barren scenery. It looked like he felt. Empty, wasted. He knew his place too well. He was a bastard, with nothing. His place was sucking on a beer at the local tavern.

Since when had he had a choice? Go to school, go to prison, live on the Rez, drink himself numb, take care of Zach. Those had all been chosen for him.

Nobody asked him what he wanted.

CHAPTER THIRTEEN

SILKI STEPPED out onto the sidewalk. The night air wrapped around her like a soft blanket. The gentle breeze was warm enough that her short-sleeved t-shirt was enough to keep her comfortable but it wouldn't protect her from the cold later when they passed through the Badlands. Thank goodness she'd thrown her sweater in the car that morning. She'd wrap up in it and take a nap while Jesse drove them home.

Mariah was dead and nothing was going to fix that. She tilted her head back and gazed up at the heavens. A clear night, not a cloud in sight. The stars had free rein to litter the heavens over the Black Hills. In her heart she knew they were shining over Texas, too. She blinked back the tears that threatened to well up in her eyes. This was not the time to cry.

How many nights had they twinkled above the Jeep casting their peaceful spell? How many nights had Zachary laid on his back in some gutter never seeing their beauty, like the empty sockets in Mariah's skull. He was breathing, but he'd been just as dead.

There had to be a crime in all that, somewhere. Someone had shot Mariah Blue and killed Zachary's spirit. They'd murdered Jesse's hope and turned love into despair. She had a bone to pick with someone. And God have mercy on them when she found them, because she would not.

The air smelled fresh and dry. The breeze had carried away the exhaust fumes that might have accumulated during the day. The Black Hills loomed in the distance. What a beautifully sad place.

She said, "I need to get out of here." She swiped at her eyes and sniffled.

They'd finally been told they could go. The FBI agent in charge wasn't the least bit happy about the three-ring-circus that had landed in his lap. A wealthy Texan shot dead on the Rez was bad no matter how they looked at it. With a loud, living relative stirring up the press it looked worse. It hadn't taken him very long to decide that she, Jesse, and Zachary weren't murderers.

So that left the skeletal remains and the Jeep to tell the story.

Silki promised the agent in charge she'd come back if this case wasn't solved quickly while he shoved them out into the street with a tired promise to call when he knew something. Yeah, sure, as if any of them really believed that.

Zachary said, "The car's over there," and nodded to a small parking lot across the street.

Silki didn't move. The lump in her throat made it hard to talk and her feet had turned to stone. The search was over. They'd found Mariah. She'd been ambushed, murdered on her way back to Martin from Rapid City. That was it, the end of a legend. It wasn't fair. Tears rose up and spilled over. This was how it ended, with Silki standing in the street crying over something that couldn't be changed, couldn't be fixed. If this is what defeat felt like, it was no wonder Mariah had sworn vengeance on the culprits who had taken Zachary and Jesse from her.

Jesse stepped up alongside of Silki and looked down. The girl looked dead on her feet. Then he noticed something shiny trickling down her face. Damn. He wasn't good with crying women. He had no idea what to do for her. He looked at Zach and shrugged his shoulders. It was a question and a plea for help.

Zach glared back at him, like he expected Jesse to know better.

Well, tough, he didn't. It didn't fit his image, his happy-go-lucky attitude. He didn't even have a handkerchief to hand her like they did in the movies. He was useless.

In desperation Jesse said, "Look, we don't have time to stand here boohooing over this. We need to put some gas in the car and get home. There's still that stuff in the trunk. There might be something mixed up in that mess that can help us."

It was dark, but not dark enough to hide Zach's irritation. Jesse saw him roll his eyes. Okay, so he had sounded a little gruffer than he'd intended to. Was he supposed to wrap his arms around Little Red and tell her everything would be all right? That would be a lie. It was probably going to get worse and it might never get better.

"You look tired. I'll drive." Jesse put his hand on Silki's shoulder and started moving toward the road steering her ahead. "I'll need money for some gas."

Silki tried to speak but in came out garbled. She cleared her throat and tried again. "It's in the glove box."

"You left your wallet in the glove box?" Jesse sounded a bit shaken.

"Yeah, it was the only place where you guys could get to it if you needed it."

"We could have taken off with it and the car. Weren't you worried?"

"No," Silki answered in a voice devoid of emotion. "I'd have found you."

~

She told herself she only had to get to the car for now, keep moving and she'd be okay. Mechanical legs carried her to the faded relic of what had once been a fine automobile. She was going to get through this and what came after the same way Mariah had. She might be down, but she wasn't out, not by a long-shot. Somebody was going to pay for this.

Zach smiled into the darkness. As he followed along behind them he said, "It's been a long, sad day, but we still have each other, we're still alive. There's still hope. We'll make it. You'll see. Mariah was too smart to let death slow her down."

Jesse whirled around and snarled, "She's D. E. A. D., dead, not coming back, can't do anything from the grave." He shook his head and ranted, "Or from her customized Jeep coffin. That's it, the end. It's over."

Silki reached the passenger side of the Buick and placed her hands, palms down, on the roof. The metal was cool. Her head hung low between her shoulders as she prayed silently for patience. She refused to fight with Jesse again. He'd been through enough, so had Zachary. She could beat Jesse black and blue and he would still use stark, unemotional reality to shield himself from anything that required him to feel sorrow or pain.

Her heart bled for all of them. They were caught in a storm that made the Galveston nineteen-hundred hurricane look like a spring rain. They were going to have to be stronger and smarter than Harvey Warfield to survive. But they would survive if she had to drag them kicking and screaming all the way to Texas. They were going to succeed in putting the final nails in the Warfield-Hardcastle coffin and write the final chapter in Mariah Blue's legend.

Zachary stepped up beside her. "He'll come around. You'll see. Give him time. He's never had anything or anyone to believe in. This is all new to him."

Silki glanced at Jesse, who was unlocking the driver's door, then back at Zachary. She didn't understand how anyone could be so hopeless. "I don't get it. Everything she did was for both of you. She always loved you and Jesse."

"He never really knew her. He was too young. Then life on the Rez and years in prison taught him not to hope, not to care."

～

Jesse opened his door and looked across the roof of the car at his dad and Silki with their heads together whispering secrets to each other. They thought they knew so much. Man, were they in for a surprise. The dead couldn't do a damn thing to help the living.

He grumbled, "Hey, are you two getting in or what?"

Two sets of eyes fastened on him making him a little nervous. They saw too much.

Zach answered, "Yeah, we're getting in as soon as you unlock the doors."

They stopped at the first gas station they came to and gassed up the car. Jesse steered them onto the interstate headed back to Martin with Zach dozing in the back seat and Silki huddled up in the passenger seat. She had slouched down, pulled her sweater tight around her shoulders, and rested her head in the space between the seat and door, half hooked on the window ledge. She was going to have a sore neck in the morning.

Jesse didn't want to examine why that thought bothered him but it did. Zach snored, turned and went back to sleeping quietly. The wind blew through the car ruffling Silki's hair. Jesse wanted to reach over and touch it, smooth it, caress it. He wanted to throw her out of the car, and leave her on the side of the road. He hated these feelings. He didn't know what to do with them. He wanted them to go away, and he thought he might die if they did.

Silki gave a little huff in her sleep and wiggled a little lower in the seat. Oh, hell, what was a man supposed to do when a woman did that? He'd probably get his hand torn off but what the heck. Jesse reached over, wedged his hand under her shoulder, dragged her away from the door and toward himself.

He watched her eyes flutter open. The question was there but he didn't have an answer. He mumbled, "Lie down, you're getting a crick in your neck trying to sleep like that."

He watched her lips form a silly little grin. She quietly said, "I promise not to bite."

"Yeah, good." He pulled her closer and patted her shoulder as she settled her head on his thigh. "Try not to drool."

He heard a strangled noise from the back seat. Great, Zach had heard every word. Now, he'd think there was more to this than just not wanting to put up with a cranky little witch with a stiff neck.

The road stretched on forever, at least it felt that way to Jesse. Endless miles listening to Zach snoring softly in the back seat and feeling every warm breath Silki exhaled on his thigh. He breathed a soft sigh of relief when her head slipped down the outside of his leg so that she was breathing on the seat instead of on him. Trying to drive with that girl's mouth a few inches from his cock had been torture. A little bump in the road and she'd have been on top of it. Oh, man, he could only guess what that would feel like.

He bit the inside of his cheek and tightened his grip on the steering wheel. It took everything he had to keep his foot on the accelerator. He had visions of pulling over, unzipping his jeans, grabbing her by the back of the head, and finding out how her mouth would feel wrapped around his throbbing cock. He might not belong between her legs but that didn't mean she didn't belong between his.

He whispered softly into the night, "Yeah, baby, suck me."

Silki dozed on and off. The seat was lumpy and Jesse squirmed incessantly. He obviously wasn't comfortable with her touching him. To say she was disappointed didn't begin to cover her feelings on the subject, but she didn't want to look too closely at that. Some feelings weren't meant to be acted on. She wasn't Mariah Blue; she didn't step over the lines.

And that wasn't exactly true anymore. Ever since she'd found her way home to the Ruins, she'd been changing. She didn't step over the lines, she stomped on them and marched past the shattered remnants. She'd never be the same helpless girl sitting on the curb, evicted from her townhouse, and crying while the leasing company towed her car away.

Mariah had wanted Zachary the minute she'd laid eyes on him, and Silki wanted Jesse since the first time she'd stood over him trying to wake him up. But she wasn't telling anyone. That secret would go to the grave with her. It had taken a little longer than first glance, but not much. She'd refused to admit it to herself for the longest time, and she was never, ever going to admit it out loud. Sick, sick, sick. That's what she was. He was no good, and she was every kind of fool for even briefly contemplating a very casual relationship with the man.

He didn't have anything to offer her, not a darn thing but misery. That, he had lots of, as if she didn't have enough of her own. Charley the Weasel had offered plenty to hide his true nature. He was a taker, good at taking and taking, like all the way to the proverbial cleaners.

She was better off with Jesse than another Charley. At least Jesse was warm.

She wasn't sure if it was her imagination or the wind but she could have sworn she heard Jesse say, "Yeah, baby, suck me."

Her eyes popped open. She stared at the bottom edge of the dashboard. A dark well with a nest of tangled wires, a place no one wanted to look unless they absolutely had to. Sort of like looking inside one's self. Well, now there was a revelation she didn't want to think about. She closed her eyes and exhaled.

A couple hours later and running on empty, Jesse pulled up at the apartment. He shut off the engine and sat listening to the night. A few crickets chirped in the weeds that clung to life along the concrete foundation and dry leaves rustled on the trees. It got cold out on the prairie at night and he'd turned on the heater coming across the badlands. It had blown enough warm air to keep him from having to stop and roll up the windows the last few inches. But now it was cold, and he was too tired to waste energy shivering. It took serious effort to reach for the door handle, but he wasn't about to sit outside in the car till dawn. Nope, he was going inside and taking Little Red Drooling Queen with him. He was too exhausted to drive her to the motel, so she'd just have to slum it for one night.

After walking around to the passenger side, he opened the door, rolled up her window and reached for her. Doing the considerate thing, he shook Silki gently, saying, "Come on, we're here. Let me get you inside so we can get some sleep."

When she stirred and struggled to push herself up off the seat, Jesse caught her by the arm and steadied her while pulling her to the edge of the seat. "I'll get you there. Lean on me."

"Hmm, okay," and a yawn was what he got for his efforts.

Well, it was a start. At least she wasn't threatening to tear off any of his body parts.

She actually did lean on him wrapping an arm around his waist and resting her head against the side of his chest. It felt good. Kind of warm and comfy. He had to remind himself it wouldn't last; but for one night only, it wouldn't hurt. He heard Zach close the car door and his footsteps climbed the stairs behind them. She was safe from him and his wayward thoughts. He had some pride left.

He felt her pull away. She was half-asleep but stumbling well enough to make it to the bathroom. He knew better than to get between a woman and the bathroom. They could turn into raging monsters when they were on a mission.

Jesse waited for her just outside the door. He didn't want her slipping out the front and trying to drive herself to the motel. She'd no sooner cleared the door than he had her by the shoulders steering her toward the bedroom and his bed.

It surprised him when she didn't protest. He'd expected to at least get kicked in one shin for his trouble. But no, she crawled into bed, dirty clothes and all, then buried her head in the middle of his pillow. No sharing, she commandeered the whole thing. He stood at the side of his bed and wondered what the hell he'd been thinking. Since no good answer came to him, he bent over and struggled with her boots.

He drew the line at wearing boots in bed. They came off and he dropped them at the foot of the bed. He wasn't about to try and get her socks off. Nope, not without an invitation. He'd be fine as long as his skin didn't touch hers.

Sleeping double in a single bed with her was going to be a problem. They'd be touching in a horizontal position, under a blanket, in the dark. Maybe this wasn't the best idea he'd ever had. He pictured the lumpy couch. No, no way was he passing up an opportunity like this. He'd probably never get another one, ever.

"Scoot over." He nudged her hip with his hand trying to make a space for himself on the edge. "This is my bed, mine. You don't get to hog the whole thing." He pushed a little harder.

Silki muttered and moved slightly away giving Jesse a whopping six inches to lay on. He glared at the miniscule space.

"Get over." He reached out and shoved hard. "First you take the pillow, then you take up the whole bed."

"I like lots of space," came a muffled reply.

She was speaking into the pillow and it was all Jesse could do to make out her words. He'd give her lots of space if she didn't move her butt. The floor had lots and lots of space. He shoved again, she scooted over a few more inches and rolled farther onto her side away from him.

He eyed the area like it was the demilitarized zone of a border war. Maybe it was safe and maybe it would blow up in his face. He was too tired to spend any more time worrying about it. He spread his thin blanket over her, pulled off his filthy t-shirt, and flung it across the room thinking he'd really like to fling her right along with it. With an exhausted sigh, he eased down on his side facing away from Silki. It might help if he didn't have to look at her.

Who was he kidding? Not himself, no, not with her butt pressed up against him. She was trying to kill him. That's all there was to it. If she couldn't cut his guts out one way, she'd do it another. She didn't have to bash his brains out with a rock because she could drive him crazy instead rubbing up against him.

Texans were devils in disguise, he was absolutely sure of it. This one was just smaller than most, and prettier, and sexier, and he couldn't sleep. He sat up on the side of the bed. She'd won. His shoulders drooped in defeat; over his shoulder he eyed the fiend who was sleeping in his bed. He had to get away from her.

The lumpy couch hadn't improved any over the years. In fact, it was worse than he remembered, but at least he had it all to himself.

CHAPTER FOURTEEN

ZACH LAID ON HIS BACK, eyes closed, listening to Silki sleep. She sighed from time to time in between soft feathery breaths, just like Blue. It could have been yesterday that she was there with him, and not all the empty years that had crawled by. He could still see her, feel her, hear her. Sometimes he could even smell her. She didn't have to haunt him because in so many ways she'd never left him. But then she'd promised to stay forever and she had, just not in a way he could touch.

Then she'd sent Silki, the spitting image of his Mariah Blue; before the pain and vengeance took hold and changed her. It didn't take a genius to know Silki had come to take him and Jesse away from the hopeless existence of their lives.

Blue had sworn she'd get them out of there if it was the last thing she ever did. From where he was laying on his sagging mattress, it sure looked like she'd kept her word.

Silki had only begun to fight, and it was going to be a long and ugly battle. But Blue had sent the best. Not an experienced warrior, but Little Red was all heart and she'd do fine. She needed to learn patience. That was something he could help her with.

She muttered in her sleep. Zach heard her say, "My feet are cold."

She had every right to be screaming in her sleep, or crying, or chewing on the pillow. Instead she sighed, "Jesse."

The boy had good hearing. Zach heard him get up and pad across the apartment. As small as the place was, it wasn't far. When Jesse slid into bed behind Silki. He breathed easier knowing his son had made the right choice. The man was finally coming to his senses. Zach closed his eyes. Now, he'd be able to sleep.

~

Jesse slipped into bed behind Silki, he had more room if he molded himself to her. It was harder on his mind and body but at least he wasn't hanging off the edge. He put his arm around her shoulders and waited for her to bite him. It was the kind of thing she'd do. No warning, just sink her teeth into his arm clear up to the bone. He waited for the pain to shoot through him. When nothing happened, he relaxed, let out the breath he'd been holding, and closed his eyes.

Sleep was what he needed. Thoughts of the last few days rolled around in his head and they led to thoughts of the past. His clothes were worn thin, and either too small or too large. He ate whatever he could find or whatever anybody gave him. It was better at school where they fed him lunch. In jail and prison, he got three meals a day and his uniforms were clean. There were chains on his ankles and wrists if he was being transported. Bars for doors and concrete walls. Then there was the pretty lady. He'd been so young then, so small he'd sat on her lap and they'd laughed when she'd pointed at the tops of the pine trees. He'd seen birds and clouds and maybe heaven. But she'd been taken away by the bad men.

He shuddered and tightened his hold on Silki. He could feel her ice-cold feet through her socks when they rubbed against his legs. Damn, he pressed closer sharing his heat with her. Maybe she wouldn't go away. Maybe if he was good, she'd stay. Or maybe he'd end up in prison again. That's what happened when you weren't good enough.

~

Silki snuggled into the warmth surrounding her. Her pillow was soft, the bed lumpy, and she felt fine. She was waking up slowly, stretching

104

her legs and wiggling her toes, feeling her body slowly coming back to life. She must have slept like the dead. Dead, oh god, Mariah was dead. The bed moved under her and she clutched at the pillow and mattress. It took a minute to register that she wasn't alone in bed and the tilting was someone moving, not the earth shaking.

It was Jesse. She opened her mouth to cuss him and then shut it firmly. It was okay, for now. A quick glance across the tiny bedroom to the empty bed that was Zachary's sent her mind racing. It didn't take long for the previous night's events to come roaring back. She'd been so tired. She'd let Jesse put her to bed and fallen asleep to dream of Mariah and Jesse.

Her dreams had been peaceful. She'd sat next to Mariah in a shady spot not far from a dark-blue lake. Mariah was at peace and Zachary was headed for something better. Mariah told her, "Don't worry about Zachary, take him with you. I'll be right here waiting for him when he's ready."

That was easy enough to do, so she'd said, "Sure. I like him. I wish I'd known him when he was younger, when you were still with us. Things could have been different."

"That wasn't what fate had in mind. But it's not too late for you to make a life with Jesse."

"He's been in prison. That scares me.

Mariah tilted her head back and closed her eyes. "If something scares you, look closer, see it for what it really is. Then decide."

Mariah disappeared and Silki was left gazing at the peaceful scene surrounded by pine trees high in the mountains. She would look closer.

Now that she was awake, she had a dozen questions starting with looking closer at what? What was she missing? Where should she look? She had to talk to Zachary.

Jesse was half-laying on her. He should weigh a ton, but he didn't feel heavy to her. Hmm, that was different. Charley always felt like a granite slab mashing her flat. Always leaning on her, pushing her, squashing her, pawing at her with his cold clammy hands. She really hated him, and the reasons were getting clearer.

She tried slipping out from under Jesse but she wasn't having much success. He might not feel heavy, but he didn't budge easy. Finally, in desperation she pushed at his shoulder. "Get off, I need to find Zachary."

His shoulder moved slightly then settled back against her. He mumbled, "Why Zach? What's wrong with me?"

"Nothing." Everything, but she didn't have time to discuss it. "I need to talk to Zachary right now. We've got to look through the papers we found yesterday."

"We didn't find anything. You stole it." Jesse rubbed the side of his face against the pillow, the tiny patch he'd been able to worm his way on to.

Silki watched him trying to wake up. He stretched his legs and yawned. He looked so innocent in his sleep. She was tempted to lean over and kiss him. *Wrong, terrible bad idea. Forget that.*

She said, "I did not steal anything. Aunt Mariah wanted me to have her stuff."

"You're a thief, robbing from the dead. Is that something you learned in Texas or is it just your way of doing things?"

"Live in Texas long enough and you learn to survive any way you can. Now, get off me." Silki fixed him with a move or die stare.

Silki sounded so sure of herself that he had to grin. His efforts at goading her into wrestling with him failed. It was the only time she'd touch him. When it came to her, he'd take what he could get.

"Okay, since you asked so nice and all." Jesse rolled back a fraction and let her wiggle out from under him. Damn, some of his parts were awake and getting excited about it. He groaned as she crawled over him and dashed from the room. She was obviously in a hurry to get to Zach, and away from him. His one-night-stand with Little Red was over.

He could hear her voice, smell her on his pillow, and still feel the warm imprint of her body against his. He could hear her talking to Zach while he stared at the empty space in his bed. What would it take for him to find the courage to be a better man? One that she'd want. There was no point in wishing for the impossible. He turned over and stretched. He'd get up in a minute.

~

Silki landed on the couch next to Zachary. Curling her legs under her, she leaned over staring at the papers fanned out on his lap. She was excited and anxious and wanted to know what was in them and afraid to find out all at the same time.

She asked, "What have we got?"

It wasn't polite to grab, but if he didn't tell her fast she was going to do exactly that. She glanced at him and caught the seriously sad expression that rested on him like the worst kind of bad news. "What is it? What do they say?"

~

Jesse dragged himself out of bed and leaned heavily against the bedroom door frame. He couldn't take his eyes off the girl. She was something else. Her hair was a wild tangle and her t-shirt a wrinkled filthy mess that did nothing to hide the finest tits in South Dakota. Her jeans were worn so thin they molded to her thighs like tights and he could imagine the way her legs would feel wrapped around him.

There she was all but falling into Zach's lap and there he stood, forgotten. In a voice still rough with sleep and some stronger emotion he didn't want to examine, he muttered, "Yeah, what do they say?"

~

Silki tried hard not to notice Jesse's smooth muscled chest and his bulging biceps. He was a sculptor's dream. He was her dream, but a dream was all he could ever be. Damn the bad luck.

Look closer.

Hell no, she wasn't going to look closer. If she looked closer, she'd see the bulge in his jeans and the powerful legs that could really take a girl places. Nope, not going to go there.

Look closer.

No, then she'd see the grim set of his mouth, the pain in his eyes, the severe line of his jaw, and the color riding his high cheekbones. No, no, and hell no. If she saw all that she'd want to do something about it, and then there be no end to all the trouble she'd be in. She didn't need any more trouble.

Silki forced her eyes back to the papers. They were trouble too, but at least they didn't bleed.

She'd made Jesse bleed, and she shouldn't have done that. That roll down the hill had cut and scraped him up pretty badly. That was her doing. Of course, he'd stabbed her in the heart with his hateful words. She'd gotten even, but that wasn't feeling like such a good thing.

Zach stared at the papers until they blurred in front of his eyes. He couldn't believe it, didn't want to believe it. Things like this didn't happen in real life. He'd reread them to be sure he had the words right. What would he do with it?

He didn't know the right answer so he blurted out, "She left us the Rocking T."

Silki shrieked, "Oh my god!" She grabbed the papers out of Zachary's hands and fixed her gazed on them. She had to read it for herself. But the second she got focused, they were snatched away. She snapped, "What the hell? Give me those." She looked up to see Jesse backing up and holding the papers clutched tightly in both hands.

He snapped, "You're not getting your hands on these. If they really say we get that place, you're not ripping them up. You don't get to screw us out of what's ours."

If he'd punched her, he couldn't have hurt her any worse. "What are you talking about?"

"There's nothing you'd like better than to go home with these and keep them from ever being enforced. The last thing you'd want is for a drunk and an ex-con to get your precious aunt's ranch." He stalked to the kitchen and put them on the table.

Zachary said, "That's not true and you know it. Listen to what you are saying."

Jesse's eyes flew to Zach. "No. You listen for a change. They're sneaky, greedy people. Her father probably sent her." He nodded in Silki's direction.

"Nobody sent me, you fool." Silki wanted to scream but she didn't want to give Jesse the satisfaction of knowing he'd hurt her. She kept tight control of her voice and emotions. "I came here trying to save the ranch from my dad. He wants to sell it. Aunt Mariah would hate that. I knew she'd have made some kind of arrangement to keep it out of his hands. I needed to find her."

"Well, you found her and she's dead, and the ranch goes to the low-lifes."

Silki aimed a disgusted glance at Jesse, who'd lost his mind as far as she was concerned. Zach on the other hand looked like he was still hanging in there mentally. "Zachary, what did the papers say exactly?"

"You get the hunting cabin and the land around it. She wanted you to have a roof over your head. He patted Silki's hand and said, "She wanted you taken care of."

"Yeah, great, but I can take care of myself. What about you?" Silki wanted the details. Needed the details.

"The house, land, cattle, horses are for me and Jesse. It's what she promised us." He looked first at Jesse, then at Silki. "She kept her promise."

Silki didn't feel well. There was this sinking feeling in the pit of her stomach and it wasn't from not eating. She really didn't want to be the one to tell them, but they'd find out soon enough when they got to Texas. It wasn't fair to let them walk into it unprepared. "There aren't any horses or cattle on the place. I walked it from one end to the other myself. There's nothing there."

She was still looking at Zachary, waiting for his reaction when Jesse's hands gripped her arms like steel vices and ripped her off the couch. She'd never considered herself a lightweight, but Jesse was strong and she was a rag doll in his hands. One that was being held tightly and pulled into the middle of the room. It was hard to hear what he was saying because her brain was arguing with her first-instinct to fight back. "Stop," finally fell out of her mouth. She refused to take him down again.

At the same time, she was wrenched out of Jesse's hands and wrapped in Zachary's arms. At least she wasn't moving. She clung to the solidness of the man wishing that she could stop shaking.

Zachary yelled for the first time in years. "Don't ever treat a woman like that!"

He rubbed Silki's back and murmured softly as if to a child, "It's okay, he won't hurt you. I won't let him. You're all right. It'll be all right."

She gulped deep breaths and snuffled, "It'll never be all right, you've been cheated."

Silki struggled to gain control and gave an inelegant sniff. She could hear Zachary's heart beating under her ear. He was still alive; she wasn't too late to do something to help. "We can't let them win. I'm going to help you."

He nodded gently. "Of course you are. We won't let them win."

∽

Zach shook his head in disbelief. She was still worried about him. He rested his cheek on the top of her head. So like Blue. She was right, he'd been cheated. Jesse had been cheated and so had Silki. He whispered calmly, "She wouldn't leave us without some way to get by. We just have to find it. It's bound to be in these papers somewhere."

Zach fixed a hard gaze on Jesse. He was his son, but he'd done the unthinkable. Jesse was too big, too strong to ever handle a woman roughly. He didn't want to fight with his son but there were limits.

Still holding Silki, more to reassure himself that she was okay than anything, he said to Jesse, "I watched that man backhand Blue so hard her head snapped back and I thought he'd broken her neck. It almost killed me. She wanted to stay with us. Hitting a woman in anger is not something a man does. I don't want to see it again, ever. You're too strong to lose control."

Jesse tried to defend himself. "I wasn't trying to hurt her. I didn't hit her, but damn, she could tear up those papers and we'd have nothing. She doesn't really care about us; nobody cares about us. Why can't you see that?"

Silki picked her head up and turned red-rimmed eyes on Jesse. She looked like something out of a bad sci-fi movie and Zach wasn't about to stop her from ripping his son to pieces. Jesse would have to stand there and take it.

She sniffled again and said, "Mariah died because she cared about you. How much more do you want? How much more do you think you're worth?"

Jesse stood there open mouthed for a second before turning on his heels, stomping back to the bedroom, and slamming the door shut. He didn't have an answer. His mind replayed the whole lousy scene and he still didn't have an answer. Her boots were laying on the floor at the foot of his bed. Yeah, whose bed had her boots been under? Wouldn't the world like to know the lovely Miss Silki Warfield had shared a bed with a bastard. He swept them up and chucked them out into the front room before slamming the door shut a second time. There, that made him feel better.

Jesse sat on the edge of his bed resting his head in his hands, elbows braced on his knees. He was the biggest loser ever born except for maybe Zach. He couldn't win. Nothing he did was ever right. For the first time in his whole rotten life, he'd found a woman that he honestly wanted. Not just a fast fuck, or a temporary place to crash. But a woman who could keep his attention, his interest, make his cock hard without even trying.

So, what had he done? Gone and screwed it up. Wrecked his only chance at something decent. Seeing her all over Zach had set off something inside of him that he couldn't control. He wanted to yell at her, "Look at me. Jesse. I'm the one who wants you. I'm the one who can love you." Oh shit! There it was, the L word. Now it was out in the open and he'd have to pay for it. He'd been paying all his life so this wasn't going to be a big change, it was only more disappointment he'd have to live with, because she'd never love him back.

He heard the front door open and close. A heartbeat later, the rez-ride growled to life and drove off. She was gone. His fingers dug into his scalp; she'd left him. Well, why not? After all, he was so fine. Yeah, he didn't need her, there were plenty of others.

The shower turned on, so Zach must have stayed. Okay, he could make things right with his old man. Apologize. He'd been wrong to grab her like that, but he'd never hit a woman in his life. This time he'd come close. Closer than he wanted to think about, and closer than he ever wanted to come again.

It scared him. No matter how bad things got he wasn't going to start down that road. Some men did, but not him. The thought made him sick. He'd be more careful. He'd get cleaned up, talk to Zach, set things right.

They could go see what was left of this so-called ranch. Maybe they could do something with it. Maybe pigs could fly in Texas.

CHAPTER FIFTEEN

ZACH WALKED into the bedroom with a towel wrapped around his waist. Jesse glanced at him long enough to realize that eating for the last couple of weeks had put a little weight on his father. He almost looked like the man he used to be. He didn't have the muscle, but he was slowly getting back to his former size. That was good. The muscle would come later. The man was looking healthy for a change.

"Look, I'm sorry for being rough with her. I didn't mean to do that, but she has a way of pushing me." Jesse waited for Zach to say something, anything. When he didn't, Jesse said, "I'm sorry if I spoiled things for you."

Zach dropped the towel on his bed and took a clean pair of jeans from the small four-drawer dresser next to his bed. Then he rummaged around for a clean shirt. Finally, he answered, "You haven't spoiled anything for me. You're my son and I've always loved you. Blue loved you, wanted the world for you, and did her best to get it for you. When you're through being angry, you'll be able to see the good that's waiting for you with that girl."

Jesse sneered, his lip curled and his white teeth gleamed in the morning light. "What good? There's never been anything good for me, or for you, for that matter. You were always the town drunk and I was always your throwaway son."

"You got that college scholarship. Where do you think that came from? Aren't many of those around for kids living out here. Blue fixed that for you. And yeah, I'm the town drunk. I did that to myself. I drank to forget. Nobody made me do it. But it's time to move on. We have a chance to get out of here. You can take your education and finally do something with it."

"Don't forget I went to prison. No one's going to let me do anything but sweat like a dog in the sun at some dirty job nobody else wants. I'm an ex-con, a piece of human garbage that no decent person wants to even know." Jesse hung his head and stared at the scars on the floor. He was scarred like that from people walking on him all of his life. "I'll always be some low-life ex-con living from one day to the next with no future, no way to ever be anything respectable.

"You're right. As long as you believe it, everyone else will too. But I don't believe it and Blue didn't either. She pulled every string she could, paid every official she could get to take the money, and got you the best lawyer in the state to try and save your sorry ass. She paid your fine. You'd still be in prison if it weren't for her. You played right into old man Warfield's hands. What did you think you were doing, getting drunk and fucking a judge's wife? Did you think the man was going to let you get away with it?" Zach sat down on his bed and pulled on his socks, followed by his jeans. He stood to fasten them. "You were lucky the only thing they could make stick was the drunk driving and stolen car. The damn thing was in the judge's name, not his wife's, and he wasn't going to admit he'd let anyone not even her, have permission to drive it after Warfield made an impressive donation to his campaign."

Jesse mumbled, "She said she was leaving him. She was afraid of him and wanted me to drive her to her mom's. She hid in the back seat so no one would see her."

"Yeah, and she said all that to the lawyers. For all the good it did you. At least they didn't try you for kidnapping the woman. They stuck you in a hole for three years. The way you act tells me you don't want to make any effort to crawl out of it. This isn't what we are. We're warriors, fighters. We don't lie down and die because some white bastard says to. We wait and when the time is right, we turn on the son-of-a-bitch and show him what we're really made of."

Jesse spat the words at Zach. "I didn't see you turning on anybody. You laid down drunk in the gutter and let them spit on you."

"They had to think they'd won. It was the only way to make them leave you alone." Zach buttoned his shirt and tucked it into his jeans. "I had to stop being a threat. I had to be a loser no decent woman would want. It was the only way to win in the end. Everything I did was to protect you." Zach turned and walked out leaving Jesse staring after him.

Jesse spent the rest of the morning thinking over all the things Zach told him. Then he got cleaned up and walked into town to get lunch. He wasn't going to sit in the lousy apartment and wait for Zach to come home and chew him out again.

He had clean jeans and a t-shirt that fit. He looked good. He'd find someone to party with and have a good time. He'd forget Silki and Zach, and all his old dreams that were never going to come true. He still had some money he'd gotten from Silki for gas. It wouldn't hurt her to pay for his evening's entertainment. After all, he'd walked miles looking for her dead aunt. She owed him something for that.

After lunch he stopped at the pawn shop and got his watch back. He'd thank Little Red for that later.

He pushed open the door to the Country Acres tavern and walked up to the bar. He hitched his hip onto an empty stool and waited for the bartender to take his order. He pulled out some bills from his pocket and placed them on the bar showing everyone he had the money to pay for his drinks and theirs. He knew that would get things rolling. People loved the sight of money, especially in a place like Country Acres where money was tight.

It worked, as usual. In a few minutes Jesse had a beer and company approaching on his left. He smiled invitingly at the woman making her way toward him. He'd seen her before, maybe even fucked her; he couldn't remember right off hand.

"Hey Jesse, how've you been?" she asked, flashing him a big smile.

She wasn't bad looking, kind of tired around the eyes, but all right.

Long black hair parted in the middle and held back with beaded barrettes. Her jeans were too tight and so was her red t-shirt. It didn't leave much to the imagination. He knew what he'd be getting.

"Fine, how about you?"

"Yeah, okay. My kids are with my sister so I've got some time to myself." She perched on the barstool next to his. "I just stopped in here to visit, you know."

Yeah, he knew all about it. Too bored to stay home so she'd gone down to the local watering hole to see what she could find for company, start something with somebody, find her dream lover.

"So, can I buy you a beer?" He could play along.

"I don't know." She sounded uncertain. "I mean we had a good time last time, but I don't know."

Jesse watched as she looked around the room and chewed on her bottom lip.

"Are you with someone?" He didn't want to fight with a jealous boyfriend. He was looking for some easy company, and a fast fuck to get Little Red out of his system.

"No. I don't know is all. I heard you've been with some white girl, and you beat her up pretty bad. I don't need that trouble."

Jesse coughed. He'd almost choked on his swallow of beer. He glared at the woman whose name he still didn't remember. He watched in fascination as she inched away from him to the far edge of her barstool, putting a couple inches more between them. Did she think he was going to hit her right there in the bar?

He cleared his throat and asked, "Where'd you hear that?"

"I don't know. Around. I guess your neighbors heard you and Zach fighting over her this morning and then they saw her stumble out of the apartment and drive off. One of the maids working the morning shift at the motel saw her and she was all messed up. Her clothes were torn and she looked bad."

Jesse took in the tight grip her left hand had on the edge of the bar and way her upper teeth bit into her lower lip. She wasn't going to have a lip at the rate she was chewing. He was starting to remember her. She wore cherry lip gloss so thick he got a mouthful of it when he'd kissed her. Okay, no kissing, he could get off without kissing her.

Silki didn't wear lip gloss. She didn't waste time biting her lips either. He didn't want to think about Silki and her kissable lips. He was out on the town trying to forget her.

"Believe what you want. If you'd like a beer, I'll buy you one."

She looked around the room and glanced at the money on the bar.

"I guess it'll be okay. You were always real nice to me."

Jesse signaled the bartender for another beer. He smiled at his nameless companion and said, "Yeah, and you were always real nice to me."

She giggled at that. Nobody giggled anymore. What the hell was the matter with him? He needed a woman, not some giggling, silly girl who wanted to fuck him for a few beers and pretend it was love. Hell, he still couldn't remember her name.

He wanted Little Red. He wanted her to love him. He wanted to fuck her, call it love and have it be love. That's what he wanted. Man, he was in bad shape. He chugged the rest of his beer and signaled the bartender for another. It was going to be a long night.

It was funny what a few dollars and a couple cans of beer would buy. It hadn't taken all that long to get SuAnne to go home with him. After a couple beers she was tough enough to throw him on his ass if he even thought about hitting her. She didn't take that shit from anyone. Self-confidence in a can, what a deal.

It had been easy enough to get her over to the apartment and flat on her back on top of his bed. He didn't want her between the sheets he'd shared with Little Red. SuAnne's inebriated voice carried like a bull-horn. The neighbors were gonna have plenty to talk about. He squeezed her tit through her clothes and she moaned. He pressed his half-boner against her pelvis and his zipper chewed into his cock. She moaned louder. Loud enough that neither one of them heard the front door open.

Silki and Zachary stopped in at the diner for dinner, but before they could sit down she noticed the silence and the stares. Something was up. They'd been eating there for days and hadn't gotten that kind of attention before. Something had definitely changed. She didn't like the vibe, caught Zachary's attention and suggested they get their food to-go.

After the short ride back to the apartment, Zachary had his hands full getting the plastic bags of food through the door without dropping everything. Silki followed close behind juggling their drinks.

Zachary said, "Let me put these down and we'll eat. We can talk about what the papers say over dinner."

Silki followed him toward the kitchen. She was thirsty and hungry. It had been a relief when Zachary knocked on her door and asked her to go to dinner. He had great timing and knew what a girl needed after the rough start to her day. There was a lot to like about Zachary. Mariah had seen the good in him.

He was looking healthier. She could see why he'd been a heart-stopper in his younger days. A few more pounds, a little muscle and he'd be a fine-looking man. Middle-aged but very fine.

She said, "I don't know what was wrong with those people at the diner but something was off. I didn't want to sit there getting indigestion waiting for the ax to fall. I can't explain it, but I had a real bad feeling."

"You're smart to follow your instincts. This is better. We can relax and take our time."

A groan issued from the bedroom. Silki spun around and glared at the closed door. Her head snapped to Zachary and her smile turned to a frown. Her jaws clenched and she glared at the bedroom door. Jesse was home and not alone. Hell and be damned. The man was shameless. What was he thinking bringing his hook-up home with Zachary living there?

Zachary's eyes followed her every move. She'd been slammed with a lot unpleasantness recently and hadn't handled it all that well. He was probably worried she'd do something unladylike. She said, "Ignore it and it'll go away in about twenty minutes."

Zachary suggested, "Let's get out of here."

"Hell no! I'm not carting our food back out to the car. I'm hungry and I intend to eat my dinner while it's still warm." Silki glared at Zachary daring him to make her leave.

"Are you sure?" he asked, and raised an eyebrow.

"Absolutely. Now unpack the food and let's eat." She smirked. "Our chicken-fried steaks are better than whatever's going on in there."

Silki pulled out the kitchen chair dating from sometime back in the sixties and settled herself on the cracked vinyl seat.

She was going to eat first and kill Jesse second. A wicked grin spread across her face. Mayhem was better on a full stomach. She reached for her boxed dinner as Zach pushed it across the table. She waited for him to sit down before opening it.

She ignored the occasional noise that drifted through the room and watched Zachary focus on his meal like he hadn't seen food in a week. The whole scene was too bad to be real. Silki had trouble keeping her laughter from spilling out.

She and Jesse had no commitment to each other. He had every right to do what he was doing. That didn't mean she wanted to listen to it. She was tempted to bang on his door and tell them to hurry up or shut up.

They finished their dinners quickly and put the carry-out boxes in the trash. Silki wiped off the table, and spread out the papers she'd spent the afternoon studying. She'd found a way for them to survive.

Zach pulled up his chair next to hers, leaned over the table and studied the paragraph she pointed to. The silence caught her attention first. She stopped following the sentences with her finger and stared at the bedroom door.

The apartment was momentarily quiet, then a resounding string of curses filled the small space.

The female voice yowled, "What the hell is wrong with you? You can't even get it up."

Jesse shouted, "Get out. Go back to the bar and find some other bastard to fuck."

Zachary's face turned red from his neck to his hairline. Silki's mouth dropped open while her eyes stayed focused on the bedroom door.

"Get your lazy ass out of here," boomed through the apartment.

After some scuffling the bedroom door opened, Jesse's guest stomped into the living room looking over her shoulder and grumbling,

"Guess you need that biker chick to get you hard." She turned her head forward, came face to face with Silki and shrieked, "Ah!" Then she added, "Oh shit!"

Nose to nose Silki glared daggers at the black-haired woman with cherry-red lips and smeared mascara creating the traditional 'racoon eyes' that commonly accompanied the walk of shame.

Her voice lowered to a feral growl, "Get your skanky self out of this apartment, stay away from Jesse, and don't come back."

Silki watched the girl turn a dark scarlet before blurting out, "You're the one he beat up. Everybody knows you're fucking both of them."

"That's right and I keep what's mine, both of them." Silki crossed her arms over her chest and tucked her fists out of sight.

Silki snarled, "The door is right over there. Get your ass through it."

Bolting for the door, Jesse's latest bed partner shouted, "Fuck you," over her shoulder as she scampered from the apartment.

Zachary crossed the room and stood next to Silki. "I can see you're a tyrant. What's yours is yours. Good to know." He sauntered back to the kitchen and sat down. He met her eyes. "Can we get back to these papers now?"

Silki shrugged, she didn't want to discuss it either. She walked to the front door and closed it. "Yeah, sure." She returned to the kitchen table like nothing unusual had happened. If she let it bother her, she'd have indigestion and ruin a perfectly good meal. Jesse's hook-up wasn't worth it.

Jesse sat at the head of his bed with his back against the wall, his knees pulled up to his chest, and his arms wrapped around his legs, trying to hold himself together.

He wanted to die.

How was he going to face Silki after she'd heard everything that had just happened? She'd know he was no good. He reasoned he hadn't been cheating on her since they weren't together but somehow it didn't feel that way. He had secretly hoped he could change that some-day. After what she'd just witnessed that would never happen, and he had no one to blame but himself.

He rested his forehead on his knees and closed his eyes. He could see himself clearly. This was the end, the bottom of the pit, there was no place left to go. He'd hit the hard rock bottom of his life. The landing had broken what little self-respect and pride he had left and he knew it.

It would be a long, long time before he could even begin to put the pieces back together, and he wasn't sure he wanted to. He'd have to face what he'd become. That was a look in the mirror that would be hard to take and he wasn't that strong.

Under the dim kitchen light, Silki and Zachary went over the documents one by one. She pointed at the bottom of the page. "Right here is where it says there's money set aside for the running of the ranch and each of us has an account for living expenses. We need to find these accounts. I know she had an attorney, a bookkeeper and an investment broker. We can start with them."

When Zach didn't answer she looked over at him to see what was going on. He'd been too quiet. There was nothing she could say about Jesse that she hadn't already said. She'd really gone and stuck her foot in it. Sleeping with both of them. Were the people in this town crazy? There wasn't a woman alive that could take on both Zachary and Jesse.

She could see his thoughts were a thousand miles away.

She questioned, "Zachary?"

No response.

"Zachary, are you all right?"

"All right? No girl, I'm not all right. I've been accused of some bad things in my life, but sharing a woman with my son. That's low, even for me."

"Don't pay any attention to that nonsense. It only goes to show you how bored these people are. Jesse wouldn't beat a woman and you know it. And we know I'm not sleeping with either one of you. It sounds like a really bad X-rated movie. I doubt we could sell that story line to a porn producer. Come on, we've got important stuff to take care of here." She squeezed is arm gently and patted it. "We know the truth, that's all that matters."

"What is the truth? In a town like this, you can't be sleeping with two men at the same time without being talked about."

"I don't care what people say. They don't know anything about us. It's not worth worrying about. Let's get on with what's important." Silki didn't take her eyes off Zachary. He still hadn't moved. He still wouldn't look her in the eyes. Well, that wasn't a big indicator because staring someone in the eyes at a time like this could be considered rude and he wasn't a rude man. But he needed to stop staring at the table and see her.

"Grandpa and Daddy called Mariah every bad word they could think of, and I think they even invented a couple new words. It didn't bother her. She knew who she was. She was good with herself, and I'm good with who I am. I don't measure myself by what other people think. I have to live with me, so it's what I think that counts."

"How did you get so strong?" Zachary glanced at Silki and then looked across the room at the closed bedroom door.

"I'm not strong. I'm following in Mariah's footsteps. If she made it, I can make it. I have to, you need me."

Zachary finally turned his head toward her and met her gaze. His shoulders slumped and he folded his hands on the table. His voice cracked when he asked, "And what about Jesse?"

Silki put her elbow on the table and rested her head in her hand. She could see he thought she didn't care about Jesse.

"Jesse doesn't need me right now. He's trying to prove something to himself, and maybe to me. He has to live with the consequences, and so do I, and so do you. We all heard it. What we do about it is something else."

Zachary raised an eyebrow in inquiry. "What are you going to do about it?"

"I keep what's mine." Her gaze bored into his.

"And he's yours?"

"Yeah." She sounded sure, like it was something everyone knew. "Until he tells me differently."

"How do you know? He's doing everything he can to push you away, or haven't you noticed?" Zachary wrung his hands.

"I noticed. But it doesn't matter. I guess he's a little scared of me. It'll take him a while to get over that, but it's going to be fine." She smiled, "You'll see." Jesse was his son; all he had left in the world. She'd do her best to help him.

Zachary blinked and his brow wrinkled. "But how do you know?"

"Because Mariah told me." She softly smiled, reached out and put her hand over his. "Give him time."

CHAPTER SIXTEEN

THE NEXT MORNING, Silki got their breakfast at the diner along with a few sly looks from the men and condemning stares from the women. She didn't have time to waste on them. They could think what they wanted. She gathered their bags and walked out with her head held high. She had nothing to apologize for and nothing to be ashamed of.

A few minutes later, sitting across from Zachary at the kitchen table she could see the worry lines etched on his forehead, and that was more important to her than anything else. She shoved the thought of wringing a few necks out of her mind and concentrated on the man in front of her.

There were dark circles under his eyes, he ate slowly, and kept glancing toward the bedroom. He had every right to be preoccupied, but it wouldn't solve any of their problems and the list seemed to be growing. Hell, thinking about it made her tired.

Jesse's food sat untouched. The bedroom door remained closed. Looming silence eclipsed their meal and unduly influenced her inclination to whisper. It wasn't like one of them had died.

Putting her fork down, she modulated her voice to gently ask, "Are you all right? Is the food okay?"

Zach stirred the scrambled eggs with his fork and looked up.

"Food's fine. I've got a lot on my mind." He went back to poking at his breakfast.

He still wore the same clothes he'd had on the day before. That told her he hadn't gone in the bedroom to change, hadn't seen Jesse. Her arrival in Martin had turned their world upside down. Zachary surprised her with how well he dealt with the changes, but Jesse was having a tough time of it. Zachary had every reason to be worried about his son. She got that.

"I know you're worried." Well, duh, that was brilliant. She tried again. "It's only natural for you to be concerned about Jesse. If we give him time to come to terms with what happened, he'll be okay. He's smart. He'll figure things out."

Zach kept staring at his cooling food.

She should say something comforting or reassuring. She stared at her toast. No answer there. She wasn't much into sharing, some things a girl really didn't want people to know. But if it would help Zachary, just this once, she'd go ahead and blab.

"I know it's hard to see him like this." Not that either one of them had laid eyes on Jesse lately. "It's tough to know someone you care about is hurting and you want to rush in and fix it for them. That isn't always the best idea. Sometimes a person has to make their own way through the rough stuff in order to learn and move on."

Zach glanced her way, and she caught his eye. Good, now she could try to explain.

Silki sat back. It was hard to look at Zachary, but if she didn't, he wouldn't be able to see what this was costing her and he wasn't going to get off that easy. If she was going to go through this, so was he.

"I'd known something was wrong with my marriage almost from the start. Like a couple hours into the honeymoon. But there I was, and there was no getting out of it. So, I told myself to make the best of it. Charley was probably suffering from a case of honeymoon jitters." She took a deep breath. This was the hard part. "I was fooling myself." There, it was out in the open. "We both worked. He worked late a lot. It didn't really bother me because I had the townhouse to myself, and I could go out with friends after work without having to think about Charley."

Silki gave an inelegant snort and drew circles on the table with her index finger before continuing. "We were at one of his company parties around the holidays when the truth finally came out. He'd been drinking and he bragged to some younger executives that the right marriage would take them farther than all the talent in the world. Guess he didn't know I was standing right behind him."

Silki's hand stilled before she put it palm down on the worn table. The poor thing had been wiped so many times the gray and white swirled pattern was totally white in places.

Zachary waited for her to go on.

"He continued his affair with his secretary after we married. You don't have to say it. It's the oldest story out there. I really didn't care. Not until he divorced me, had me evicted from the townhouse, and stole all our assets. He left me sitting on the curb. My car was leased to his company so I couldn't even drive away. I traded my Rolex and fur coat for the gardener's truck. It got me to the Ruins and the rest as they say is history. I could sit there and starve or get off my butt and do something about it. Here I am."

Silki shifted in her seat. "The point is, I had to hit rock bottom before I could make myself face facts and climb out of the hole I was in."

"Do you think Jesse's hit rock bottom?" Zachary raised an eyebrow.

"Yeah, I do. If not, he'd be out here eating breakfast and showing us his I-don't-care smug attitude." Silki eyed Zachary and added, "You know you're going to have to change clothes sometime."

Zach eyed her back. "Yeah, and you could go tell him his breakfast is here."

"Somehow I don't think he really wants to see me." Silki gave a wry grin. "He probably thinks women are pretty awful right now and this is mostly my fault. If it wasn't for me, you wouldn't have been here and nobody would have heard a thing. Well, nobody except the neighbors."

Zachary glared at the far wall. "The neighbors hear too much."

"It doesn't matter. We're not going to be here much longer." Silki tapped her fingers on the table. "We should start planning how we're going to get home. We won't all fit on the bike."

Their eyes met and they both started to laugh.

Jesse stumbled out of the bedroom and into the bathroom without saying a word or looking in their direction. He'd heard them talking and laughing. Hell, they were probably still laughing at him. The whole stinking town was probably laughing at him this morning.

He flushed the toilet and turned on the shower. Kicking off his jeans he stepped under the spray. He bowed his head to let the water soak his hair and run down his face. He wished he could wash away the past, the mistakes, the stinking shit-pile he'd made of his life.

He grabbed the soap. He could still smell SuAnne on his skin. It was going to take more than soap to get rid of the stench. He rubbed till his skin was half raw, and he could still smell the cheap perfume.

His stomach curled. He shut off the water and staggered to the commode barely in time to hurl what little there was in his stomach. He continued to wretch even after there was nothing left to come up. He was so sick. Sick of his life, sick of meaningless empty sex, cheap whiskey, and warm beer. He didn't want to live like this anymore. He didn't care if he had to crawl to Texas. He was going to start over. He would beg Silki not to tell everybody what a piece of shit he was. There was a remote chance she'd keep quiet. She probably wouldn't want anyone to know she'd ever met him.

All he needed was a chance, he could change. He could leave the beer alone and find a nice girl who wouldn't expect too much from him. He hung his head over the sink. He'd leave the beer alone and never mind the girl. The only one he wanted wouldn't touch him with a long, pointed stick, never mind any part of her body.

He brushed his teeth and rinsed his mouth. He needed to finish getting cleaned up and crawl to her on his hands and knees. If he begged, really begged, she might let him go with them. He'd never begged for anything and he have to figure out where to start.

They stopped laughing as Jesse staggered from one room to the next. Looking at each other they silently acknowledged the fact that he was alive and looked like death warmed over. The sounds of the shower followed by Jesse's vomiting filled the space between them. They couldn't help him, not this time.

Zachary was the first to speak. "He has to come with us."

"Absolutely, it's what Mariah wanted. It's only fair. Do you think he will?"

"If we don't make it too hard for him."

Silki said matter-of-factly, "I wasn't planning on making it hard for him." One side of her mouth curved up.

"He won't make it easy for us. He's never made it easy for anyone to care about him." Zachary released a sigh of resignation. "It's always been that way with Jesse. I don't know why he won't let anyone get close to him. I've never been able to get him to explain it to me."

"It's his way of protecting himself." Silki sipped her lukewarm coffee. "If he doesn't care, he won't feel the hurt so bad when he gets rejected. I'm pretty sure you have some first-hand knowledge about that."

"I must have missed that lecture in school. I had to learn it the hard way."

He got up and walked to the counter. Picking up the coffee pot he brought it back to the table and poured some in both their cups. "Do you think he'll want some?"

Silki cocked her head to one side listening to the sounds coming from the bathroom. He was back in the shower. She glanced at Zach. "Yeah, he'll want some but he won't ask us for it. He won't ask us for anything."

"How about we go out and leave his breakfast here?"

"Works for me." Silki got up and stretched. "Let's go see a man about a horse. I wouldn't mind keeping the Regal. I've sort of gotten attached to it."

A slow smile spread over Zachary's face. "Huh, okay, guess that's fine with me."

It took a fair amount of haggling to get the garage owner to part with the rez-ride, but in the end the money had been too good for him to resist, and they had a deal. The Regal was going to Texas. It wasn't a fancy way to ride anymore but it would get them there. It wasn't as if they had a lot of stuff to take with them.

Cruising down the road headed to the apartment, Zachary glanced at Silki. He said, "It's kind of like the old days, we loaded what we had on our horses and moved. All we could take with us was what we could carry."

Silki kept her eyes on the road. "The old days were tough on everybody. It's up to us to decide what kind of new days we're going to have. It's time to rethink a few things."

Zachary's brow knit and the skin around his eyes wrinkled. He asked, "What things do you have in mind?"

"I want to get things right so Mariah can rest in peace. I want to be at peace with myself. I'm tired of never being able to please anybody no matter what I do. I think it's way past time I got my priorities straight." Silki tightened her grip on the steering wheel. "We can't make Jesse do anything. He's got to want to come with us."

As they pulled up in front of the apartment, Zach said, "We'll talk to him, explain that we want him, that we need him."

Silki heard the words and knew they came from the man's heart. Jesse was his only child. They weren't going to leave him behind.

If she had to get on her knees and beg him to come, she'd do it for Zachary. If that didn't work, she'd hog-tie the stubborn mule and stuff him in the back seat. He could cuss and complain all the way to Texas but he'd go. He could do it the hard way or make it easy on himself. It really didn't matter to her.

Zachary led the way up the stairs and through the door. They needed to start gathering up their stuff. Jesse looked up from his seat on the couch, coffee cup in hand and the empty breakfast container open on the coffee table in front of him. He had some color in his cheeks, and his eyes were clear. His damp hair hung in soft waves around his shoulders.

Look closer.

Silki focused on his eyes, the windows to the soul some people called them. Of course, some people could look you in the eyes and fool you. They could make you see anything they wanted you to see. They didn't have a soul. Kind of like Charley the Weasel, the conniving, soulless son-of-a-bitch. Catch him off guard and his eyes were black vacant holes.

Jesse's eyes weren't vacant. They were shuttered. In that moment she understood how close he was to falling apart. She could break him into a million pieces. All the glue in the world wouldn't be enough to put him back together again, not ever.

This was her chance to destroy him. She could get even for everything he'd ever said or done, or neglected to do or say. She could make him pay for the rest of his miserable life. It would only take a few simple words.

This was it, her big chance. She fixed her gaze on him so he'd know she was talking directly to him, seeing him.

"We really want you to come with us. We need you. Please, Jesse. We can't do this without you."

She watched his mouth open and close without making a sound. He looked first at Zachary and slowly turned back to her. His eyes shifted to the side and his eyelids fluttered. He looked at the floor and then at the door behind her. She could tell he wanted to run. And she saw it when he realized he had nowhere to go.

His eyes finally settled on Zachary. "Are you sure?"

Zach nodded. "We're sure. We gotta stick together. It's going to take all of us to make this work."

They weren't making him beg. He wasn't going to have to crawl to her on his belly like a whipped dog. All he had to do was say, yes. So, why was it so hard? He didn't want to be left behind. He wanted to go. They were offering him a way out. He had to take it any way they offered it to him. He had to.

"I guess so. It'll be easier with more of us to drive. We can get there sooner."

Zach smiled. "That's great. We ought to go out and celebrate. Get us a real good meal at the diner."

Jesse blinked and looked at the bedroom door. "Sure, we can go out tonight and have steaks."

Silki's eyes followed his line of vision. She said, "Why not? Sounds good to me."

To Jesse, it sounded like horse pucky. She didn't care what excuse he used to get his butt in the car as long as he got in. He had no idea what Zach had said to get her to agree to taking him, but it didn't matter. They weren't going to get there any faster because there were speed limits and she could only ride so many hours a day.

They couldn't go ahead of her because they had no idea how to find the ranch once they got to Texas. She had them there. Without her they'd be wandering the Hill Country for a long, long time. Jesse kept all that to himself. This was not the time to screw up.

In the meantime, they put what few things they wanted to keep in a pile by the door. They'd pack the car right before leaving. Everything else had to be hauled out to the dumpster on the side of the building.

Silki picked up another bag of discarded items and headed out the door.

Jesse watched her go. Everything had been quiet while they'd sorted and packed. Maybe too quiet. He still couldn't believe he'd been asked to go with them after the scene they'd witnessed the night before. He didn't understand it and he didn't want to question it too closely. If they changed their minds, what would happen to him? He'd be left behind, again.

But still it bothered him enough that he had to ask Zach, "Is everything okay with her?"

"Depends on what you call everything, but yeah, she's okay." Zach went on stacking his clothes on top of the dresser.

Jesse rubbed a hand over the top of his head. "I don't know why I brought SuAnne here. I didn't think you'd bring Silki back here after what happened earlier."

Jesse realized he was rambling and the words weren't coming out right. Quiet, he needed to shut up before he screwed things up again.

Zach's focus remained on the clothes in his hands. "Yeah, there were times I didn't mean for things to happen, but they did, and I paid for them over and over again. I'll pay for them till my dying day, but I can't make them go away. I should have been a better husband, and a better father. But I wasn't, and now it's too late."

"I'm sorry." Jesse looked down and turned away.

"We have to live with the things we do." Zach's hands rested on the clothes. He took a deep breath, and said, "I want a better life for you, but I can't make you live it."

"Don't you want to get out of here and go to Texas? You talked about doing this for years." Jesse stopped packing and waited for Zach to answer him.

"What I want is my life back. I want Blue and all the years we should have had together. But this is what I get because I didn't have the courage to fight old man Warfield for what was mine. Don't make the same mistake I did."

"He's dead. I can't fight him. There's nothing to fight over."

"You're wrong. He's dead, but his son is still alive and carrying out his father's wishes. We're just starting to fight and it's going to get rough before it's over. You'd better be thinking about what you want and what you're willing to do to get it."

"What I want, I'll never have. I already know that."

Jesse sounded defeated even to himself so it surprised him to hear his dad say, "What makes you so sure that you won't even try?"

Jesse could barely bring himself to speak the words that would condemn him forever. "She'll never want me, not after last night."

Jesse turned and wandered out of the bedroom leaving Zach alone and staring at the empty space. He needed air; he needed his heart to quit hurting so bad. He wanted Little Red.

He was almost to the front door when it opened and she walked in. She smiled at him and he forgot to breathe for a second. How did she do that to him? How was he going to make it through the rest of his life with her smiling like that and him not being able to touch her, hold her, love her? Oh, hell, he didn't want to admit that, not even to himself. He'd never really loved anybody and now was not the time to start. No, not now, not when it wasn't going to go anywhere. He didn't need the disappointment.

Jesse grumbled, "What are you smiling about?"

Flipping her hair over her shoulder with a toss of her head, Silki smiled bigger and said, "It's moving day, we're all going home at long last."

From behind him, Jesse heard Zach's footsteps and then his voice.

"Those are the best words I've heard in a long time. We've waited a long time." Zach put his hand on Jesse's shoulder. "We're all going home."

Seeing their meager things sitting by the door reminded Silki all too well of her last days in the townhouse. She'd managed to pack a few boxes of her personal things and mail them to her folks before the sheriff had come knocking on the door. The court order read, "all contents of the townhouse to be removed," and movers had taken everything in the name of Charley the Weasel, even the toilet paper. She hadn't had to pack any more boxes because there was nothing left when they pulled away from the curb with the moving van.

This was better. They were taking what they wanted and leaving the past behind.

Silki thought they looked good standing there together like that. They were both tall, slender men with broad shoulders that looked like they could carry the weight of the world without straining. Damn good thing because it would take big strong men to carry the load that was about to land on them like a ton of bricks. They were going to need all their strength and then some. Her father, Harvey Warfield wasn't going to stand still for this, not for one single second. War was going to come at them hard the minute he found out they were in Texas.

"You know something, all this packing has made me real hungry. How about we take a break and go have some dinner?" Smooth, she was so smooth it kind of scared her sometimes. "We can finish up the last of this later."

Zachary took his hand off Jesse's shoulder and moved toward the door.

Jesse didn't budge.

Zach turned and asked, "What's the matter, aren't you coming?"

Silki took Jesse's hand. "Come on. I've got your back."

$\sim$

Oh man, he didn't want to show his face in town. People would be staring and laughing at him. He didn't think he could stand it. But how could he explain that to Zach and Silki? He saw it in her eyes the second she realized what he was thinking, and he knew he'd never be able to fool her; she'd always be able to read him like a neon sign. He was so doomed it wasn't even funny. Before he could open his mouth to spit out some lie, she already had him pegged.

"In all that commotion last night nobody will have the slightest idea what was going on. They're all going to think it was another family squabble. A cat fight over me wanting to keep both of you all to myself." She grinned. "All you have to do is keep smiling and they'll be fit to be tied. As long as we look happy, their curiosity will be killing them. And remember they'd give anything to be in your place. You're living their fantasy." With that she turned and headed out the door saying, "Now, let's give them something to talk about."

CHAPTER SEVENTEEN

Riding long hours and keeping to the speed limits, it took Silki four days to get over the Comal County line. They were on the home stretch with only five more miles to the Ruins. She rode like the devil was chasing her. And he was. Behind her, Jesse barreled down the highway with the hot Texas wind whipping his hair, sweat running down his back, and his t-shirt sticking to his skin. She knew because he'd complained about it at the last four rest stops. Imagine that.

It was too hot in Texas even for the Devil, but there he was. Silki glanced in her left side mirror. Yeah, she could see the horns sticking out the sides of his head. She checked the driver's window to be sure his tail wasn't flapping in the breeze. No, no tail, yet. Man, she needed to get a grip on herself. Her imagination was getting the best of her. Or maybe it was the heat.

According to the calendar, summer was on its way out and fall was coming in. That didn't mean the temperature went down in Texas. Nope, it could stay hot for months. The weather was the least of her worries. They were on the last of the money she'd gotten from selling her Harley Sportster and her credit card was reaching its limit. She needed to find the operating accounts Mariah had set up for them. They needed money soon.

And that was only the beginning. She was going to have to get

Zachary and Jesse cleaned up and present them to everyone as Mariah's husband and stepson. Man, oh man, was that going to heat things up. The fur was going to fly in all directions.

Maybe she could eat rat poison, die and avoid the whole ugly mess. They could go it alone and she could rest quietly in her grave. Of course, she'd miss the look on Charley the Weasel's face when he got the news that the Warfield empire was going down like the Titanic and taking Hardcastle with it. What a shame, hmm, she really wanted to stick around for that. It would be worth it to watch the mighty Hardcastle fall on his ass. Yeah, she'd hang in there for the show if nothing else.

Silki rolled on the throttle and the Heritage roared in response. She couldn't outrun the wind but she could lead the Devil on a merry chase and make it home before sunset. This time Highway 46 looked a lot better. It was taking her home, really home. This time she had a place to call her own. It wasn't much, a water well and the old hunting cabin, but it was hers along with ten acres around it. For a girl who started with nothing a few months ago, she was doing good with her own house, truck and Harley. She was aces now.

Zachary and Jesse had the main house along with everything else. The land and barns were all theirs along with all of Mariah's assets. She'd always kept her business and estate in order and that was going to eat Harvey Warfield's lunch. His sister was getting even with him big time for everything he'd done. Only he didn't know it yet.

Silki roared past the Highway 46 Tavern and waved to the fellas sitting on the front porch. Same old bunch. Some things didn't change. They'd been drinking, visiting and gossiping there for as far back as she could remember. She'd have to remember to stop by and introduce Zachary and Jesse. The thought of it made her smile. She smiled all the way to the front gate.

～

Jesse hung on to the steering wheel trying to ignore the cramped muscle in his right leg. The Regal didn't have working cruise control. He'd been behind the wheel since they'd left Martin. The job of driving had fallen to him, and he'd done his best to keep up with her. But following Silki down Highway 83 had been like following a tornado across the plains of Nebraska, Kansas, Oklahoma and Texas. She'd only stopped for gas, food, and a little sleep. This last stretch had been the worst. Hot, sweaty, dusty. Jesse rolled his shoulders and then stretched his legs as much as the tight space would allow. It didn't help.

"I've got a cramp in my foot," he muttered to Zach.

"We're almost there."

"How do you know? We've been driving for the last two days in Texas. How big is this state anyway?" Jesse glanced at Zach, who was watching Silki wave at some scruffy looking guys outside a tavern. "Do you think she knows them? Everybody in this place waves at everybody else."

"Hard to say, but we're almost there. I can feel it. This looks the way Mariah described it. That's the Highway 46 Tavern. They have music and dancing on the weekends. We were going to go, have something to eat and dance. She liked to dance."

Zach sounded like a man who'd lost his last friend, given up on his last dream. Jesse didn't like the sound of it. In the past it was usually followed by a drunken binge that only ended when Zach passed out. It wasn't supposed to be like that anymore.

"Are you sure you want to do this? To be here? If it's going to make you sad all the time, it's probably not a good idea. We could sell the place and move somewhere else."

Jesse watched Silki disappear over the top of a hill. Heaven only knew what was on the other side. He had to be ready for anything. When he heard the anger and hurt in Zach's voice, he knew he'd hit a nerve. By then it was too late and he couldn't take back the words.

"She dreamed this dream for the three of us. She spent her whole life building this and we will not run away. I'm not going to let her down this time." Zach drew in a ragged breath. "Do you understand?" This time I'm going to be the man she needed me to be."

"Yeah. Fine, I understand." He said the words but he didn't understand at all. What kind of man had she needed? Mariah Blue was dead. It was way too late to do anything for her.

Jesse turned right and followed Silki up a narrow two-lane road. He wanted to get out of the car and hold still for a week. His whole body vibrated with the hum of the engine and wheels rolling over the black-top. He'd never been on the road like this and he never wanted to do it again. It hurt. His back ached, his legs were stiff, he hated sleeping on the front seat, and his tailbone would never be the same. He swore if he lived through this, he was never going on another road trip.

He followed Silki into a driveway and stopped. *Oh please, let this be it.*

He leaned out the window and yelled, "Is this it?"

Silki kept digging in her jeans pocket. "Yeah, this is it. Welcome to your new home," she shouted over the noise from the Harley and the car.

∼

Finding the keys, she walked stiffly over to the gate. She checked the dirt for signs of intruders. She'd locked the place up when she left, and it looked like it hadn't been disturbed. She hadn't told anyone where she was staying, where she was going or why. That didn't mean her father wouldn't come around snooping.

The gate swung open and Jesse pulled through stopping when they came even with her. Silki knew she should say something to Zachary, but what do you say to a man who has arrived too late. *Sorry old boy, but she'd dead. Here's what's left.* No, that didn't sound right.

Instead, Silki said, "Welcome home, Zachary."

Zach blinked. "Yeah, we made it. She said the house was on a hill. How do we get there?"

Silki pointed to a dirt road on their left. "That way. It's kind of bumpy so go slow."

"Okay."

She watched them start up the hill. They had a long way to go and bumpy didn't even begin to cover it. She pulled through on the bike, closed the ranch gate and clicked the lock. No uninvited guests for now.

The Harley rolled to a stop and she parked beside the car when she

138

reached the house. It was good to be back on familiar ground. She could see Zachary and Jesse stretching their backs and legs. It had been a long, long ride. Longer for some than others.

Standing over six feet tall, the two of them had no doubt been cramped in the mid-sized car, leg room notwithstanding. Yeah, it had been a long ride home for Zachary. Damn, she wished it didn't have to end this way. Why couldn't Mariah come running out of the house and throw her arms around Zachary and kiss the man senseless? That was how happy endings were supposed to be.

She'd get her stuff out of the saddlebags later; she was stiff and doing a darn good job of walking with the old-biker-limp as she ambled toward the garage door.

Passing Jesse, she glanced at Zachary and said, "We used the back door the most."

He fell in beside her.

"She always left the garage door open except when the weather got really bad. The front door takes some doing to open and close. It's heavy. This is easier."

Silki reached down and pulled up on the handle. The gears screeched and the chain clanked. The door moved up slowly, protesting every inch of the way. Mud dauber nests cracked and crumbled, raining dust down on their heads. Silki's hair was protected by her doo rag, but Zachary had to brush the dirt out of his with his hand.

Not exactly the welcome home he'd hoped for, but then he was a few years late. That was enough to piss off just about every woman on the planet. He kept quiet and followed Silki up the steps and onto the back porch. This was it. He was finally going to see the house Mariah built. His house, his house of broken dreams.

He stepped into the kitchen behind Silki. It was big and made him feel small. The outside appearance was misleading but that was the beauty of it. The woman he remembered never did anything in half-measures but she didn't flaunt it. You had to get up close to see the quality. That was one of the things he loved about her. She believed in doing everything the right way.

Silki kept walking. She reached up and flipped the light switches on the living room wall. The place lit up like high noon. She turned to Zach. "This is the living room and dining room. The bedrooms are at the other end. I've been staying in my old room. I'll get my stuff out and Jesse can have it."

Zach kept staring, his eyes blinked occasionally and his chest moved with each breath. He was still alive, but he didn't feel good. Men weren't supposed to faint but the lightheadedness reminded him it got like this right before he'd pass out. If his eyes rolled back and he keeled over he'd crack his head on the tile floor and then what would Silki do? Oh no, he wasn't going to leave her high and dry. He sucked in a deep breath.

"I'll show you to your room and you can lie down if this is getting to you." Silki stepped toward him. Taking his arm, she guided him to Mariah's bedroom. She pushed open the door to a huge room and pulled Zach in behind her. She nodded toward the massive four-poster bed. "There, you can rest a while. Jesse and I can bring in the things from the car."

Zach watched in silence as Silki turned around and disappeared the way they'd come. He was all alone. Him, the empty room and a bed he never got to share with his Blue. He would have to be dead not to feel her presence. She was there, waiting for him. What could he say? What could he do to make things right? He stepped over to the closet and opened the door. Everything was there, exactly the way she'd left it.

He reached out and ran his hands over her clothes. He was still standing there fingering the garments when Silki walked in carrying his belongings in a green plastic garbage bag. How appropriate. The garbage man was home. If she thought it was odd for him to be brushing his hands over the clothes in the closet, she didn't say so.

He was all but crying. If she'd thought he looked lousy before, he probably looked worse now.

She said, "I brought your stuff. You can put it away anywhere you want. You can move her things over. I didn't move any of it before in case I found her and she came home with me. I wanted everything to be where she'd left it."

Zach mumbled, "It's not fair."

His voice came out all choked up. The tremor indicated he was on the verge of losing it. He didn't know how to stop it. He needed to get through this, not avoid it.

She quietly asked, "What's not fair?"

"I'm finally here and I can't hold her, can't touch her, can't be her husband. What good am I?"

A scalding tear rolled down his cheek. He wiped it away but another one quickly followed.

Silki had never seen a man cry. She had no clue what to do. She guessed maybe you did the same as with a crying woman and children. She walked over an put her arms around Zachary and murmured, "It's all going to work out. We're going to get even with the bastards who did this to you and Mariah."

CHAPTER EIGHTEEN

DURING THE NEXT WEEK, Silki cleaned the old hunting cabin and moved in. Zachary lived in the main house with Jesse and held himself together with sheer willpower and nothing else. He'd lost some weight, which wasn't surprising since he wasn't eating much and nothing she or Jesse tried seemed to appeal to him.

He hadn't had a drink and that was a good thing, but that didn't stop her from worrying about him. There was no telling how long he could go on the way he was.

The hunting cabin resembled a rock shack with a metal roof and indoor plumbing. Most importantly, it had a door she could lock and a propane stove she could cook on. It also had hot and cold running water and that was a blessing. Losing everything could make a person grateful for the things everyone around them took for granted.

An odd assortment of dishes, utensils, and cooking pots littered the shelves. After she'd washed them and the shelves, she got busy turning the place into her home. In time, she could paint and replace the ancient linoleum. For now, she had her own cozy cabin. She owned the rusty roof over her head.

She had contacted Mariah's attorney, H. Davidson. He had a reputation for being a very meticulous man. He'd gotten them access to the accounts Mariah had put in place for them. He was also a very ethical man. It followed that he had all the paperwork in order to transfer the Rocking T to Zachary High Horse. He filed Mariah's will with the Comal County Clerk and they were going through probate according to the book. The marriage license was checked and rechecked. It was legitimate. Zachary High Horse was Mariah's legal spouse. He and Jesse inherited the ranch with the exception of Silki's ten acres. Harvey was out of luck right along with Warfield Enterprises in all its forms.

The not so good news was that Harvey's lawyers were fighting every inch of the way. The inventory of the estate was another matter since most of it was missing. No cattle, no horses, no agricultural equipment, but the bill for the livestock manager had been paid every month and he was now in one hell of a bind trying to explain where the livestock, tractors and hay equipment had gone.

The private investigator Silki hired was getting a few bald spots from raking his fingers through his hair. She felt a little guilty about that, but the animals had gone someplace and four-wheel drive tractors didn't up and vanish. She wanted to know where it all went. Somebody had profited and it was time for them to pay up. She didn't care if they went to jail; she'd kind of like it if they did. They'd known better than to steal from Mariah Blue.

Jesse disappeared every evening after dinner and didn't get home until after midnight. He was no help, and Zachary was lost in his own misery. She was in this alone for the most part. She kept sifting through the papers in the ranch files. The clues had to be in there somewhere. She looked up at the sound of Zachary shouting, "Silki, that lawyer is coming up the drive."

"Okay, Zachary. I'll go see what he wants." She put down the file she'd just pulled out and closed the drawer. "It's almost lunch time. I'll fix us some sandwiches and we can eat and talk at the same time."

"I'm fine. Not really hungry."

"You've got to eat something. You can't help me or Mariah if you're too weak to stand up. I'm telling you, we're going to have a fight on our hands any day now and we need to be strong."

"I know, but food just sits in my stomach like a lump."

"It's called depression, and you've got it. It will get better, it takes time. Right now, we need to see what Mister Davidson has been up to. This is about you and Jesse, not me."

"I'm not worth it. I never was. You might want to keep that in mind."

They'd had this discussion before. Silki reminded him, "It's what Mariah lived and died for. If you won't do it for yourself, do it for her and Jesse. Come on, let's go put on a united front for the lawyer. Don't want anyone to see any weakness. Not that Davidson isn't on our side, but we don't want him to feel like he's representing a bunch of quitters."

They both walked out through the front doors putting their best face on a bad situation. They could still come up losers in many ways but victory starts before the battle.

Silki blinked at the spotless new Lexus SUV sitting in their driveway. The caliche dust would dull the sparkle by the time he left. He fancied himself moving to the country the minute this was over. His fees would put him in high-cotton as he liked to say. He had big dreams of moving to Montana. She could hear the country music playing on his radio as she and Zachary walked up to the driver's door.

The pristine white door opened and a very expensive, suit-covered leg stepped out. Silki caught the fine pair of cowboy boots peeking out from under the pant legs. Oh, boy, it was getting worse.

"Hey, Davidson, are those Luchese boots?" She shuddered to think what they cost.

"Yes, aren't they great? Real comfortable, too."

She'd never seen the man so happy. Hell, if a new pair of boots could do that, maybe she'd get some for Zachary and Jesse.

She beamed her best smile at him. "That's great. What brings you out to see us? I've got sandwiches if you're hungry."

"Are you sure I'm not imposing?"

"I'm sure. Come on in."

Davidson followed her and a silent Zachary up the front steps. His eyes traveled over the arch and hanging custom cast-iron porch light. "Wow, you've got these doors working. It's a miracle. They haven't opened in years."

"Yeah, it took some serious cleaning and lots of lubricant to get the hinges to give. They were on the heavy side of rusty." And that was putting it mildly.

Davidson took a seat at the dining room table while Silki put their lunches together. Settling in for a nice afternoon visit, he eyed Zachary who took the seat across from him.

He intoned, "It's good to have you here. You know I've been worried. Harvey's like a woodpecker, he never gives up. He's been after this place for years. Even before Mariah left."

Silki caught the disdainful stare Zachary fixed on Davidson. Mariah could take care of herself. Harvey had every reason to worry, then and now. He'd lost any rights he'd ever had the day he didn't help Mariah escape from their father's greedy, manipulative clutches.

Zachary looked away, and said, "He's not going to get it."

"No, he isn't. But he's got his lawyers digging through Grandma Drew's will with a fine-tooth comb trying to find some way around Mariah. They've even gone back and pulled the great-grandparent's wills. They're desperate, that means they don't have much to run with. That's bad because desperate people do desperate things."

Silki put their lunches in front of them and went back for hers letting it all sink in.

Returning to the polished oak table she sat down and said, "Grandma Drew left this place to Mariah. Her will was very clear. George Warfield, tried and tried to take it from her and couldn't. I don't think Daddy will have any better luck."

"No, not with Drew's will. Mariah's is a different story. It's good, don't get me wrong. That attorney in Rapid City did an air-tight job. But it's Zachary they're aiming at now. It's a question of how married were they."

Jesse's voice boomed across the house from the doorway of his room. The words echoed off the walls. "How damn married did they have to be? They were married by a Justice of the Peace, said the words, signed the papers. They fucked each other, that's as married as it gets."

Silki went scarlet from her head to her toes. The mouth on that man was a nightmare. She shouted, "Shut up!"

145

Zachary reprimanded, "Never talk about her like that. Show some respect."

"Not for Warfield. No nice words. Let's have the truth for once." Jesse stalked across the room. "She was a white woman sleeping with my father. That's it, all there is, beginning, middle and end."

Silkie did her best to ignore Jesse. He might never get over being angry but today was not the time for her to deal with it.

Looking at Davidson, who appeared to have been struck speechless, a terrible problem for an attorney, she said, "They were married by a Justice of the Peace in Martin, South Dakota. They occupied an apartment on Third Street. Mariah paid an attorney in Rapid City to draw up her will. She was there and she was in her right mind."

"Uh, well, good. That's good. But was Zachary in his right mind?" Davidson grabbed the sandwich off his plate and took a big bite.

Jesse stood looming over all of them. He was tired of the lot of them. All this legal mumbo-jumbo and nobody could give any of them a straight answer.

Silki hadn't made him a sandwich. Some things never changed. He didn't exist in her world. Every day she came to make sure Zach was okay, that he was eating and had everything he needed.

She never checked to see if he was okay. He'd had enough. "Hey, girl, where's my lunch?"

Davidson flinched and took another bite.

Zachary held his breath.

It's right here." Silki picked up her sandwich and flung it at him. Pieces of it flew in all directions. Some of them even hit Jesse.

"You little witch. Get the hell out of this house. You don't live here anymore." Jesse brushed at the mess clinging to his shirt. "And you owe me a clean shirt."

Silki was on her feet, heading around the table straight for Jesse.

Davidson popped to his feet holding his hand out in Silki's direction. "Hang on now. No assault and battery where I can see it. At least wait till I'm gone."

Silki stopped just short of running into Davidson's arm. "Fine, but as soon as you're down the road all bets are off."

"Okay, that sounds reasonable. Now can we sit back down and talk about keeping this place in the High Horse family and out of Warfield's assets?"

On the way back to her seat, Silki turned and muttered, "Yeah."

Jesse glared at her, nodded his head and sat down next to Davidson.

Zachary nodded. "I was very sober when we got married. Mariah sat with me through the shakes. She said I was suffering because of her. It wasn't pretty but she wouldn't leave me."

Davidson focused on Zach. "That sounds like her. I want to be ready if there are any questions raised about the two of you being under any artificial influences at the time. How about Mariah, was she sober?"

Jesse answered before Zach could get a word out. "Saint Mariah was always sober."

"Well, yes, she told me there was nothing more disgusting than a sloppy-drunk woman." Davidson glanced quickly around the table. "So, um, that just leaves one last thing. I already told you that Harvey sent a PI to South Dakota to dig around. I heard there's a story, a rumor really, not something anyone could prove, but it might make things look bad if it gets out in front of a judge. I don't believe it of course, but I do need to, uh, ask, you understand, that way I have an answer, in case it comes up."

Silki huffed out a breath and grumped, "Quit dancing around what-ever it is and spit it out. What do you want to know?"

"They're saying Silki is sleeping with both of you. That could make it look like she's got ulterior motives. You know, trying to get something for herself out of this."

Jesse launched out of his chair. He glared down at Davidson, barely able to keep from grabbing the man up and breaking him in half for even thinking about Silki that way.

"She isn't sleeping with either one of us. Zach is too old and I'm not her type. She's trying to do what her aunt wanted. That's all."

"Well, of course. Anyone who knows her would know that."

Davidson took a sip of the iced tea that was sitting in front of him. He smiled. "Silki wouldn't be interested in any casual relationships."

Resting one hand on the table top, Jesse leaned down so he could look Davidson in the eyes. "She doesn't fuck men like us."

~

That did it. Silki sprang to her feet, stuck out her chin and announced, "I might, if I felt like it. If I knew a good one worth fucking!"

All eyes were on her, and they were all the size of silver dollars.

She went on, "I am divorced." She waved her hand in the air like she was shooing a fly. "I can do what I want these days."

So much for lunch. Family meals were always prone to these fights. No wonder they were all suffering from indigestion.

She crossed her arms over her chest. "And I'm sick of fighting every time we try to sit down to a meal. I'm not eating over here anymore. I'm going home."

With that she turned away from the table, stalked out, and slammed the back door shut behind her. They could figure it out without her if they couldn't act like civilized human beings, at least at meal times. She'd go home and fix herself a sandwich since her last one was scattered over half of South Texas and Jesse. *Men! Most exasperating creatures on earth.*

She eased up on her stride, marching slowed to stomping, which slowed to something resembling an afternoon stroll. Letting herself be goaded into an unladylike outburst was too tiring, and too much effort to waste on the likes of Jesse High Horse.

She spent the rest of the day puttering around the cabin including cutting and chopping some branches into small pieces of firewood for her wood burning stove. The nights would get cold in the coming weeks and she wanted to be ready. She hated being cold.

After sunset, she ate her dinner in peace and spent the evening reading. Occasionally, she glanced at the light bulb illuminating the porch. Moths flitted around it giving off fluttery noises and the occasional ping from hitting the bulb.

She half-expected to see Jesse standing at her screen door but no such luck. He wasn't coming to apologize or ask her to come back. Well, good. She didn't need him getting under foot. She could do fine without him.

Her eyes got tired and she shut the door, clicked the lock and went to bed. She wrapped her arms around her pillow and whispered, "Good night, Jesse."

CHAPTER NINETEEN

JESSE SAT across the table from Zach with the morning sun lighting the dining room. He watched his dad with a practiced eye. No, he wasn't drinking, yet, but he was thinking about it.

Zach was lost without the little redheaded witch. They both were. They hadn't seen hide nor hair of Silki in a little over two weeks. Every now and then they'd catch sight of dust and a quick glimpse of the RAM truck on the ranch road leading to her place, so they knew she was still alive.

The silence was overwhelming. It would have been better if Zach would have yelled, told him he was an idiot, anything but the condemning silence that said a lot more than angry words ever could. He took another bite of his congealed sausage and egg breakfast and decided he'd had enough. They needed something decent to eat, and she was the only one who could cook anything remotely edible.

Jesse put his fork down on the edge of his plate and muttered, "I'll go apologize and ask her to come back."

"Might not be that easy. She was way past angry, closer to raging mad. I don't think she's going to get over it any time soon." Zach sipped his coffee. "We got any whiskey around here? I could use a shot."

There it was. The beginning of the end, again. "No, we don't have any. And I'm not going to go buy you some. She damn near beat me to death once, I'm not giving her another reason to try again over a bottle of booze."

Zach returned Jesse's gaze, cocked his head to one side and grinned. "She gets kind of worked up over things."

"Yeah, you could say that." Jesse's lips curved into a thin smile. "She's kind of hot tempered."

"Too bad you can't get all that energy headed in a different direction." Zach continued grinning.

Jesse caught the look in his eyes and knew what he was thinking.

He said, "Yeah, sure, as if anything I can do would get her interested in me. I'm used toilet paper to her. Only good for flushing down the crapper; the sooner the better."

"You could show her you've changed; you're trying to do better. I'm not saying it would be easy, but Mariah forgave me. Little Red might forgive you, if you ask her real nice."

Jesse felt the heat creeping up his face. He didn't want to be forgiven. Why should he have to ask forgiveness for living the only way the world let him? "I didn't do anything to her. I don't need her forgiveness. She needs to see life the way it really is."

"I think she expected more from us. We haven't made things easy for her."

Jesse groused, "Tough, she's the one who came looking for you. She can't complain about what she got. We didn't ask for any of this. So far, I'm not real impressed."

"It's not over yet, and you gotta admit this is better than anyplace we've ever been." Zach looked around the enormous room. "Our whole place would fit in this room with space left over."

Jesse wasn't going to admit a damn thing. "So, that doesn't mean this is better."

"What did you expect it to be?" Zach took another sip of coffee and peered over the rim of his cup.

"I don't know, but not like this. Not big and empty." Jesse's eyes traveled around the room.

"So, you think it's empty. There's plenty of furniture. What's missing?"

Jesse had the answer but he'd eat dirt before admitting it. "Lots of stuff."

～

"Let me know when you figure it out." Zach got up, picked up his plate and headed for the kitchen sink. He'd had enough. If Jesse didn't go apologize to Silki, he would. Then he'd stay for lunch.

Jesse disappeared into his room while Zach dumped the scraps into the trash. They'd hardly ever had enough food, so throwing it away went against everything in him; he had to keep reminding himself things were different now. Right about the time he had the dishes piled in the sink Jesse reappeared looking like he was ready to take on the Seventh Cavalry. Great, he was going to go talk to Silki.

Zach drawled, "See you later."

～

"Yeah, see ya." Jesse strode past Zach on the way to the back door wishing he didn't have to go face Little Red. But he didn't want to go through another two weeks like the last two.

Some things were simply too hard on a man. He couldn't sleep, the house was too quiet. He could barely eat, the food he fixed didn't taste like hers. He didn't want to get drunk. The last thing he needed was a hangover. He was miserable and it was all her fault. Life was really going to hell fast. He kept that thought all the way to the dilapidated hunting cabin.

The place was a shack, a run down, rat trap, with lacey curtains hanging in the windows. Now, what was that all about? Oh yeah, a girl thing. Hang some frilly stuff and everything got better, wrong. Well, he'd come to apologize and he'd get it done, then he'd leave as fast as his legs could carry him.

Coming around the side of the cabin, Jesse spotted a silver

152

Mercedes sedan. Nice car. Not Silki's style at all, which meant she had company. As he got closer to the front porch, he heard angry raised voices. Livid shouting from a male voice that he didn't recognize and a screeched reply from Little Red. That, he recognized. He was on his way up the stairs when he heard her holler, "No, I won't help you cheat them out of what's theirs. What part of that don't you understand, Daddy?"

"It's not theirs. It should never have been Mariah's. If Granny Drew hadn't been senile, this never would have happened. All this should have been mine and I want it. I've earned it."

"Well, that's too damn bad because you're never going to get it."

Jesse ripped open the screen door in time to see Harvey Warfield do a quarter turn and back-hand Silki across the face.

She stumbled backwards hitting the wall. She pushed herself away from it, fists raised and ready to come out fighting when Jesse found his voice.

"Son-of-a-bitch." Jesse grabbed Warfield's shoulder from behind, spun him around, and planted his fist in the man's face. "Don't ever lay a hand on her." Wrapping his other fist in the man's shirt he began dragging him toward the door. At the threshold he snarled, "Get off my land. You're trespassing." A shove sent Warfield stumbling out onto the porch his nose dripping blood on his pressed, stark-white dress shirt.

Harvey cleared the porch steps, staggered a safe distance away from the house, and yelled, "Silki, don't think you can come crawling home when these two are through screwing you." He made it to his car, yanked open the driver's door and got in. Before pulling it closed, he added, "I don't care what happens to you."

The Mercedes whirred to life in between Jesse's shouts and curses.

Silki called out, "Jesse, please, give it a rest. I can't hear myself think."

He turned away from the front door. His eyes landed on her leaning against the wall. She looked pretty shaken. He'd seen her take a hit that would have knocked most men down but Little Red was still standing. Wobbly but standing. How did she do that?

He demanded, "What the hell was going on here? What'd your old man want?"

"I had the radio on. I didn't hear him drive up, next thing I knew he was standing there." She nodded to the same spot where Jesse was standing. "He wanted me to help him take the ranch away from you and Zachary."

Jesse closed the distance between them. She wasn't all that tough and she wasn't all that strong; nobody was supposed to hit her, ever. Before he knew what he was doing, he reached out and wrapped his arms around her. He felt her trembling and asked, "Are you all right?"

"My eye hurts. I think it's gonna be a shiner." She rested her head against his chest. That surprised him. The only other times she touched him were when she was beating him or sleeping with him. She added, "I should have seen it coming but I never expected my father to hit me like that."

"How about putting some ice on it? That might help." He held his breath waiting for her to tell him what he could do with his ice.

"Yeah, it might." She tightened her hold on him. "I'm okay here for a minute. This is nice."

Neither one of them moved.

Jesse didn't know what to make of it. She might be going into shock or something. "You took a pretty hard hit; you should lie down for a while. I can get you some ice to put on your eye."

"Yeah, that would be good. There's ice in the freezer."

Still neither one of them moved.

This was an excuse to hold her, and there was no telling when he'd ever get another one. He'd imagined doing it enough times, relived the few times he'd gotten to touch her. What would it hurt if he hung on a little longer? "I came by to apologize for what I said back at the house the other day. Zach isn't doing too good without you. We need you to come back."

Yeah, good, he'd blamed it on Zach. She'd go for that.

"What's wrong with Zachary?"

"Ah, well, he's not eating right, and today he asked me if there was any whiskey to put in his coffee. I'm afraid he's going to start drinking again."

She tightened her grip on Jesse. He could feel her trembling getting worse.

She clung to him tighter and said, "He's come so far. I'd hate for him to lose it now." She sucked in air and confessed, "Jesse, I don't feel so good."

Jesse felt her knees start to give out. He scooped her up, carried her to the bed along the wall at the back of the cabin and put her down. "Here, you get comfortable and I'll get some ice for your eye." He turned and darted back to the kitchen. He didn't know anything about taking care of women. He'd been having sex with them since he was fourteen, but he didn't know anything else about them, really. What was he supposed to do now?

The refrigerator was old, it had ice trays. Those, he knew how to use. He broke out some cubes, piled them on a thin dish towel and carried it back to Silki.

Sitting on the edge of the double bed, he tentatively reached toward her eye with his small bundle. He lowered the make-shift ice pack over her left eye and he let her hand guide his. She was letting him touch her a lot more than usual. Of course, her usual was not at all, so this was a big change. She'd said it herself; she wasn't feeling too good, her brains were probably scrambled.

She continued to hold onto his hand, and he wasn't volunteering to remove it. He might never get this close to her again. He scooted his hip a little closer toward the head of the bed. He'd started at arm's length in case she decided to punch him for sitting on her bed. He proceeded to slowly inch nearer, presumably to get a better angle to hold the ice. Yeah, right. He couldn't resist the urge to get next to her. He'd wanted her from the minute he'd set eyes on her. It didn't do a thing for his ego that she had to be half unconscious for it to happen.

With his free hand he brushed a strand of hair away from her face. She was so beautiful. He'd seen Mariah years ago and there was one hell of a resemblance. They could have been mother and daughter. Zach had fallen hard for the old lady and now here he was all but crawling on his hands and knees after the meanest little devil that ever came out of Texas and who looked like an angel.

Her skin was warm and soft; he brushed his fingers over her cheek one more time while he still had fingers. She was probably going to bite them off any second.

"Silki, are you okay?"

He was worried; she hadn't moved. The girl was constantly in motion and this wasn't a good thing if you asked him.

CHAPTER TWENTY

SILKI MURMURED, "THANKS FOR HELPING ME." The man had great hands. Long tapered fingers, wide palms, smooth skin. He was so fine in some ways. It was the other ways that scared her. She opened her right eye and peered up at him. He was so damned handsome, it hurt to look at him. She slammed her eye shut and sighed, "I'm fine."

Oh, yeah, she was fine. So fine, as long as she didn't open her eyes again. She wanted to hold still and pretend a little longer. If she moved, the spell would be broken and she wasn't ready for that. Who'd have guessed the roughest man on the planet could have such gentle hands. And the closer he came, the better he smelled. It was so not fair. And his voice. Why did Native American men get the best voices? So soft and low and comforting, when they wanted to be. Of course, they could let out a whoop that would scare the bark off a tree.

She couldn't blame the pioneers for being scared to death of them. She'd probably have turned-tail and run all the way back to the Atlantic Ocean in the old days. Unless, of course, she'd been out there on the prairie with Mariah; then they'd have crept toward the drums and snuck up on them to see what the noise was all about. That was the way Aunt Mariah did things. The woman had never run from anything, ever. Silki smiled to herself and the movement sent a pain shooting across her eyelid and temple. "Ow."

~

Oh hell, he had to get ready, she was going to beat him for sure. Jesse winced in anticipation. "What's wrong?"

She sighed, "I had this crazy thought. I smiled and it hurt my face."

"Oh." Jesse was afraid to ask what might have crossed her mind. He said, "Seems like your dad and Mariah fought a lot."

"You could say that. But that's not what I was thinking about. It crossed my mind that while the rest of the pioneers were running in the opposite direction, she'd have been busy sneaking up on your people to see what they were doing."

"What brought that on?" He didn't know whether he wanted to laugh or argue.

"You did." Silki smiled again. "Oh, this really hurts." She raised her hand and touched his hand holding the cold compress. "Pain is good, it lets me know I'm still alive."

"Me? What'd I do?" He sat back in case this was her way of suckering him closer. She was sneaky that way.

"It's your voice. I was thinking how easy it is on the ears, except when you guys get to beating on drums, singing, and dancing around the fire. Then you sound pretty scary. Anyone with any sense would have run the other way, but Mariah would have gone to see what was going on."

Silki inhaled and added, "I think it's the drums. Imagine how it sounded in the dark, rolling across the hills and valleys. I think I'd have run."

Amazing, the things that went through a white girl's mind. The old days, hmm.

He teased, "In the old days, I'd have been waiting in the dark to catch you." Oh, shit. What was he thinking? Had he lost his mind? His legs tingled with the undeniable urge to run for his life before she could pound him into the floor.

Since she wasn't moving, he hung there on the edge of the bed with his hand still trapped between her eye and her fingers.

"Then what, Jesse? What would you have done with me?" Her

good eye remained closed. He figured it was a trap. She was trying to get him to say things he'd never be able to forget or take back. His ass was in trouble now.

"I'd have held on real tight," to keep from being clawed and beaten to death, "and carried you off into the hills on my war pony." What the hell he'd have done after that was anyone's guess.

"I think you'd have killed me, scalped me, and hung my hair on your war shirt. But I'd have given you a couple of good scars to show for your efforts. You'd remember me."

Only a crazy man would have killed her. She was strong, brave, and beautiful. Any warrior worth his feathers would have kept her for his very own.

"No way, girl. You'd have been living in my lodge. I'd have been coming home to you every night." Jesse gulped. Just shoot him now before she killed him for real in this life. She still had him by the hand but she might as well have had him by the balls because he wasn't up and running, couldn't get up to run, even now when his life depended on it. His eyes were glued to her face hoping for a hint of what was to come.

"Hmm."

"Hmm, what? Things were different in those days. I'd have taken you so far into the hills nobody would have been able to find you. It would have been you and me, babe."

Now there was a thought. He liked that idea.

She asked, "I wouldn't have had to share you with anyone else?"

Oh man, there it was. The major fuck up of his life. He'd been available, willing and easy; now his past was biting him on the ass.

"Hell no, no sharing. And I wouldn't have been sharing you with anyone either. You'd have been mine."

These days it wasn't going to happen. She'd never be his.

"Wow. I guess we're living in the wrong time."

Jesse thought he'd heard wrong. Her head might be hurt worse than he'd suspected. She was talking crazy. If all she wanted was to have him to herself, all she had to do was say so. He could do that. It didn't matter what century it was.

"What's wrong with now?" Stupid question, but it shot out of his mouth on its own.

Silki's face crinkled up in a half-grin, half-smirk. "Now? Well, let's see. How about you've got the fastest zipper in the West? You're so damned handsome at least half the women in North America want to do you and you're willing to give it a go. And let's not forget I'm such a cold bitch that my poor, neglected ex-husband had to get sex from his secretary. I'd say we're not a good match, but other than that, nothing's wrong with now."

"Well, if that's all, we're in good shape."

"Oh, yeah, great shape, Jess."

It was the Devil that made him do it, or maybe it was Mariah dressed up like the devil, but either way, it was the same result. Jesse leaned down and tentatively touched his lips to Silki's.

His lips lingered on hers and his tongue gently skimmed along the seam of her mouth. He licked again, requesting entrance. He groaned when her lips parted under his. His tongue penetrated her mouth and it was all over for him. He'd died and gone to heaven or he was falling into the depths of Hell. Either way, he'd spend the rest of his life remembering this and knowing he'd never get to taste her again.

His one hand still held the ice pack and the other stroked her cheek before it tangled in her hair to hold her head at the perfect angle to deepen their kiss. Harder, heavier, deeper, he needed this like he needed to breathe. Even knowing he'd pay for it the rest of his life, he couldn't stop.

He crawled onto the bed, and stretched out beside her. His body aligned perfectly with hers. For the first time in years every nerve ending he had was on full alert. He felt the heat where they connected and the cool empty spaces where their bodies didn't touch. He moved, struggling to close those spaces until she was solid against him. His heart beat frantically, trying to get out of his chest and he ached deep down inside. Nothing in his past experiences had ever been so overwhelming. He wanted to see it through; see where it would take him.

He gasped for air. He looked at her flushed face and slightly swollen lips and knew he'd done that. At long last, he'd kissed her and she'd kissed him back. He'd been lost and she'd found him. She still held his hand and wasn't letting go. She'd also managed to get him by the shirt and he was so not able to pull away.

He begged, "Don't hurt me, Silki. Please don't hurt me."

"Kiss me again, Jess."

~

Silki kept her uninjured eye closed. She didn't want to see the expression of horror that was surely plastered on Jesse's face. The concept of fidelity was something he didn't know anything about. She liked the idea of having him all to herself under different circumstances. But this was the here and now. She could look closer, but it wouldn't turn him into a faithful partner for the long ride through this life.

She couldn't bring herself to open her eyes and look at the one man who made her feel alive. It would destroy the fantasy.

She'd see him the way he really was, and not the way she wanted him to be. Fine, she was being selfish, but for once she wanted to have Jesse all to herself, make believe he loved only her, wanted only her. She wanted to touch passion, live it, breathe it, be consumed by it. Tomorrow she'd figure out how to get over it.

She felt him moving next to her. The bed jiggled and his leg slipped over hers pinning her underneath him. He was so smooth with the moves. The ice pack moved away from her face and his hand was back running up her leg, wrapping around her hip, his fingers digging their way under her. He had a solid grip on her as she felt him firmly pressing his body to hers. Good God in Heaven, he was hard and big, too damn big for her. And strong, he had her pinned under him with all their parts fitting together perfectly. The only thing saving her from being impaled on his erection was two pairs of jeans.

She didn't want him to stop, but she was too scared to go on. He was too much for her, and she didn't have any appropriate way to explain it to him. She couldn't do it; she didn't have the words to tell him she wasn't built for a man like him. He was too damn big.

"Aww, Jess, stop, please, we can't do this. I can't do this." She pulled at the back of his shirt. His face was buried in the vicinity of her jugular where he was kissing, licking, and biting her neck. Oh, yeah, it felt so good. "Oh, yeah, Jess. Oh, hell no. We can't do this." Her fist hit his shoulder. "Listen up, stop. I can't do this with you."

That must have penetrated the mush his brain had turned into. He didn't look at her, moved his head to the side of hers and buried his forehead against the mattress near her shoulder. "Why? Why, Silki? Why can't you do this with me? What's so damn wrong with me?"

Oh no, this wasn't the way it was supposed to go. The truth could really suck some times and this was one of those times. It was something a girl never admitted to anyone ever, but then Jesse had been through worse. She'd been there, heard it for herself, so on this one score they were even.

"I can't do this with you because you're too big or I'm too small. It doesn't matter how you say it, we're not going to fit together."

"And just how the hell do you know that?" He still didn't look at her.

"Well, let's see." Silki reached down between them and gave his cock a gentle rub from base to crown through his jeans. "Yeah, it's as big as I thought from the way it felt against my thigh."

"And it won't fit because why?" He was still struggling to catch his breath. "Women want guys with big dicks, or haven't you heard."

"I have heard that, and it's probably mostly true, but not for me. I can't. You're too big."

"No. That's not right. Men and women have been managing to put things together for a long time. You're no different. Not unless there's something wrong with you."

"Um, Charley and I didn't have a good sex life. He said it was my fault. It wasn't comfortable for me. He had to use lots of lube." She inelegantly snickered, "One night he went to the bathroom and didn't turn on the lights, he reached into the cabinet and grabbed the first thing he came to." Silki started to laugh, first a little snort, then it grew to a genuine laugh with her eyes scrunched shut. "When he was walking back to bed, he started screaming. He ran back into the bathroom and slammed the door. I heard the shower turn on and him cursing. He blamed me." She was still laughing between sentences and gulps of air. "He'd smeared himself with Ben-Gay and it was kind of hot."

"Oh shit!" was all Jesse could say as he started to laugh. "Bet that was one hell of a surprise."

"Yeah, I'm afraid so. But the point is, I couldn't look at the man without laughing after that and then we really had no sex life. Sex with him was kind of painful and he said it was because I was too small. You're so much bigger, I can't have sex with you. It won't be good for either one of us."

Jesse raised up on his elbows and took in the honestly sorrowful look on Silki's bruised face. She had to know he wouldn't do anything to hurt her. "You're built to stretch, that's how it works. It'll be fine."

"No, it won't. I went to the doctor and she said I was normal, nothing wrong with me, but it still hurt with Charley."

He'd finally found someone he could love, be faithful to, and fate was going to snatch it away from him because his dick was too big. Oh, hell, no, this wouldn't be happening. He'd find a way to fix it.

He could plainly see he wasn't going to win the battle today. But by damn, he would win. He had been kissing and tasting her, lying horizontal in a bed with her, while she kissed him back and explored his body with her hands. She'd been willing up until she'd felt his size and hardness. *What the hell?*

He sat up on the side of the bed and ran his fingers through his hair. He was still hard, but he could live with it. What he didn't want to live without was the woman who'd given him the erection. Her, he wanted, for all time, any time, whatever time, past, present, future. It didn't matter as long as she was his.

"I'd better get back and check on Zach. Can I tell him you'll come by and fix us some dinner tonight?"

"Yes, and warn him about my black eye. And Jess, it's not your fault, really. I'm sorry. I didn't realize. I wouldn't have let you get started if I'd known."

"It's okay. Don't worry about it. It's nothing I can't handle." He got up slowly, rearranged his slowly receding semi-erection and walked out. It was going to be a long slow walk back to the main house.

By the time he stomped through the back door and slammed it shut, he was in one lousy, piss-poor mood.

Zach who'd been watching TV, looked over his shoulder at him and reached for the remote control. The TV blinked off and silence fell over the room for a hot second before Jesse exploded.

"That stupid little rat-bastard she was married to didn't know what he was doing!" Jesse flung himself into the easy chair at the end of the coffee table.

"Are we talking about Charley the Weasel?"

"Yeah, Charley the stupid fucking Weasel that doesn't know shit about women."

"Hey watch your mouth. Have a little respect here. Start at the beginning. What are we talking about? Do we need to go skin this creep alive? What did the stupid weasel do?"

Jesse hit the arm of the chair with his fist, wishing it was Charley the rat-bastard instead. "He messed her up. He hurt her trying to have sex with her."

~

Zach sat forward resting his arms across his knees. He focused on Jesse. His son was partly angry, partly worried. And that was a big change. Jesse got angry, that wasn't anything new, but the worried part, that was a High Horse of a different color. Usually, Jesse didn't give a shit about anything.

After sitting there in silence for the better part of a minute, Zach broke down and asked, "What happened?"

"It's hard to get a straight answer out of her, but it sounded like he didn't get her ready, in the mood, you know, he was too fast. He'd get lubed up and go for it. She said it wasn't comfortable, which in her language probably means it hurt like hell."

"And so, she doesn't want to have sex again?"

"Yeah, that about covers it. She's not interested in anything bigger than a pencil dick."

"Hey, stop the gutter talk. And how do you know any of this anyway? Were you over there trying to get her into bed? I thought you were going to apologize."

"I did. I apologized after I punched her old man in the nose and threw him out of her shack. He hit her before I could get to him. She's got a black eye. She wanted me to warn you about that before she gets here tonight. She's going to fix us some dinner, and things can get back to the way they were."

"If her father was here, things are ramping up. He's coming for us. You don't know the man like I do."

"I don't want to know him. He said she couldn't come home after the two of us get through screwing her. Nice guy, huh?"

"He was never a nice guy. So, he's still going with both of us sleeping with her. What a prince? Her reputation in this town is going to be ruined beyond repair. He'll make sure she never gets a decent job. She's a CPA, and she has a business degree, she can do things with numbers, she's making a business plan for this place. She's a real smart girl, but she needs a reputation people can trust. They won't want her near their money, and the banks won't lend on her business plans when Harvey's through spreading his lies. She probably won't be able to stay here and make a living."

"Fine, I'll take her away from here. We'll go someplace high in the mountains." Jesse was now in sulk mode.

Zach all but fell off the couch. Jesse was going to take her away. Since when had that become a possibility? Was his son finally turning into the man he'd always known he could be? Was he going to take responsibility for another human being? There was the possibility he'd heard wrong.

"What makes you think she'd go anywhere with you?"

Jesse glared at him. "I don't know. I guess I was hoping she might love me enough someday."

165

CHAPTER TWENTY-ONE

SILKI SPENT the next month digging through ranch records, hanging on the phone with Attorney Davidson, and questioning the accountant who handled Mariah's affairs. She tried not to think too much about her close encounter with Jesse but it kept popping up and eventually she'd have to deal with the feelings that had come with it. He smelled wonderful, fit against her perfectly, and he made her tingle in all the best places. Jesse was all man.

She wanted him to be her man. That was the catch and she hadn't been able to find a way to tell him they could try to work it out between them. The words kept getting stuck in her throat because for the first time in her life she was afraid of failing. It wouldn't be fair to put Jesse through that.

Sometimes the things a person didn't say were the things that hurt others the most. From the look on his face, she'd hurt him badly, and every passing day the silence increased the distance between them. In the meantime, she went to sleep reliving Jesse's kisses and woke up feeling like her life was a bad soap opera.

Jesse came and went from the ranch. They'd smile and wave and keep going on about their business. She'd make their breakfasts, Zachary's dinner, and leave a plate for Jesse.

Zach worked on the barns and corrals fixing what had been left to fall apart. It gave him something to do and made the place look like it might get back on a paying basis eventually. Judging by their condition, the ranch manager had been paid largely to look the other way.

She'd gone to see the bank manager who had been politely unhelpful. Most likely her father's influence was at work there. In the end, Silki moved the account Mariah had left her to another financial institution that was new in town and more cooperative. Taking control of her life was a lot of work, but she owed it to herself and Mariah to get it done.

She set up an appointment for Zachary to consult with Attorney Davidson to discuss moving his and Jesse's accounts to a more neutral institution. That was their business, not hers. She stepped back letting them take control of their futures.

She'd listened in on the call when they reported the missing livestock to the county sheriff, but since there was no telling exactly when the animals had disappeared it was a lost cause.

The missing tractors were a different subject. They had serial numbers and cost one-hundred fifty thousand dollars each, and Mariah had two of them. They'd turn up eventually when they went in for repairs or service. As soon as a dealer punched them into a computer the trail would heat up. She had to be patient.

The ranch manager left town without a forwarding address, and there were precious few records to be gotten from his file cabinet. It was hard to follow a paper trail without any paper or computer files without the computer. Mariah would have fired his ass on the spot. He'd probably had an escape plan ready in case she came back.

There was nothing pointing to Harvey Warfield, but Silki would have bet her last dollar he was at the bottom of all of it. He'd been stealing from Mariah for years, she just couldn't prove it, yet.

This morning she'd helped Zachary pack and load his new suitcase into his shiny red pickup truck. He was going to Oklahoma to look at some horses. Harvey hadn't been able to stop the transfer of funds to her, Jesse, and Zachary. His attorneys had tried but couldn't stop Zachary from spending the money that Harvey coveted.

After lunch, Zachary shut the driver's door and started the engine.

"You look mighty fine sitting there. Drive careful and call when you get to the motel." Silki stuffed her hands in her back pockets to keep from hanging on the window ledge. It wouldn't do at all to have him think she was worried. He was sober and he could go anywhere he wanted with his Texas driver's license in his wallet.

"I'll be careful, and I'll call as soon as I get checked in. Don't waste time worrying about me. I'm only gonna look at some horses. I'm not gonna buy any this trip. This place isn't ready for livestock, but I want to see what's out there. I'll be home in a few days and we'll talk about it. Okay?"

"Okay. You've got a deal." She said it, so why didn't she feel it? About half a second later she had her answer in the form of Jesse.

"Have a good time. I'll keep an eye on things around here." Jesse winked and added, "Everything is under control."

She tipped her head back, glanced over her shoulder and caught the smirk on his lips.

Familiar hands rested on Silki's shoulders as they both watched Zachary head for the road. Jesse gave her shoulders a light squeeze. "Hey, I got some things to do in town, but I'll be back in time for dinner. You cooking tonight?" he asked.

"Yes, I'm cooking. Can we eat at my place so I don't have to run back and forth all day? I'd like to get some things done at the cabin."

"Sure, your place it is." Jesse brushed a kiss across her cheek, turned and walked back into the house leaving Silki standing in the road.

She pressed her fingers over the spot on her cheek still warm from Jesse's kiss. Winter was coming on. The leaves were falling off the oak trees and the air was getting cold at night. She needed to winterize the cabin as best she could. Caulking was high on her list of things to do. Silki checked the sky for signs of rain and headed back to her place.

Jesse watched from the kitchen window as Little Red disappeared up the hill. She was too damn stubborn for her own good. She'd come back and started cooking, cleaning, and in general keeping Zach company and running the house. That had been a month ago. She never mentioned what had happened between them at the cabin, and neither had he. Mostly because he didn't have any idea what to say.

But tonight, Zach was out of town making this his golden opportunity to spend time convincing Silki to take a chance on him. If it took all night, it would be fine. If he was still working on it tomorrow that would be fine, too.

She could fix dinner and anything else she wanted, but he was going to fix her. She was going to learn a few things about men and women and how it all fit together. He did know sex, love was a foreign subject to him, but he'd start with what he knew and work his way through the rest. Charley was an idiot. If he ever met the man, he was gonna have to thank the jerk for dropping Silki into his lap right before he gut-punched him for hurting her.

Jesse smiled; he couldn't wait for the twilight to shine orange fire on the horizon. Yeah, he was gonna start slow but before Zach came home, he'd show her how to sit on his lap the way he liked it and ride him as far as he could take her.

He went through the rest of the day waiting impatiently for dusk. That easy time of day between daylight and dark when he could relax and put the day behind him. He wandered the path to the cabin running the possibilities around in his head. He shouldn't push too far, too fast. No, he needed to let her get used to him being in her place. He'd move in on her easy, not scare her. Damn, he had zero experience with this kind of thing. His dates had always been ready, fast, and to the point.

This time he had to mind his manners, had to speak softly and touch gently. Shit. He was hard already and he wasn't even through the rickety door.

Silki stood over the sink draining the noodles and glanced quickly over her shoulder when she heard the screen door open. She had the radio playing a local country station to keep her mind from dwelling on things that couldn't be helped.

She said, "Hey, you're right on time."

He looked wonderful. He'd put on a little weight and his color was a healthy glowing tan. She was honestly glad to see him.

"It's almost ready. Get yourself something to drink out of the fridge."

"Sure. You need help with that?" He tipped his head toward her batch of noodles.

"No. I've got it. You can turn off the radio so we can eat in peace. It's mostly commercials."

A couple minutes later, she put their plates of beef stroganoff on the tiny table that barely fit in her miniscule kitchen. Its round wooden legs rested on mismatched, chipped linoleum tiles over concrete. She looked at the faded pastel yellow paint on the walls and then at Jesse. "It's not the Ritz but the food is good."

"Looks good, smells wonderful. Hey, thanks for feeding me." Jesse reached for the serving spoon.

"Not a problem." Silki watched Jesse load his plate. "Hope you like it."

It was foolish to wish for more, but right then she wished it could be like this always. Having him near brought her a sense of security. He'd fought for her, something Charley never would have done. She was safe with Jesse. But meals and companionship were only a small part of a relationship. Intimacy connected people on the deepest level. She wanted that with him, but taking the risk and failing would be horrific. She wasn't sure she had the courage to face that. A long road trip to the Badlands had rebuilt her self-confidence and being unable to meet Jesse's needs would be a screaming downward roller-coaster ride of a lifetime.

It would be better to stay on the safe side and live with what could have been. Her pride and self-esteem could stay intact and nobody would ever have to know she'd been in love with Jesse High Horse.

With the radio off, the sound of flatware on the plates was the only sound in the cabin. If she'd had a clock, she'd have been able to hear it ticking. She hated this uncomfortable truce they were trapped in. She gave up and asked, "So, do you think Zachary will want to raise horses here?"

"He might but this land isn't the best for that. It would be expensive, especially in dry years." He took another bite of his dinner.

"It's good that you got a degree in agriculture and land management. You'll be able to help him." She looked across the table and got a nod in response.

The elephant in the room that nobody wanted to talk about was taking up more space than the people.

"After I get working, I'll fix this place up. It could be really cute with a little help." More like a complete remodel but that was a thought for another day, and it got zero reaction from Jesse. His mind was somewhere else. The soft rustling of leaves on the trees outside the kitchen window filled the tiny kitchen.

It didn't take long to finish dinner. Silki washed and Jesse dried the dishes with only a few words passing between them. When they were finished, he turned to her and put the dish towel on the old-fashioned tile counter. Before she could get away, he reached out, wrapped an arm around her middle, and pulled her close.

"I want to thank you for cooking and taking care of Zach." His head lowered and his lips covered hers. He pulled her up against his body. The hard planes of his body warmed her and tiny shivers and tingles skittered all the way to her toes.

Strong arms held her tight but not too tight. He lifted her as he'd pulled her closer. Her toes were barely touching the floor and her arms were around his neck before she knew what was happening. She wanted this. She wanted his kisses, his hands touching her, and his body pressed tightly to hers.

She wanted the man Jesse had become. He wasn't the same messed up loser she'd encountered on the streets of Martin. He'd cleaned himself up and showed signs of using the education he'd earned from Mariah's scholarship. He was intelligent, when he wanted to be. It was his personal life that was a screw up. But that seemed to be getting straightened out.

This man she could love a lot if she could get her body to cooperate.

Jesse moved his lips from her mouth to her neck. His hands moved as well. One hand held her firmly against his chest while the other had taken a hold of her butt and was urging her up against his erection.

"Silki, let me love you, please. We can go slow, real slow. I won't hurt you. Let me show you how good it can be."

"What if it doesn't work? You'll make fun of me." Silki let her head roll back, so Jesse could keep seducing her neck.

"Never, I'd never make fun of you. This thing with us is private. Let me hold you. It'll be good. I won't do anything you don't want. We can stop anytime you say. I promise."

They'd never talked about that night from hell back in Martin. She'd kept her mouth shut and never made fun of him. It wouldn't have been right to add to his pain. This sounded like his way of telling her they'd be even.

"I'm scared, Jess. I'm not as brave as Mariah." Silki moved her head till it rested against Jesse's chest. "I want to be with you. Mariah said it was meant to be, but I'm not as tough as she was. What if I'm not strong enough?"

"Strong enough for what? What do you think I'm gonna do to you?"

"I don't know. It always hurt; I didn't like it. I don't want it to be like that again. You're bigger and stronger. What if I can't handle it?"

"It's not about handling it. Trust me. I'll never hurt you that way. I can't promise not to make you mad, or disappoint you, but I'm done sleeping around. You're the only one I want." Jesse pressed his erection against the warm space between her legs. "This isn't for causing pain. It's for showing you how much I love you, how much I want you. It's the first time in my life I want to share myself with a woman. Give me a chance."

"Trust me, is like the worst thing in the world a man can say to a woman. We know better than to ever fall for that line." Silki reached up and gently cupped the side of his face.

"You've changed a lot. I like this new Jesse. It would be so easy to fall in love with you." Her eyes searched his. "Is that what you want?"

"I've never been in love before. You'll have to take it easy on me because I'm bound to make mistakes." Jesse rubbed her back and tightened his embrace. "But I'd like to try with you."

It was a miracle. She wasn't screaming and throwing him out into the night. She hadn't ripped his hair out by its roots, kneed his balls, or stomped on his feet with her damned boots. This was more than he'd hoped for.

He'd never been honest with a woman before. Never trusted one enough to share his innermost feelings. He was in uncharted territory. It would either save him or kill him.

Little Red had no clue that she was holding the rest of his life in her hands.

She asked, "Are you going to take me to bed now?"

"Yeah, we're going to lock the door and go to bed."

He let her slide down his front till her feet were firmly planted on the floor. Then he took her hand and led her to the front door while he turned off the outside lights and locked up. He wasn't letting go. No interruptions. No intruders. No nothing to interfere with him making love to the hottest babe in the universe.

CHAPTER TWENTY-TWO

JESSE LED Silki to her bedroom and slowly removed her clothes. He didn't rush, he took his time first with hers and then with his own. He had to remind himself to take it slow and let her get used to the idea of being with him; of seeing him naked, body and soul, and letting his hands touch her intimately. He was putting her heart on the line and if he messed this up, he might never get another chance.

Jesse leaned over, pulled back the covers and put a condom packet and small tube of warming sensation lube on the bed by the pillows. He needed the large version to be comfortable and he'd made a habit of carrying a couple with him in case he got lucky. The lube was something new. He desperately wanted to put the odds in his favor and make it especially good for her. This could be his one and only chance to show her how good it could be with him.

He turned and caught her deer-in-the-headlights look. Without thinking he reached out to her. "Take my hand and we'll do this together. Don't give up on us. We'll take it slow."

He held on to her while she moved to the edge of the bed. He could only imagine how it would feel to kiss her all over all night long. But more than anything, he wanted to feel her soft lips kissing him anywhere and everywhere.

Standing there naked in front of her was the sexiest man on earth. Broad shoulders, narrow hips, long lean muscular legs. Oh, and the big attraction jutting out from his pelvis. Yeah, well, that was another subject altogether. One of her hands would not go all the way around it, her two hands wrapped around it would not begin to cover the distance from base to tip. It was the kind of cock she'd heard women whisper about in the bar at the country club and over long lunches with dry martinis.

She'd never seen a so-called 'magnificent one', and hadn't been particularly interested in seeing such a prize considering the fact that she had absolutely no use for it. What was she going to do with it? She should run while she still had the chance. Great, she'd be chased out of her own house by a giant cock, and she didn't mean rooster. This was so not a laughing matter.

What was Jesse going to do with her?

Silki took his hand and crawled into the double bed that suddenly seemed to have gotten smaller. He knew about this stuff, she didn't. In this modern day and age, it wasn't the kind of thing she'd want to admit. Charley was the only man she'd ever been with, that wasn't saying much and she didn't want to think about him. She was starting over with a new man, a better man.

She watched Jesse turn off the bedside lamp. Her chest tightened and her pulse quickened. His knee landed securely on the mattress. He was coming to her. What would she do if this went badly? It would be all her fault. She had to stop thinking like that. It was going to be okay if she could get her hands to stop shaking. She had to trust Jesse. Talk about taking a risk. Why not grab the fox and throw him into the hen house and get it over with?

Jesse slid in next to her, pulled the covers up around their waists and turned toward her. "Come here, babe." He held his arms out to her. "I need to hold you, feel you next to me. I've waited so long." He wrapped an arm around her as she settled in next to him with her head resting on his chest. "I've imagined this night since the first time I saw you. We've got as long as it takes to get where we want to go."

"We slept together in your bed before." She snuggled into the warmth coming off his body.

"Not the same thing. You were trying to torture me that time." His hand slowly skimmed down her side to her waist. His fingers urged her to slide closer.

She wanted him to kiss her like the last time they'd shared her bed. That had been so good. She'd been ready to let him do anything he wanted until her past brought them to a screeching halt. That wasn't happening this time. She softly said, "Jess, I like it when you kiss me. It's always perfect."

He tightened his hold on her and urged her over on top of himself. "From up there you can take me any way you want me." His lips curled up invitingly. "Soft and slow kisses are the best. I'm yours tonight and every night from now on. Show me what you want."

Her legs straddled his waist as he moved under her making room for her to position herself comfortably and lean over his chest. His eyes watched her every move as she lowered her lips to his.

He had the softest, warmest lips. She could see spending hours kissing the man. It didn't take long before she wanted more, she wanted to taste him. When she ran her tongue over his lips, he parted them in open invitation. Her tongue found his and the dance was on. He tasted like she remembered. He had his very own flavor and she craved it.

Somewhere along the way she inched higher and tightened her thighs against his waist to get better access and leverage. She discovered the rush and heightened sensations that rubbing her breasts against his chest created. More, she wanted, needed lots more.

His hands gripped her hips and guided her lower. He must have read her mind and more came when she realized his cock was centered between her legs, tucked in the space between her clit and his abdomen. An easy rub back and forth sent the most delicious sensations cascading through her. She'd never felt so damn good, and they were just getting started. If it got any better it might just kill her and then where would she be?

His hands gripped her waist guiding her movements back and forth, helping her stroke him. Good, that was good. He needed to feel good, too. She kissed her way down his neck and came up for air. Oh, but that was a mistake. Without her mouth keeping his occupied, he found something else to do with it. Jesse fastened onto her nipple and sucked.

Silki gasped and moaned and gasped again. "Jess, yes, Jess, that feels so good, don't stop."

~

Hell no, he wasn't gonna stop, but his mouth was full and he wasn't about to let go long enough to answer. From the sounds coming out of her, she liked what he was doing and that was all that mattered.

He had one hand on her other breast and one hand on the very fine cheek of her very tight ass. And it was all his. He was getting hotter by the second and he couldn't get any harder. If she kept rubbing his cock, he was gonna come without ever getting inside of her. And she wouldn't get to feel his release. He wanted her to feel them completely joined, how perfect it would feel when they came at the same time, the way it felt when it was done right. They'd be able to make love to each other many times before morning but the first time had to be the best.

He let go of her breast and reached down between them. It was a tight fit but he managed to slip a finger past her clit and inside her opening. She was wet. Tight and wet. Okay, she'd warned him. He could work with it. First one finger sliding in and out letting her get used to the feeling. Then he added a second finger. Silki was making soft little whimpering sounds. Damn, "Babe, tell me how it feels."

"It's good, really good. It's never felt like this before." She sounded breathless.

Hearing that confirmed that she was still with him.

"Okay, babe, raise up for me." When she did, he tore open the condom and rolled it down his length, applied extra lube to make it slide easier and positioned his cock under her and said, "Okay, lower yourself down on me. It's going to feel warm. Relax and let yourself stretch a little at a time. Take what you want, the way you want it."

~

Silki felt Jesse positioned at her entrance. He was huge. She wanted him, but how to do it was the problem. She pushed against him and he moaned. She exhaled and told herself to relax and let him in. She pushed down a little harder and felt him sliding past the tight muscle guarding her entrance, stretching her. The pressure gained delicious intensity. She pushed again and he slid deeper.

She was moaning and whimpering and gasping for air. It was too much; he was too big. The pressure continued to build. Her thighs quivered. She'd never felt that before and it was enticing and unsettling at the same time. She didn't know what to do. She wanted more. She wanted all of him. Silki raised up and sank slowly down willing herself to relax. She moved from side to side taking more of his length till there wasn't any more to take. She was full and pushing against his shaft with all her inner muscles. Out, she needed that damn thing to move. She raised up, pushed down, and let out the first full throated groan followed by a loud wail, "Jess". The first man made orgasm of her life hit her full force.

Jesse's hands fisted in the sheets and he bucked under her as she pressed down harder. Hovering over him, she cried out in completion and he followed.

In a mind-numbing haze, she felt him pumping warm fluid inside the glove covering his cock. She relished the pulsing caress of her body surrounding his. She didn't have the strength to move. So, she eased down on him and listened to his heart beating like thunder in her ear. His chest was rising and falling with every breath he took. His hands slowly released the sheet and moved to her hips. His fingers pressing into her soft flesh and holding her in place felt right.

She hadn't killed him, but she thought she might have come pretty close. They were hot and sweaty. There was goo between her legs and Jesse was still inside her. She'd never been that wet before without half a tube of coconut smelling lube. This was totally different and totally wonderful. It smelled like Jess with a hint of some exotic spice.

"Jesse, are you okay?" He still hadn't moved.

"No, babe, I'm not okay."

Silki's head jerked up. "What's wrong, did I hurt you? You didn't say anything."

"Shh, it's not like that." He reached up, caught her head with his hand, and pressed it back down against his chest. "I've never felt anything like that in my life. I think that's how it's supposed to be when it's really right."

"Then what's wrong?"

"You leave me weak. That's what's wrong, babe. I've never been this weak."

"Are you sure your middle name isn't Samson?"

They both laughed, and Silki felt that amazing part of Jesse still inside of her receding but still there. He was soft but he was still tucked up safe and sound.

She whispered against his chest, "You were right. You did fit."

"Yeah. A tight fit, but that's good, nothing wrong with it at all."

Silki asked, "So, now what? Where do we go from here?"

"Now? Now, we're going to do whatever we want, whatever feels good." Jesse held the condom in place and pulled out before he rolled Silki under him. "You tell me."

Only moments ago, he'd strangled the sheets to keep from grabbing her by the waist and impaling her on his shaft out of sheer desperation. She was so damn tight. He'd never been so desperate to come. She'd done that to him.

He dropped the used rubber on the floor. Then he braced his arms on either side of her shoulders and looked down studying the soft features, the trusting face of the only woman he'd ever love. Heaven help him, he didn't have the courage to say the words. The best he could do was lower his lips to hers and silently commit to loving her the only way he knew how. He'd finally found what he'd been searching for and he swore to himself he'd do whatever it took to be enough for her.

CHAPTER TWENTY-THREE

ZACH WALKED into the same house he'd left five days earlier finding it suspiciously clean and quiet. Jesse wasn't home and Silki wasn't fussing in the office. So, this is what happened the minute his butt was off the place for a few days.

He smiled. Good. It was time the two of them did something besides worry about him and the ranch.

Once Mariah's will was settled, they'd all be able to get on with their lives.

The back door opened and Jesse walked in with Silki right behind him.

Jesse was the first to speak. "Hey dad, how was Oklahoma? Did you see anything you had to have?"

"Hi! How was the truck? Did it give you any problems?" Silki hugged Zach and stepped back. "We missed you."

"The truck ran fine and there were a couple of fine horses a man would be proud to own. It's real green in that part of the country, kind of pretty." Zach sat down on the couch keeping an eye on Jesse and Silki. "Okay, so what's going on around here?"

It's been quiet, but I got a call from my cousin Elizabeth Gail. She's coming out this evening after work. Said it was important." Silki shrugged her shoulders. "I remember she was a very quiet girl when we were younger. We got along okay. She went to work for Warfield Enterprises right out of college. Her dad has a small share in the company. I haven't seen her since my wedding to Charley. It's all a mystery to me, but she sounded like it was serious."

Zach didn't say anything, but his eyes stayed focused on Jesse.

Jesse looked back meeting his gaze. "I've been helping Silki fix her place up and get it ready for winter."

"Yeah, it's coming along and Jesse is really good at fixing things." Silki's cheeks turned pink and she smiled at him.

Jesse's chin dipped down and he rubbed the back of his neck.

If Zach wasn't mistaken, his son was embarrassed by the praise. He looked back and forth between the two of them, before commenting, "He was like that when he was a kid. He liked the classes at school where he got to build stuff."

Silki could see the looks going back and forth between Jesse and Zachary. The two of them had something they wanted to talk about and it didn't include her. She had plenty to keep her busy at the cabin.

She said, "Look, I'm going to go back to my place and let you two visit and catch up on Zachary's trip. I'll be back in plenty of time to fix some snacks before Elizabeth Gail gets here."

"Good, that's good," came out of Zachary's mouth at the same time as Jesse said, "Okay."

"See ya later." She gave a little wave and turned toward the door.

She could feel both pairs of eyes watching her go. Men were so strange. One minute everything was fine and the next the tension in the air was so thick you could cut it with a Bowie knife.

Charley was an expert at that tactic. She hadn't liked it then and she didn't like it now, but they had a right to have a private conversation. Stuff between a father and son was none of her business.

She and Jesse had gotten along fine together. He told her things about himself that she was pretty sure he'd never told anyone before. She was somewhat surprised with how much there was to admire about him when he let it come to the surface. He was a good guy way down deep inside. After listening to him talk about his past, it was understandable why he'd hidden parts of himself away from the rest of the world. What people didn't know; they couldn't use to hurt him.

She sure wasn't the same silly fool that had married the wonderful Charles Hardcastle who morphed into Charley the Weasel, while she sat there like a passive lump letting him rob her blind. She'd done everything she'd been told to do by her parents and Grandpa Warfield. She had retraced her journey from meeting Charles to where she was now without finding any surprises. Only now she had a better perspective of what had happened. How she'd ended up used and broke wasn't a mystery to her any longer. No, it was all pretty darn clear.

She'd fallen asleep a lot of nights staring at the ceiling of the cabin replaying her mistakes. One thing she knew for sure was that her ceiling was in worse shape than the ceiling of the motel. She was on a steady downhill slide habitat wise, but her love life was aces. Jesse was amazing; at least a three Margarita lunch, Martinis wouldn't cut it when it came to describing him. The ladies at the country club would overheat in their oh-so-tiny, but very chic tennis outfits at the thought of enjoying Jesse. Silki frowned, no way were they ever getting their manicured claws on him.

The door was no sooner closed than Zach turned to Jesse and asked, "What's going on here?" He could guess but he'd rather hear it out loud.

Jesse walked over to the easy chair and sat down. Leaning forward resting his elbows on his knees and hanging his hands between his legs he said, "I've been staying at her place. I don't like her being there alone."

"I've seen her place." Zach kept his voice even and stated, "She hasn't got a couch."

"Yeah, we kind of worked things out. She doesn't think I'm so bad."

Zach didn't like asking but it was important for his peace of mind. "You didn't push her into anything, did you?"

"No. I didn't. She'd have beat me senseless if I'd put the moves on her without her consent. She might be little, but she's still meaner than the Devil when she wants to be."

"I wouldn't exactly call her mean. If a man called you out, you'd say he was strong and independent. A woman does it and she's a bitch or she's cold and mean."

"Silki told me about her marriage to Charley. She said she did her best to stay out of his way." Jesse sat back. "Their parents wanted the picture-perfect marriage to solidify their business partnership. She let him do what he wanted with no-questions-asked to keep the peace."

"There's no such thing as picture-perfect marriages. You're gonna have some fights that'll make that nose dive you two took out there on the side of the road look like a minor tussle. You'll want to kill her and she'll be fixing to beat you black and blue with a skillet." Zach rubbed his hands on his thighs. "Get out of this now, if you're not up to it."

"I've spent plenty of nights thinking about that. I've thought about how it would be if I didn't see her, couldn't sleep next to her, how I'd feel. I can't do it, can't imagine sleeping without her next to me."

"Oh, it's only the beginning." Zach laughed softly and sat back making himself comfortable. "Let me give you a few thoughts on the subject. Mariah and I had a short time together but I remember every minute of it."

By the time Elizabeth Gail arrived, Silki had Margaritas, iced tea, chips, salsa, and a hot cheese dip ready. Elizabeth Gail took a seat on the couch. She had her Margarita glass firmly in hand and sipped on it while she'd carried it from the kitchen. If Silki didn't know better, she'd say the girl needed a drink.

Elizabeth Gail looked at Zachary and Jesse one more time before speaking. She'd been eyeing them since she'd arrived and been introduced. What was she looking for?

She turned her attention to Silki. "It's been a long time. I wasn't sure you'd remember me."

Silki sat next to Elizabeth Gail. "We used to keep each other company at Grandma Drew's family dinners. It was years ago, but it's the kind of stuff that sticks with a person. We hadn't been reshaped by our parents into the people they wanted us to be. We still had our own ideas and plans for our lives. I used to call you Ellie."

"You got the wealthy husband and I got the family company book-keeping job and a desk in the back office."

"You didn't miss anything worth crying over. I got set out on the curb when Charley had the sheriff evict me from the townhouse. Be glad you missed that."

"Mariah was afraid it would go badly. She didn't like Sneaky Little Charley. That's what she used to call him."

A bell went off in the back of Silki's head. Mariah was talking to Ellie. That was interesting. "I didn't listen to her like I should have. She had a way of knowing what was inside of a person. She was right about Charley."

"She told me things would have been different if Zachary and Jesse could have come here like they were supposed to. She made a point of getting even with your grandfather and dad for that."

Ellie made eye contact with both Zachary and Jesse.

Silki noticed her cousin included them in her story without requiring them to say anything. Silki nodded in agreement. "He and Dad never could figure out how she knew so much about what was going on inside the office."

Silki took a closer look at her cousin. Her tasteful and understated makeup didn't call attention to her, but Ellie was pretty behind the black-rimmed glasses perched on her nose, hiding her very deep blue eyes. Of course, you had to get past the long straight, dark brown hair hanging like a curtain around her head and shoulders. Her soft voice and gentle manner made her almost invisible. She could easily go unnoticed as she went about her work.

"It was you, wasn't it? You're the mole."

Ellie hung her head hiding behind her hair. Silki wasn't fooled.

"I'm not smart enough to do anything like that. I keep the books and files straight. I'm a bookkeeper."

"Your quiet, unassuming appearance is the perfect disguise. You blend in with the furniture. I can see where Dad and Grandpa missed it.

I can also see where Mariah saw the advantage. What did she promise you?"

Ellie steadily sipped her margarita and stayed silent.

Silki knew it took time to come up with a good lie. "Don't bother trying to lie. Zachary and Jesse can pick out lies at a hundred yards. What did you get out of it?"

Ellie finally moved, picked up her head and brushed her hair back over her shoulder.

"I got an investment account. She made me financially secure. I don't have to worry about eating dog food in my old age."

"Okay, that's good. Dog food isn't what it used to be. That brings us to why you're here today. What is so important that you needed to drive out here?"

"Warfield Enterprises is going under. The bank is calling in their loan, no more extensions. Your dad's been on the phone to Hardcastle all day. It looks like they're not in any better shape. They're coming after you," Ellie chewed on her lower lip and added, "And Zachary and Jesse. They need this place to get them out of the hole."

Silki caught Zachary's eye, he was doing his stoic resigned to his fate thing. Jesse looked like he was building up a head of steam and getting ready to blow sky-high. She turned back to Ellie.

"How exactly are they planning to pull off this little coup?"

Ellie took a big gulp from her glass. "By getting you to sell out real cheap."

Silki quirked an eyebrow. "And why would we do that?"

"To get information from them."

"Come on, Ellie, what kind of information? Quit playing this cat and mouse game. Say what you came to say."

"They've been trying to get Mariah's will nullified claiming she wasn't mentally capable of making a will. But their lawyers have warned them it won't fly once it's in front of a judge. So, they've been working on this new angle. The livestock are gone, the place has been let go for years, and it'll take a boat load of money to get it back on a paying basis. You won't be able to get a loan anywhere, the fix is in at the banks. Zachary's an alcoholic, Jesse's an ex-con, and you're unemployed and going to stay that way as long as you're in Texas. The three of you are playing house together." Ellie's grim frown and sympathy laced tone of voice clearly conveyed her displeasure at delivering the news.

"None of that is enough to make us sell out cheap." Silki's patience was running low but she kept her voice composed.

Ellie fished in her tote and pulled out a handful of papers. "I brought you these. I think they can help you prove Harvey stole the livestock and sold the equipment." She held them out to Silki.

Jesse's fidgeting increased and Zachary leaned forward waiting for the punch line.

Silki took the papers, tucked them in her lap, then took Ellie's hands in hers. Looking at her, she implored, "Please, tell us why we'd sell to them."

Ellie looked beseechingly at each of them. Silki could see she was looking for something, forgiveness or understanding, but whatever it was they couldn't give it until she told them the secret she was keeping.

"Zachary got Mariah pregnant. If you want to know what happened to the baby, the price is the ranch."

Silki's forehead wrinkled, her eyebrows lowered and knit. "No, the baby wasn't born. Grandpa Warfield had Harvey take her to a private clinic where they drugged her and aborted the baby." Silki looked Ellie in the eyes. "Mariah begged Harvey to help her get away but he refused. He was afraid of Grandpa. She never forgave him for that. It's why she went after him right along with Grandpa."

Ellie confided, "Silki, they don't know you know that. They're going to tell you the child is alive; all grown up, and for a price they'll tell Zachary where it is."

"It was a boy. Mariah got that out of the doctor who performed the procedure. He confessed everything to her in an attempt to save his son's college education fund. She exposed his under the table operations and wiped out his practice. His medical license was revoked. She put him in bankruptcy."

"I know they're planning on hitting you with this at the Livestock Raiser's Charity Ball next week. I wanted you to know so you could be prepared. Your dad took the event coordinator to lunch to find out if you were attending. She told him Mariah always got an invitation and she'd sent it to the ranch in order to carry on the tradition. The Rocking T always made a nice donation."

"And the Rocking T will make a nice donation again this year. We might be down on our luck but we're not out of the game."

"I'm so sorry. I've been keeping quiet and waiting. I didn't know what else to do. Mariah has been gone so long, and I've been so scared. It was like your dad knew she was dead. He'd say things like, 'the bitch isn't coming back,' and 'she's never gonna set foot in Texas again.' I think he's known for a long time."

"Yeah, I think you're right. We have to give the FBI time to prove it. Can you hang in there a little longer? You don't have to do anything but stay put so they don't get suspicious."

"Sure, I can do that."

Silki walked Ellie out to her car and waved goodbye as the Silver-Sky colored Rav4 disappeared down the driveway.

CHAPTER TWENTY-FOUR

Silki turned and walked back inside in time to catch sight of a tight-lipped Jesse shaking the last drop of tequila out of the bottle into the sink. Zachary wouldn't be getting drunk on it tonight. But she would have liked to take it back to her place. There were times when she could have used a drink, especially when the lights went out and the night closed in on her.

The scowl on Jesse's face and the foreboding quiet gave her pause. She stopped in her tracks and said, "Well, that solves one mystery. We know how Mariah was getting the inside scoop on things at the office. Who'd have thought Ellie was capable of it? She was always so quiet, never gave anyone any trouble."

Jesse put the empty bottle in the trash and turned; his eyes cold and hard. "You knew about the baby. You knew your old man helped kill my little brother."

Silki glanced in Zachary's direction. He sat motionless on the couch. His eyes staring straight ahead and his face bereft of emotion. She wished she had something comforting to say but nothing could soften the devastation of losing a baby.

She hid the instinctive wince Jesse's words generated and squared her shoulders. "I found out when I read Mariah's journals."

Jesse's color rose right along with his voice. "And you didn't think you needed to tell us?"

Holding her ground, Silki replied, "I didn't know what to tell you. I didn't know how Zachary would take the news. He needed to get sober, that's what we needed most. There would be time to sort the rest out later."

"It's always about you, what you want, what Mariah wanted. What do you think, we're all here to serve the great and mighty Warfields?" Jesse planted his hands firmly on his hips waiting for an answer.

"No. It's not all about me. It's about getting you and Zachary what was yours. If some of it hadn't been about me, I wouldn't have been hiding here, going through my aunt's belongings trying to find a way to survive, and ending up looking for you. You'd still be a couple of losers dying slowly in some rundown bar." Silki felt her heart sink a little at the ugly words. She was hitting low and she knew it. It might be true but that didn't make it better. It did make her small for saying it.

"So, now we can die here on your rundown, Texas ranch instead. Great, what a deal."

"It's not about dying. It's a chance to change the way you live. You have choices now, better choices. A chance to do something besides piss your life away in some back alley in a one-horse town."

"Like what, spend it scratching at the rocks and cactus around here, trying to get a blade of grass to sprout out of limestone. This might be your idea of a ranch, but it isn't mine." He ran his fingers through his hair. "I've been hanging around the Highway 46 Tavern and getting acquainted with the guys. They're barely hanging on. Harvey and the ranch manager siphoned off the livestock and sold it at the stockyards in Seguin and Nixon."

"Well, I'm sorry this isn't the ranch you want it to be, because this is the one you have. You can either do something with it to get you where you want to go, or you can do what you always do. Here's some news for you. Nothing's fair in this world. It's a struggle every day to survive. But the good news is, if you can make it here in Texas, you can make it anywhere. This is where we separate the men from the boys."

Jesse reached Silki in three steps. Grabbing her by the shoulders, he looked into her eyes. "I think I've proven I'm man enough for you."

Silki's eyes narrowed as her chin jutted out. "God knows you had plenty of practice before we ever met."

Zachary's voice reached between them. "Mariah told me about the baby. I knew it a long time ago. It broke my heart right along with hers. We loved each other so much and planned to have a big family. Being so young and not knowing any better, we didn't believe hate and Warfield's insatiable greed would motivate him to justify murder. George Warfield would stop at nothing to destroy us and protect his image."

Silki broke away from Jesse. "I'm so sorry, Zachary. I always knew Mariah hated Grandpa and Grandma. She had no use for my dad, but I never knew why until I read her journals. She'd have done anything for you."

"She did. She died for me. That's as good as it gets. No one can love you more than to give up their life for yours. I'm the one who let her down."

"Well, this is your chance to even some scores." Silki rubbed her arms.

Zachary sat back and sighed, "It's time to bury Harvey, that's what she wanted."

"We're getting there. Dad and Charley are going to pay for what they did to Mariah, you, Jesse, and me," Silki reassured him.

"Not if you and Jesse don't stop fighting with each other."

Silki cringed. "We're not fighting. It's Jesse's way of getting his point across. He's a little hot blooded is all."

Jesse's lips quirked up in a lopsided grin. "Yeah, I get a little worked up around people who lie to me. It's nothing to worry about."

He stepped up behind her and slid his hands down her arms brushing her hands away. He wrapped his arms around her locking his hands together in front of her midriff, effectively trapping her. Holding her close, he rested his chin on top of her head. "See, we're fine. She's not scared of me."

"Of course, she isn't afraid of you. She's like Mariah, she'll meet you toe to toe and heaven help you." Zach closed his eyes, opened them, and stared at Jesse and Silki. "So, we're going dancing at the Charity Ball. This ought to be good."

~

Good or not remained to be seen. Silki's mind reran the conversation with Ellie while she walked back to her cabin. Harvey had known Mariah wasn't coming back. It had only been a suspicion but the more she thought about it, the more she realized it was true.

She tried to ignore Jesse walking along beside her looking like he was lost in his own thoughts. She'd really gotten herself into it this time. When they got home there was no telling what he'd have to say.

That was another thing. Since when was her cabin their home? Since Jesse had moved into her double bed and hadn't gone back to the queen-size one in Zach's house. He'd have more room in his bed. She'd half expected him to stay with his dad for the night, but no, here he was walking along in the moonlight with her. Life was so twisted. She was going to have to send him away. She couldn't fight a two-front war. Harvey and Zachary were the priority.

"Jesse." She stared straight ahead.

"Hmm?"

"You don't have to walk me home. I know the way."

"What are you saying?" He kept walking alongside of her.

"I'm not doing this anymore." She couldn't bring herself to look at him. "I can't take away all the hurt and ugly things that have happened to you. It wasn't me and I'm not going to let you keep punishing me for the wrongs those people did to you. You're a good guy, but not the right one for me."

"What the hell? I was the right guy this morning."

"That was this morning. Things have changed. I'm doing my best to do what's right for you and Zachary." This was it, she wasn't going to take the coward's way out. She looked him in the eyes. "You've shown me you're never going to trust me and I can't live like that."

"So, that's it. We're finished?"

"You can't make a life with someone you don't trust." She sniffled quietly.

191

"You're more like Mariah than I gave you credit for. You're throwing us away, same as she did." He ran his hand over his head and looked up toward the sky. After inhaling, he met her gaze. "Okay, we're done."

"We need to go to the ball and keep up appearances. Once this is settled, you and Zachary can do whatever you want with the ranch."

They'd reached the bottom of the cabin steps. Silki stopped and turned as Jesse's foot hit the first step.

He kept his foot on the step and settled his weight on it.

"Silki?" He implored, "Don't do this."

She said, "I didn't see this coming. Guess I've still got a lot to learn about relationships." She swayed on her feet. It felt like she'd been hit in the chest. She had to catch her breath. "I wanted to believe this was all going to work out okay."

"Hey, there," Jesse reached out to steady her, "Whoa now, babe. Are you okay?"

Silki steadied herself. Looking up at Jesse, she said, "It never occurred to me that you'd hate it here and want to leave. I'm sorry."

"I didn't mean for it to come out like that. I look around and all I see is something that never had a chance. It's not healthy for me or Zach. It's a constant reminder of what never was." Jesse took his foot off the step and moved around in front of her. With one hand on her shoulder, he touched the fingers of his free hand along the underside of her chin, tilting her head up.

She asked, "Where will you go?"

It wasn't a question he wanted to answer. It wasn't a question he even wanted to think about. But he had been thinking about it. When the will was settled and Zach was ready to get on with his life, he'd be heading down the road. He didn't like Texas, not at all. He'd pictured her going with him. He'd be alone now unless Zach joined him.

He said the only thing he could. "I'll find a place where I can use my education. Probably a state or federal agency. Land Management and Forestry is what I'm good at. There's a lot of remote places and not too many people. Trees and animals won't care where I've been."

"That's one good thing that came out of all the misery. I can see you loving the land and taking care of it. Probably someplace with mountains and rivers. That fits."

"Yeah, that's more me. This is some tough going around here."

"No kidding." She chuckled softly. "I guess it's all in what a person is used to." She looked past him toward the stock pond two-hundred yards away. "Good night, Jesse."

"Good night, babe. I'm sure gonna miss you sleeping next to me."

"It was good while it lasted." She turned, went inside, and closed the door.

She'd shut him out of her life. There was nothing left to do but turn around and go back to Zach's. He covered the distance quickly without her short strides holding him back.

He opened the back door, crossed the kitchen, and lowered himself into the easy chair he'd claimed.

Zach's eyes followed him across the room and met his gaze. The silence stretched between them.

Jesse gave up and muttered, "She doesn't want me anymore."

"Can't say I'm surprised. It's never been about her. It's always been about George Warfield, his empire and his legacy."

"She could have said something. It would have answered so many questions. I would have understood what was going on." Jesse leaned his head back and stared at the exposed heavy wooden rafters. "You two were dealing with a murderer."

"It wasn't something I wanted my son to know. You'd have been looking over your shoulder or you'd have gone looking to kill him." Zachary rubbed his hands on his denim covered thighs. "I didn't want that for you. I knew your life would be hard enough."

"Right, cuz this isn't hard, is it? Silki is finished with me and it's a long way back to South Dakota." Jesse tilted his head back to level and stared across the room and Zach. "What am I supposed to do?"

"Give her time to get over being angry with you. Find a way to apologize and mean it."

"It won't matter. She says I don't trust her and she's right. I'm not sure how to trust anyone. It's never turned out good for me." Jesse sat up and leaned forward. "She's the closest I've ever come to anything worth having."

"You're going to be here a while longer. There's a lot to settle before we're free to go anywhere. You could try to change her mind unless you have something better to do with your time."

"Any suggestions how I might do that?"

"The same way I changed Mariah's." Zachary's mouth curved up on one side in a grin Jesse hadn't seen in quite a while. "I loved her into keeping me."

"I can try but I wouldn't count on it working." Jesse got up and went to his room. He didn't need his dad to tell him how it felt to lose something he cared about, something he wanted, someone he loved.

It didn't take him long to strip out of his clothes and step into the shower. He needed to scrub away the anger and feeling of betrayal that had washed over him when he'd heard Ellie's secret. He'd instantly taken it out on Silki. He'd jumped to the wrong conclusions without hearing all the facts. After years of being on the defensive end of accusations, he'd learned to strike first. This time it had cost him what he valued most.

Silki was the only woman who had ever truly given a shit about him. What would he do if he couldn't get her to reconsider, give him another chance, take him back?

He didn't want to go down that road, without her at his side it was a dead end. He'd been there and knew he didn't want that for himself, never again.

One good thing about the Ruins, it had a big hot water heater. He didn't have to rush; he could take his time. He could close his eyes and pretend she was there with him. It was the only way he'd be able to get any sleep.

When he was done, he dried off and crawled into bed. The sheets were cold and there were no welcoming, warm arms reaching for him. He didn't have to share the queen-size bed and pillows. One click of the bedside lamp and darkness enveloped the room. He reached out and ran his hand over the smooth empty space next to him. He didn't like the feel of it. He could hear the TV and knew Zach would stay up late watching reruns.

Eventually, Zach would get tired and go lay down in the bed Mariah used to sleep in. All of this was hard on him. Everywhere Zach looked, all he could see was what could have been. His dad needed to get out of there before he became a ghost himself. What were the chances he'd drive away and leave Silki behind? Jesse didn't need a crystal ball to know the answer to that. He closed his eyes and pretended Silki was there with him. He'd get her back, he had to.

CHAPTER TWENTY-FIVE

NOTHING LIKE A GLITTERING charity ball on a warm Saturday night to give a girl the urge to vomit. Silki sat in the comfortable back seat of Zachary's truck blindly staring at the passing highway markers and exits. Zachary relaxed in the passenger seat while Jesse drove them toward the showdown at the Crockett Hotel. She wondered if this was how the Queen of France felt on her way to the guillotine. Heads would roll. She hoped they wouldn't be carrying hers home in a basket.

Zachary glanced over his shoulder, caught Silki's eye, and said, "It's all right. We're ready for them. You look beautiful."

"Thanks." She fingered the diamond and ruby heart pendant hanging on a thick gold rope around her neck. "Mariah gave me this for good luck. She told me never to give it to anyone. Tonight seems like a good occasion to wear it."

Jesse snorted. "What's good luck about it? It's fancy glass surrounded by rhinestones."

"These aren't rhinestones, and this isn't red glass." Silki pressed the pendant against her chest.

Jesse briefly looked in the rearview mirror, his eyes met Silki's. "It has to be. It would be worth a lot of money if it was real."

Zachary shot a quick glance at Jesse then turned his gaze back to the dark road ahead. "It's real, but it doesn't matter how much it's

196

worth, she can't ever part with it. You can't put a price on someone's heart."

"What the hell are you talking about?" Jesse asked.

After Zachary exhaled a resigned sigh, he asked, "Silki, exactly what did Mariah say when she gave you that?"

"Never give your heart to anyone that doesn't love you unconditionally. That way it won't get broken."

"Yeah, and she told me to keep hers, she'd be back for it. And I've got it right here." Zach patted his pocket where he kept his medicine bag, next to his heart.

"You two have got to be kidding. You're trying to put one over on me. Right?"

"No," Silki insisted softly, "She gave it to me a long time ago. Way before I married Charley. I never showed it to him because something told me he'd try to take it. He didn't have any respect for me or what was mine. She sighed, "He would have sold it for the money. That's all he ever cared about."

Jesse tightened his grip on the steering wheel and glanced at Zach. "You've been carrying that around in your medicine bag for years. If anybody had found out it was real, they would have killed you for it."

"You and Mariah are the only people that knew I had it."

"I always thought it was a fancy piece of imitation jewelry, and Silki's is too big to be real."

Zachary smiled. "It's not too big. I think it looks perfect with that red dress." Jesse took the Houston Street exit for downtown San Antonio.

Silki looked out the window at the narrow streets. Her voice carried the stoic sound of inevitability. "There's going to be a showdown in the ballroom the likes of which has never seen before." She sighed, "It's Mariah's last stand. We have to make it count."

"Tonight's the night. It's the end of Warfield. Jesse and I will be right there next to you. We're all in this together." Zach rubbed his medicine bag.

"I don't know how Mariah did it. How she faced them down year after year." She chuckled softly, "I do know she gave them plenty to talk about."

"I know how she managed." Jesse grumbled, "She hated them. She could go to this party and see the results of her revenge."

Silki heard the conviction and understanding in his voice. He and Mariah had something in common, not that he'd ever admit it. Damn. She had misjudged him. Double damn. She needed to look closer.

A few minutes later, they pulled up under the brightly lit porte cochere. She inhaled a deep fortifying breath. The valet helped her out of the truck, and she found herself handed smoothly over to Jesse. With him on one side and Zachary on the other, they entered the lobby looking like they were walking into the O.K. Corral, but this band of desperados were dressed in Tux's and a beaded, blood-red silk dress.

The perpetual lobby noise continued with a noticeable change in the undertone. It was slightly quieter with underlying speculative whispers.

"Is that her?"

"Is that him?"

"She looks like Mariah."

Silki heard the murmurs as they passed other formally dressed patrons of the charity ball. Whoever said charity began at home had never been to this ball. There wasn't a charitable thought in the place.

Zach presented their invitation at the ballroom door and they were shown to their table. Silki didn't recognize the names on the other place cards. They were sitting with newcomers and out-of-towners. The committee wanted Mariah's money and notoriety, but they didn't want to have to rub elbows with her disreputable husband, stepson and debauched niece.

Silki muttered, "Cowards, they've seated us with people who don't have any idea who we are."

Zach leaned in her direction. In a low, smooth voice he said, "It's okay. We'll be able to eat dinner in peace."

Jesse put his hand on her thigh. "Sit still. Never let them see you're nervous. Remember we've got what they want. Zach has the ranch, and I've got you. Let them sweat."

The other guests arrived and dinner was served with all the usual meaningless introductions and small talk.

These people weren't even Native Texans. Silki blinked in confusion at their total lack of understanding of South Texas culture and environment. Jesse firmly grasped Silki's elbow when one man said, "What these ranches need is to install irrigation and agricultural sprinkler systems."

Before she could explain that water was a precious resource in the area, Zachary filled the void saying, "South Texas is unique. I understand North Texas and the Gulf Coast has been using central pivot irrigation systems for years."

Fortunately, any further discussion was cut off by the whine from the microphone at the front of the room. Instead, they were going to get to listen to endless monotone speeches about the good work of the charity committee and the ongoing scholarship program, blah, blah, blah. She looked around hoping for an avenue of escape. She contemplated the likelihood of getting away with powdering her nose for an hour.

Jesse leaned over and spoke softly. "I'm going outside for some air. I'll be back in a few minutes."

Silki pivoted on her seat, glared directly into his eyes and speared him with a move-and-I'll-kill-you grin. "No, you're going to sit right here and listen to this right along with the rest of us. This is the scholarship that sent you to college and you're not skipping out and leaving us here."

"Yes, dear. Anything you say, dear." Jesse smiled with a sarcastically exaggerated expression showing his gleaming white teeth at maximum exposure.

Silki tilted her head. "Please, Jesse."

"Sure, anything for you, babe." He planted a warm kiss on her cheek.

Satisfied he'd stay put, and mystified by his change in attitude, Silki turned away from Jesse and stared at the raised dais. She noticed the speaker busily shuffling the index cards while composing himself to begin the introductions. He appeared more nervous than the occasion called for; a clear indication it was going to be a long night.

The next thing she felt was Jesse's hand on her neck and the warmth of his breath in her ear as he whispered, "Relax, babe. You're safe with me."

Oh, no, she wasn't. She was so not safe it wasn't funny. She clutched the heart pendant for reassurance. The man was a menace. And she was undeniably in love with him. And they were absolutely not right for each other. No matter how she looked at it, there was nothing safe about any of it. And none of that stopped her from wanting him.

"Let go of that thing. Your knuckles are turning white." Jesse's free hand brushed her arm. "It's all right. I'm right here."

Silki let go of the pendant and shifted her attention to Zachary who sipped his coffee like it was the only thing in the world worth doing. Mariah would have loved it. The big boys were doing their best to impress each other with how filthy rich and powerful they were, while Zachary was deep into his coffee. While they angled to acquire the ladies with the most assets, Zachary contemplated how many lumps of sugar to put in his cup. Mariah would have been laughing her ass off and holding the sugar bowl.

By the time the speeches were over, Silki thought her spine was going to snap in half. She hated these affairs and the perfect posture required to sit through them. She'd been dragged to these types of formal gatherings all her adult life, first by her father and then by Charley. Business, it was always business. She didn't want to be in business anymore. She wanted what? To be a beach bum. The Gulf Coast had lots of beaches she could pick from. No, that wouldn't do. She liked indoor plumbing too much. Fine, she'd find something she could do that didn't require business dinners and charity balls. Definitely, no more charity balls.

"Come on, babe. Let's stretch our legs." Jesse's hand wrapped around her arm and lifted her out of her chair. "You can decorate my arm for a walk in the lobby."

Zachary frowned and took another sip from his coffee cup. His eyes met Silki's as Jesse tugged on her arm and guided her away from the table.

"What is wrong with you?" She fussed as they made their way through the tables toward the doors.

"The vultures were looking our way. I'm thinking it'll be good to keep them waiting." Jesse sauntered along like he had all the time in the world. "Let them wonder what you're up to a while longer."

"Oh, well, sure, that works." She peered over her shoulder and checked if they were being followed.

"I like that dress." The unmistakable appreciative note in his voice caught Silki off guard.

She questioned, "Really?"

"Yeah, it makes this soft swishing sound when you move. Guess it's all those beads. Anyway, it sounds nice, sexy, like in the movies."

"It's heavy," she remarked.

"It'll be my pleasure to help you out of it when we get home."

"Can we go home now?" She looked up at him hoping for a nod.

Instead, Jesse's deep chuckle filled her ears. "That's my girl, always wanting to get me in the sack. This High Horse will take you as far as you want to go, but you gotta let him rest now and then."

"Okay, fine, have it your way. Remember this is all for show." Hopefully, he didn't hear the hesitation in her voice. She surveyed the cliques scattered around the room. They would say they were networking. She called it gossiping and plotting.

"I know." Jesse tucked her arm closer to his side.

Silki's next thought was cut off by a voice from the past.

"Miss Warfield, how nice to see you."

She tugged on Jesse's arm signaling him to stop. "Mister DeLeon, it's been a long time. How is Carmela?"

"Ah, she is fine, just had my grandson." He smiled broadly looking like a proud grandfather.

Silki half-turned toward Jesse. "Mister DeLeon, this is Jesse High Horse, Mariah's stepson."

He extended his hand to shake Jesse's saying, "Nice to meet you. I miss Mariah, she always lent some excitement to these affairs. Never knew what she was going to do next. But now, young lady, when are you going to settle down and have some children? You have to think of these things."

She smiled and softly chuckled. "Well, I need a husband first."

"There are many fine young men to choose from. My son is still single." With a wink, he added, "I think he's waiting for you to notice him."

"Now that I'm home, I'll have to start thinking about the future."

He concluded, "Call Carmela, she would love to see you."

Silki nodded. "I'll call first chance I get."

He moved off and Silki turned toward Jesse. "Come on, I hear the music. We should go back. It's not good to leave Zachary alone for too long. There's no telling what stunt my dad might try to pull."

"You should listen to Mister DeLeon. If you married his son, your folks would probably take you back." Jesse didn't move.

"Look at me." She pulled on his lapel and patted it. "I don't care what my folks want." She brushed his hair back from his shoulder. "There are a hundred beautiful women here tonight who would have you in a heartbeat. You'd never have to work another day in your life. You'd live in the Dominion in a house with a pool and servants to wait on you hand and foot. You should think about it."

He frowned. "Is that supposed to give me a hard-on?"

"Well, it would work for a lot of the men here this evening."

Before he could answer they were interrupted by a joyful and loud, "Silki!" coming from a vivacious brunette with golden sun-streaked hair. Her hour-glass figure and island tan belonged on a tropical beach with palm trees swaying in the breeze and a fruity drink in her hand.

Jesse's eyes widened as the young woman rushed across the lobby in a flurry of turquoise ruffles, and flung her arms around Silki.

She chattered, "Oh my god, where have you been? I just got home from the Bahamas and heard the most awful stories about your divorce. I've been so worried." She kept on hugging and hanging on Silki. "I got so scared when Mama told me you'd lost everything and were living on the streets in Dallas. What would I do if something happened to you?"

"You'd be fine, Sunny. Honest." Silki returned Sunny's hugs.

With a contented sigh, Sunny let go and stepped back. She latched on to Silki's hand and looked her straight in the eyes. "Mama said you went looking for your aunt and met up with some rough people. Are you okay?"

Jesse lost his practiced smile and loomed over them like a gathering thunder storm. "We didn't let anything too bad happen to her."

"What?" Sunny's concerned tone deepened along with the worry lines on her forehead.

"Don't listen to him." Silki smiled reassuringly. "This is Jesse High Horse; Mariah's stepson and he has a twisted sense of humor."

"Well, if he's your cousin it must be okay."

Silki linked her arm through Sunny's. "Let's go find something to drink and see if we can find some handsome men worth dancing with."

They sauntered toward the ballroom, heads together talking quietly. Occasionally, Silki looked over her shoulder confirming Jesse was still with her. He was there, his eyes scanning ahead, watching over them. His protective nature clearly on display for everyone to see. She'd never find another man like Jesse.

She didn't know how to heal the lifetime of betrayal that had wounded him so deeply he might never recover. Spending the rest of her life with someone who didn't trust her, didn't believe in her, wasn't going to work. Letting him go was breaking her heart. It got harder every day to keep telling herself that it was all for the best. There had to be a solution they could both live with.

She might have started out like Sunny, believing the world was a good place and everything always turned out fine in the end. But she'd collided with harsh reality and it was ugly. She turned her attention to Sunny's happy chatter and kept walking.

Zach sat quietly studying the goings on around him. The sight of Silki with a gorgeous young woman strolling across the room brought an easy smile to his lips. A gentle voice from behind him softly said, "She's very beautiful."

He commented, "Hmm, they both are."

An attractive woman gracefully slid onto Silki's chair. Her powder-blue dress hung off one shoulder and draped invitingly over her feminine curves. She reminded Zach of ancient Greek and Roman sculptures. She had a classic beauty and serenity about her.

"I'm Marie Rose."

"Pleased to meet you. I'm Zachary High Horse."

Zach held out his hand in greeting.

Marie Rose gently placed hers in his for the briefest moment then withdrew it slowly.

Zach couldn't take his eyes off of her, his hand still tingled where she'd touched it. She wore her sable-brown hair pulled up and back. It fell in a cascade down her back. Her flawless ivory skin hid her age and her sapphire-blue eyes could see into a man's soul. There wasn't anything average about her. No, this one was different, special.

She said, "I've wanted to meet you since the day Mariah told me about you. I always believed you'd come and set things right."

"Oh, what things would that be?"

"She belongs in the hills with you. Take her heart and go to the place where you first loved her. Wait there."

Before Zach could say a word, another male voice cut in.

"Mary Rose, I've been wantin' to talk with you."

Marie Rose glanced up and frowned at the big bellied man towering over her. "You know my name is Marie Rose, not Mary."

An insincere grin spread across his lips. "Now, you know I'm not a fancy talkin' fella. I'm just being friendly."

"Steve, this is not the time or the place to talk about my property. I'm not interested in selling or joining our holdings." She shook her head.

Zach immediately picked up on her resigned tone that conveyed they'd had this conversation before. Although it wasn't his place to interfere, he'd back her up if it became necessary.

She said, "The only thing we have in common is a fence line and that's not enough to make us a couple."

"It's been enough for plenty of people. You're just being pig-headed. We get along good enough. Now, come on, let's go dance and we can talk about it."

"No. There's nothing to talk about. No dancing, no marriage, no combining our places."

"You're dreaming if you think some prince charmin' is gonna come along and sweep you off your feet. Hell, he'd have to use a front-end loader to pick you up."

Zach watched in amazed fascination while keeping a close eye on Steve. Besides being rude, there was an underlying hint of frustration mixed in with a worrisome note of menace in his voice.

Marie Rose was a very comely woman. Not skinny, a good handful in a very appealing way. A man would have a little something to keep him warm. No sharp bones poking him anywhere. There was a lot to be said for Marie Rose. Comfortable, a man would be comfortable with her.

She raised her chin and firmly stated, "Well, that settles that. I hear your front-end loader isn't working. I hope you can get it fixed."

Steve's face turned red and his chest puffed out. "You can't make it alone on that place. You mark my words, you'll come crawling to me. We'll see who's saying please and thank you."

Zach sipped his coffee and kept his eyes on the exasperated man stomping away.

"Well, so much for welcome to Texas." Marie Rose exhaled and her shoulders slumped. "My place is so big and my father always took care of it. I was away at the university in Austin getting a business degree when he had a heart attack and died eight years ago. I wasn't prepared to take control of a working ranch. Mariah used to help me. Sometimes she'd tell me stories about the two of you. Anyway, I'm sorry things went the way they did."

"Yeah, me too." Zach's eyes moved from Marie Rose to a place across the room. "Who's that man?" Zach nodded in the direction of a tall, broad-shouldered man who had been watching them with interest.

"The one with the black cowboy hat?" She smiled and blushed.

"Yeah."

Her eyes sparkled. "That's Randall Evans. He has a small place on the river. He hires out to make extra money. If you need work done, he won't overcharge you. His truck is old but it still runs good enough to get him around. He's always been on time when he's worked for me."

"Is he married?"

"Randall? No, he's quiet, minds his own business. I've never heard anything bad about him."

205

"I don't see anyone with him tonight." Zach set his cup on the saucer and rested his hand on the table.

"He hasn't got much to offer any of these ladies."

Zach turned on his chair and leaned toward Marie Rose. "Looks like he's strong enough to be useful on a ranch. He likely has all the working parts a man needs. How do you feel about seeing him naked? You're not gonna sleep with his truck."

Her eyes grew wide she uttered, "Well, I can't say I've ever considered he'd be interested in anything along those lines." She blushed a deeper shade of pink.

"No time like the present to find out since he's headed this way." Zach leaned against the back of his chair.

"Marie Rose." Randall tipped his hat to her.

"Good evening, Randall." She raised her open hand in Zach's direction. "This is Mister High Horse, Mariah's husband."

Randall stuck out his hand as Zach came to his feet.

"High Horse, I'm Randall Evans."

"Zachary High Horse." He grasped Randall's hand in a polite handshake. "Marie Rose says you two are neighbors."

"Her place takes up most of the valley, but I have a small patch along the river."

Zach questioned, "You got a front-end loader, Randall?"

"Yeah, I got one."

"Marie Rose was telling me she's in need of one. Don't suppose you could help her out, could you?"

"Reckon I could." He turned his eyes on Marie Rose. "What do you need done?"

Marie Rose blushed scarlet.

"Zach asked, "Can you dance, Randall?"

"Yeah, some. Why?"

"Well, where I come from neighbors get together, do some dancing, visit, talk about things. You two ought to try it. Dance, talk, you know, be neighborly."

"Well, sure. If Marie Rose wants to dance that'd be fine."

"Ma'am?" Randall held out his arm for Marie Rose.

Zach watched Marie Rose take Randall's arm and walk toward the dance floor. Good deed done, he sat down. Randall had come over to be sure Marie Rose was all right. There was no disguising his concern for her. All he'd needed was a little shove to get things started.

Jesse and Silki sauntered up a few minutes later just in time for the music to stop. Harvey Warfield arrived on their heels with a well-groomed, gray-haired man at his side. Zach was ready, had been waiting a long time for this moment.

He rose to his feet; shoulders back, his facial expression one of determination, and turned to face his adversary. This man had a lot to answer for.

Harvey blatantly ignored Jesse and stated, "Silki, you remember Mister Holdsworth, the president of our bank."

"Yes, of course. How nice to see you, Mister Holdsworth. May I introduce you to Zachary and Jesse High Horse, Mariah's husband and stepson."

"Pleased to meet you." Holdsworth reached out and shook hands with both men wearing his bankers neutral smile.

Harvey jingled the keys in his pocket and addressed Zach, "Glad you could make it this evening. We need to talk business. I don't know what shape Mariah's finances are in, but the ranch is dilapidated. We'd like to make you an offer for it. I've got something you want."

"I don't think so, Daddy." Silki edged closer to Jesse.

"This isn't up to you." Harvey turned on Silki. His eyes narrowed like he was seeing her as a serious threat for the first time. He took a step in her direction. "Where did you get that?" He reached for the diamond and ruby pendant.

Jesse caught Harvey's wrist stopping his reach midair.

With his fingers still straining to reach the pendant Harvey muttered, "That was Mariah's, she got a sapphire one when she graduated college."

Jesse let go of Harvey's arm and thrust it away while saying, "I already told you. Never, ever touch Silki. She's not yours anymore." Jesse reached out wrapping his arm around her shoulders. "She's mine."

Zach took out his medicine bag, opened it and gently shook out a sparkling sapphire heart encircled with two rows of round cut diamonds on a twisted-gold rope. A twin to Silki's except in color.

"Is this what you're talking about?" He dangled the pendant in plain sight. "Mariah gave me this when we married."

The banker gasped. "My god, they're worth a small fortune."

Harvey proclaimed, "Those are mine. I'm Mariah's nearest living relative. She was my sister. You have no right to those."

"She was Zachary's wife, and my aunt." Silki put her hand over the ruby pendant. "She gave us these gifts. They're ours. You turned your back on her. She wrote it all down in her journals. We know all about you and how you refused to help her. You're the one with no rights."

"It wasn't my fault. Nobody argued with our father. He would have ruined me, cut me off without a dime. I couldn't help her."

Zachary's cold, merciless eyes fasten on Harvey. "You had a choice. It's payback time, Warfield. You'll never get the Rocking T."

Zachary wrapped his fist around his pendant. "Mariah has always been mine. You lost your sister years ago."

Harvey blustered, "You won't get away with this. I'll see you in court. Mariah was crazy. Everyone knows she wasn't right in the head after she lost her baby. Everything she had is going to be mine."

Zachary dropped Mariah's heart back into his medicine bag and pulled the ties tight. He put it back in his pocket and patted it into place. "She didn't lose him. He was taken from her."

Jesse reached over with is free hand, slipped his fingers under Silki's and caressed the ruby heart resting in the V above her cleavage. He turned his head and grinned at Harvey Warfield. Slowly and deliberately he trailed his fingers across Silki's chest, along her collarbone then up to the curve of her neck. "This is mine now and I'm never letting her go."

Harvey Warfield puffed out his chest and approached an atomic shade of red. A vein in his temple visibly pulsed. His plan had failed.

"So what? You've both had her. Nobody will want her now." He turned and walked away, followed by Mister Holdsworth.

Jesse hugged Silki tightly to his side. "You'll always be mine."

Marie Rose's gentle voiced flowed softly from beside Zachary. "I see why Mariah hated that man."

Randall's deep voiced, southern drawl followed with, "Anything I can do to help you or your friends, you just say the word, Marie Rose."

"Thank you, Randall. I appreciate that."

"Anytime." He put his hand on the small of her back.

Zach turned to Marie Rose and Randall. "You sure looked good dancing together."

She answered, "I owe Mariah a lot, Zachary. Remember what I told you."

"Will do, Marie Rose."

Zach watched them stroll away arm-in-arm and disappear into the crowd. He turned toward Jesse and Silki. "Well, that went well, all things considered."

Silki inhaled deeply. "I'm going to the ladies room."

CHAPTER TWENTY-SIX

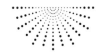

JESSE LINKED Silki's arm through his and accompanied her out of the ballroom and down the hall. He tucked her close to his side. "It's okay. Take a few deep breaths. You'll stop shaking in a minute." There was no way he'd let her go anywhere alone with Harvey loose in the building. The hall was quiet with only a few guests coming and going. He had to turn her loose at the entrance to the restroom. "Don't worry. I'm not going anywhere. I'll be right here waiting for you."

Her lips trembled and her attempt to force a convincing smile failed. She sighed, "I won't be long."

He leaned against the wall and thought how the night had gone. He'd put on one hell of a show, and Silki had let him get away with a lot. He'd probably have to apologize for that shit before the night was over, but that would be fine. He'd taken the opportunity to say all the things he'd been wanting to tell her. She didn't know he'd meant every word.

A sultry female voice interrupted his thoughts. "Hello, are you Jesse High Horse?"

Jesse turned his gaze toward the sound. "Yes, that's me."

She shifted her weight from one foot to another. Her strappy, crystal embellished sandals gleamed under the bright lights and probably cost more than everything he had on. She had every dark-brown hair in place, flawless makeup, and perfect teeth behind a scarlet smile. Her forest-green evening gown had a plunging v-neckline accentuated by enough bling to blind a man, and it fit like a glove showing off her perfect figure.

Her sensually smooth voice flowed in a practiced croon he recognized. "I saw you with Silki. Is she your girlfriend?"

This was it. He was looking at a woman who wouldn't have used him to wipe dog shit off her shoe a month ago, but all dressed up and being Mariah's stepson had put him on the acceptable to fuck list.

His casual smile didn't falter. No hint of the old flirting grin surfaced. He was so over that life. The answer was simple. "Yes, we're together."

"If it doesn't work out, look me up. I appreciate a handsome man's company. She pulled a white calling card out of her evening bag and handed it to Jesse. She sauntered off down the hall back toward the lobby leaving him staring at the gold script.

He wasn't stupid, and he wasn't blind. The ladies had been looking him over all night. Silki was right. He could find someone to keep him in fine style. It would be a better life than the one he'd left back in South Dakota, but it would come down to the same thing in the end. He'd be on call to perform on demand. Those days were behind him. He knew what he wanted and she wasn't going to come easy, but he was ready.

Silki came out of the restroom. She smiled and walked toward him like he was the best thing in the world. She stopped in front of him. He held up the card.

Her smile faltered. She took it, read it, and handed it back. "She'll take good care of you."

Jesse stepped over to the trash can and dropped it in. He turned back to Silki and held out his hand. "She wants to use me. I'm not that man anymore. I'm all yours."

He held his breath waiting for her to take his hand or walk away. When she reached for him, he wanted to shout for joy. Instead, he pulled her close, and took her in his arms. His eyes searched her face and seeing the acceptance there, he whispered, "Let me love you. There's nothing I want more."

Her eyes held his. "Are you sure?"

"Never been so sure of anything in my life. I meant every word I said in there. I don't know how to do this. I'll probably make mistakes but I'm going to try my best."

∼

Silki watched his eyelids lower and his head leaned in for a kiss. She ran her fingers through his hair and guided him to her eager lips.

She didn't want to wait; this was one time she was going to have him her way. His lips were soft and warm. He knew how to entice, tease, and coax her into giving in to his desire. He was a menace to her sanity. And she didn't care.

When they came up for air, Silki asked, "Jess, can we go home now?"

"Oh, babe, I'll take you as far as you want to go."

She'd heard that before. "That's what you always say, but will you take me dancing under the stars?" Her fingers teased the back of his neck.

"Sure." He nodded. "What else?"

She trailed her fingers along the collar of his formal shirt. "Make love to me in the Black Hills."

"I can do that." A sexy grin graced his lips.

Silkie took his face between her hands, and searched his eyes for the truth. He meant what he was saying; it was written all over his face. No lies, no being cute. This was the real Jesse High Horse.

She confessed, "I love you, Jess."

"You're sure?" the corners of his mouth turned up in a satisfied smile.

"I'm sure." She pressed her lips to his in a quick kiss.

"Let's find Zach and head for the house." He wrapped his arm around her shoulders as they strolled back to the ballroom.

It didn't take long to locate Zach, and the valet brought the truck in a matter of minutes. Silki directed them out of downtown and back on to the expressway. She was getting good at being a backseat driver. She rested her head against the window and closed her eyes.

∾

Jesse wanted to be home now, but he held the truck at the speed limit and studied the traffic carefully. He didn't need to get a speeding ticket that would slow them down. He'd worked diligently at getting back in Silki's good graces. He was only minutes away from getting her back in his arms to stay, back sleeping next to him every night.

A check of the back seat found his dream girl dozing in the corner.

Zach observed, "She's tired. That fancy party took a lot out of her."

"I know. She didn't let her old man get away with anything. She really came through for us."

They drove a few miles in silence letting the evening's events settle in. Jesse glanced at Zach who looked like he was in another world. Next, he checked on Silki. Her eyes were closed and her mouth relaxed in peaceful sleep.

Keeping his voice low, Jesse said, "She told me she loves me."

"What are you gonna do about it?" Zach blinked and glanced his way.

"What are you talking about?"

Zach repeated, "What are you gonna do about it?"

"Love her back. I don't know. What else is there?" His brow wrinkled and his mouth formed a questioning frown.

"You don't get to shack up with her. You have to do this the right way."

"We're together for as long as she wants me," Jesse replied.

"Think about it. She's likely to want you forever. She reminds me of Mariah when it comes to some things. Are you ready for a forever kind of commitment?"

Jesse lowered his voice. "That's a long time."

"Yeah, it is," Zach exhaled a slow sigh. "It's a real long time, especially for you."

The highway stretched out ahead of them. It would take another forty-five minutes to get to the Ruins. Jesse pulled his tie off, opened the top two buttons of his dress shirt, and settled in for the ride.

He'd gotten what he'd wished for. Zach had a point. Was he man enough to make the commitment? Would it be enough to only be her live-in-lover?

He admitted, "She'd be a fool to marry me. People will find out I'm an ex-con and she won't be able to get a job anywhere."

"You can't offer her anything less. It wouldn't be right." Zach shifted his weight and stared at his hands. "The night Mariah asked me to marry her, I was so scared I couldn't stop shaking. I didn't deserve her. I couldn't say no because I couldn't imagine living without her. So, I selfishly said, yes. It was the best night of my life. I didn't know it at the time, but it was the worst thing I could have done. I'm the reason she's dead."

"That's not your fault. You didn't shoot her." Jesse huffed out an audible breath. "I'm the one who didn't go look for her. Maybe I could have gotten there in time to do something to keep her alive. That's on me."

Silki's sleepy voice floated through the cab, "You couldn't have saved her, but she could have had a decent funeral a few years sooner. Her old Jeep didn't have an airbag. She had a skull fracture and her neck was broken during the crash. I talked to the FBI agent when I confirmed he'd received the records I sent him."

Jesse complained, "Damn girl, you almost gave me a heart attack. You gotta give a man some warning when you're awake."

She muttered, "I don't see why. You don't give me any warning when you wake up."

Jesse's mind clicked to all the sexy ways he used to tease her awake and he quickly tamped down a grin. He needed to change the subject fast. He asked, "What else did the agent tell you?"

"It was a high-powered Sauer hunting rifle. They got the slugs from the Jeep." She looked out the window. "Harvey has one of those. I told the agent. They'll have to get a warrant for it, so it might take a while."

"You sound tired. Do you want to stay at the house with us

214

tonight?" He wanted her to share his bed. He'd sleep a lot better if she was tucked in next to him.

"I'll be fine at my place." She sat up straighter and adjusted her dress.

The sympathetic look he got from Zach confirmed his suspicion that he'd messed up, again. It was a very quiet ride the rest of the way home. He used the time to go over all the things he'd done wrong.

For a few hours at the ball, he'd started to believe she'd take him back, but that hope dimmed with each passing mile. Who wanted a man too angry and resentful to go look for someone who might be in trouble on the lonely, snowy back roads of South Dakota?

Jesse dropped Zach off at their place and drove Silki up the hill to hers. He shut off the truck and turned to face her. "Please don't shut me out. I can't change what happened, but I can do better. Let me stay with you tonight."

Their eyes met and held. If he had to bet, she was evaluating him and weighing his words. He had no idea what she was looking for, but he had the distinct impression his future hung in the balance.

She finally said, "You promised to dance with me under the stars and I'm dressed for it. Since you're here, it only seems right. You can turn on the radio and find a slow country song." She leaned forward and softly added, "Then we can go inside and you can help me get out of this dress."

She was giving him a chance. His trembling fingers turned on the truck radio. Zach already had the local country stations programed so all Jesse had to do was turn up the volume and open the door. He slid out and hurried around to help Silki. His formal manners were lacking, but he did know he should help her out of the truck in her evening gown. And he'd get to hold her at least one more time.

∾

Silki waited for Jesse to open her door. He'd looked so devastated when she conveyed the wretched details of Mariah's last moments. Guilt had overwhelmed his features and dimmed the light that had sparkled in his eyes at the ball. He was on the verge of defeat again and she could let him drown in it or offer him a way out.

He and Zachary had suffered enough. They could have searched for days and not found the Jeep in that out-of-the-way spot buried in snow.

Her door opened, she scooted to the edge of the seat and reached for Jesse. She put her hands on his shoulders and felt him firmly take hold of her waist and lift her down. She looked up and took in the sight of him framed by hundreds of distant lights twinkling in the sky. Starlight suited him.

"The stars are so bright tonight. They must be shining for us." She touched her hand to his cheek. "I've been wondering what it would feel like to dance with you."

"You should have said something. I'm not a great dancer but I can sway to the music pretty good."

"Swaying is nice." She wrapped her arms around his middle. "Jess, did you really mean what you told my dad?"

"Hell, yeah." He inhaled and closed his eyes. "If you want me, I'm yours. All you have to do is say so."

She murmured, "I keep what's mine."

"I've been yours since the night you took me to the motel on your Harley. Why the hell do you think I ran?"

"Because you didn't want me to find Zachary." Her hand slipped down to his hip and pulled him closer. She loved feeling him pressed tight against her.

"Zach had nothing to do with it. I was scared of you, of the way you made me feel things I didn't understand." He turned them in a slow circle. "You keep rubbing against me and we're going to have a problem. How do you feel about the back seat of Zach's truck?"

She chuckled. "How do you feel about going inside and helping me out of this dress?"

"In a minute. I'm not done swaying under the stars with you in my arms. I'm waiting for you to kiss me. I'm gonna need some encouragement to get me in the house."

She leaned back enough to make room to turn her face up to his and whispered, "Come a little closer." She offered him her slightly parted lips.

He lowered his lips to hers and his tongue swept into her mouth. His hands came to her cheeks and he repositioned her head and deepened the angle of their kiss.

She melted into his deliciously enticing kisses and moaned. It was impossible to resist the warmth of his arms around her. The hard length of his cock pressed against her started a slow burn only he could satisfy.

She broke their kiss, and asked, "Is this for me?"

He met her gaze and didn't flinch when he said, "You know damn good and well you're the only one it's for."

He was telling the truth. She could see it in the dark depths of his eyes. Mariah had been right. She'd only needed to look closer.

"How about you close up the truck, we go inside and lock the door?"

"Sounds good." He released her. "I don't care where I sleep as long as you're with me."

She took the hand of the devil and led him toward their late-night, low-rent rendezvous. All that temptation wrapped up in one man was a sin. She smiled to herself. That was fine. She was on a roll where sin was concerned. No point in slowing down now.

Silki waited while Jesse closed and locked the door. The bedside lamp she'd left on earlier that evening glowed invitingly. He didn't waste any time taking the hand she held out to him.

They hurried to her tiny bedroom. She turned her back to him, slipped her hand under her hair and lifted it off her neck. His warm fingers gently grazed her skin as he unfastened the hook and slid the zipper open. She let go of her hair and brushed the straps off her shoulders.

At the sound of Jesse's indrawn breath, she looked over her shoulder. The smoldering look she got from him caused her pulse to quicken in anticipation of what was to come.

She lowered the dress revealing her scarlet lingerie-lace bra and panties and let it fall to the floor. Jesse was right. The beads did make an alluring sexy whisper as the gown pooled at her feet; her feet that were encased in red satin, high-heel pumps. She watched his eyes travel up her legs and over her sheer black stockings to the old-fashioned black garters with red ribbon trim gripping her thighs.

Cinderella was home from the ball. She stepped out of the circle of red silk and beads, picked up the dress, arranged it on a padded hanger, and hung it on the door hook. The only closet in her cabin was in the bathroom where it would be too humid for the beaded silk gown.

Jesse walked up behind her, took the French combs out of her hair and placed them on top of the dilapidated dresser. He murmured against her ear. "I think you stopped my heart just now. Damn good thing I didn't know you were wearing this under your dress. We'd never have made it to the gate."

He brushed her hair aside, leaned down, kissed and nibbled the back of her neck. His hands drifted over her shoulders, down her back, and cupped her bottom.

He said, "Let me finish undressing you." He kissed the sensitive spot below her ear and whispered. "Leave the necklace on. It's your heart and tonight you belong to me."

"Whatever you want, Jess."

She turned and took his lapels in her hands and pushed his jacket off his shoulders. Then she unfastened each button with one hand while trailing the fingers of her other hand down his chest as the shirt opened.

He boldly unzipped his pants and shoved them down, grabbing his underwear on the way and stepped out of them. His clothes landed on a plain, straight backed wooden chair.

The sight of him like that, naked and hard, took her breath away. He was so beautiful.

She took his hand and led him to the bed. She pulled the covers back and moved to the center leaving him plenty of room.

She watched him climb onto the bed and crawl over to her.

He sat back on his heels, put his hands over her lace covered breasts and gently kneaded them. "Did you wear this for me?"

"I was hoping you'd want to spend the night."

"I'd do anything to get my hands on you, sleep next to you. Tell me what you want. Anything and I'll do it."

"I want you to kiss me all over. Make it last forever."

He reached behind her, unfastened the hooks and cast the red lace bra to the foot of the bed. His lips kissed her shoulder and moved slowly across her skin to her neck. His warm breath caressed her ear as he whispered, "I never thought I could feel this way about anyone. It scares the hell outta me."

She whispered back, "You're strong. You can take it."

His hands skimmed down her arms and continued to her hips. "I think you're trying to kill me with this." His fingers slid under the edge of the panties and pushed them down past her hips.

"You're not easy to kill. I already tried once."

"Damn, I should have known you'd try again." The corners of his mouth turned up. "Let's get down to it. I'm ready for you this time."

He urged her onto her back. Slid the panties off but left the stockings and garters. He rested one knee and one hand on each side of her and caged her in between him and the bed.

"This is where I get the girl. I wasn't kidding when I told your old man that I'm never letting you go." He fastened his eyes on hers. "Are you good with that?"

"Yes, but I'd be better if you were deep inside of me where you belong."

Anticipating Jess making love to her had the moisture collecting between her legs. Her next breath was a little sharper as his hand slid upward along the inside of her thighs and his fingers trailed across her smooth skin inching ever upward. He repositioned his hand over her mound waiting for her to give him an encouraging sign. His breath caressed the sensitive skin along her neck. "Are you sure?"

She whispered, her tone tinged this time with equal parts of hope and love, "I'm sure I love you. We belong together."

His hips which he'd been rocking gently, pushing at her entrance, surged forward.

$\sim$

He'd come so hard, he'd shattered into a million pieces. His heart pounded and his breathing still hadn't returned to normal. It wasn't ordinary sex with her. There was another connection, something that started slow and grew until it touched every part of him. He could still feel the tingle in his feet. She'd changed something deep inside of him. He'd never be the same.

Jesse tucked her to his side and listened to the soft sounds she made as she drifted off to sleep. Surviving without her would be impossible. They were connected on a level he never believed existed until she'd crash-landed uninvited in his life. He finally understood why Zach had waited for Mariah.

He softly whispered into the night, "I love you. You'll never know how much."

CHAPTER TWENTY-SEVEN

THE FOLLOWING MORNING AFTER BREAKFAST, Silki cleared the table while Zachary settled in his usual spot on the couch. He stretched his legs, crossed his ankles, and looked over his shoulder at her while she loaded the dishwasher.

He casually asked, "How much do you think we could get for this place?"

She damn near dropped the dish she was rinsing and scrambled to catch the slippery stoneware. She shoved it into a slot on the bottom rack and shut the door.

Gripping the edge of the counter, she asked, "Do you want to sell it?"

"Living here in Mariah's shadow isn't going to be easy on any of us. We need to move on with our lives." Zach glanced at Jesse who was sitting at the dining table. "I can't keep fighting with the memories of what I lost. I can't turn back the clock. Jesse doesn't have the temperament for ranching." He gave her a lopsided grin.

"Okay, well, it is yours. We'd have to put pencil to paper but I'd say probably around two-million. Maybe a little more considering the outbuildings, stock ponds, two natural springs and three water wells. The pastures and hay fields have been let go so they'd need work."

Jesse's coffee mug landed on the table with a *clunk* and he stared at Silki. "You're kidding?"

"No, I'm not." She looked from Jesse to Zachary and back to Jesse. "What did you think?"

"I don't know, but not that much." He stared back at her.

"We can call a realtor who handles ranches and get them to give you an appraisal." She turned her attention to Zachary. "You'd have plenty to start over someplace where you could make new memories." She sniffed, swallowed, and cleared her throat. "I think you're right. It's probably healthier for you and Jesse. We've done what we needed to and you've both been through enough."

"We can think about it. We can't do anything until the will is probated and the place is ours free and clear." Zachary picked up the TV control.

"Right, but it doesn't hurt to start exploring all your options." She pulled her phone out of her pocket. "I'll call Mister Davidson and let him know you need names of suitable realtors. Not everyone is knowledgeable about handling large ranch sales."

Jesse cut his eyes from Silki to his dad. "Where do you want to go?"

"The Black Hills. It's the only place I was ever happy."

"Okay, I can look for work at the National parks and Bureau of Land Management."

Silki disconnected her call. "Davidson is out, but I left a message for him to call you. I didn't say why. You never know who's on Dad's payroll." She called back over her shoulder as she walked toward the back door, "I'll be back later."

"Are you coming back for lunch," Jesse asked with a hopeful note in his voice and a satisfied smile on his lips.

She noticed he had the look of a man that had been well loved during the night. It seemed that men could have that morning-after glow same as the ladies. She'd remember that for future reference. It looked good on Jesse. Maybe she'd get to see it a few more times before he left.

"There's lunchmeat for sandwiches. You can handle your lunches. I'll make us a nice pot of chili for dinner. The weather is cool enough in the evenings for that and some cornbread." She needed to get out of there, any excuse would do.

Her heart pounding in her throat was enough to choke her and she had no idea what to do about this new development. She'd never considered they'd want to sell the ranch, go away, and leave her behind.

She trudged along the dirt road to her cabin and watched the dust puff around her boots. Each step took her further away from Jesse and Zachary. The ranch could sure use some rain. She tilted her head back to look up at the clear blue sky. Nothing on the horizon at the moment but she was ready.

She had buckets stacked in the corner of the kitchen in case the metal roof leaked and there was a quarter cord of oak stacked on the porch for the wood stove. She had a roof over her head and indoor plumbing. What more could a girl ask for?

She didn't know about anyone else but given a choice, she'd ask for Jesse. How sick was that? The man was a walking disaster, a mine field that kept blowing up in her face, and she was in love with him. She'd have to get over it when he put her and Texas in his rearview mirror.

She went inside and clicked on the radio. Heartbreak Hotel came through the speakers. How appropriate. Maybe the next song would be happier.

Once Zachary and Jesse moved away, she'd need to do something to make a living. Ellie was right, nobody in San Antonio or the surrounding area would hire her. She'd have to pack her stuff into her old truck, load the Harley on a trailer and hit the road. Once again, she'd be rolling along a million miles from nowhere looking for a place to belong.

So many decisions for another day. If they wanted chili and corn-bread for dinner, she needed to make a grocery list. Pencil and paper in hand, her butt landed on a kitchen chair. The list wasn't going to write itself, but for the life of her she couldn't think what she needed to get for their dinner. Putting the pencil down, she rested her elbows on the table, dropped her head in her hands, and let the tears fall.

After Jesse finished his coffee and put the cup in the sink, he gazed out the window toward the cabin. Silki hadn't sounded right when she'd left. He needed that girl. He wasn't going anywhere without her. He wanted to make sure she understood that.

He muttered, "I'll be back," as he hurried out the door.

It didn't take him long to arrive on her porch and knock on the screen door's wooden frame.

He peered through the screen and called, "Hey, babe, can I come in?"

Her garbled answer reached his ears. "It's not a good time."

"What's wrong with it?" He didn't like the tremor in her voice. Something wasn't right. "Are you okay?"

"I'm a little tired. I'll come fix dinner after a while. Go home."

"I am home." Jesse opened the door and walked inside. He took the three steps necessary to get to the kitchen doorway and turned right. His eyes landed on Silki sitting at the table dabbing at her eyes with a paper napkin. He snapped, "What the hell is this?"

"Go away. Can't a girl even cry in peace around here?" She sniffled and wiped at her runny nose.

"Not when she's my girl and she's sitting in our kitchen crying." He walked over, pulled out the only other chair at the table, and sat down beside her. "What did I do this time?"

"What makes you think it's about you?" She blinked and dabbed at her wet eyelashes.

"It's always about me. I'm the only man you love enough to cry over." He aimed a lopsided grin at her. "Except maybe Zach."

"You really are conceited." She chuckled softly.

He reached over and took a hold of her hand. "Tell me what I did so I can fix it." His eyes met hers. "I must have done something wrong." He looked away and shook his head. "I don't know how to do this relationship stuff."

"Really?" It was a statement and a question.

"Yes, really." He stood up, took her by the upper arm, and pulled her to her feet. "You said you love me and I believe you. I also know you keep what's yours. That would be me because you said so again last night. I'm counting on you to keep your word."

Silki wrapped her arms around him and held him close while burying her face in his chest. "Zachary is right. You shouldn't stay here. There'll never be any peace and everywhere you look will be reminders of all the things that can't be fixed. Mariah named it the Ruins for a reason." She sniffled, "It sounds like you guys are going and leaving me here."

"I'm not going anywhere without you." He kissed the top of her head and hugged her tighter.

The idea of being separated from her hurt his heart. He'd admitted that to himself back in Martin and now it was worse. He'd be empty, heartbroken, and angrier at himself for not being a better man. He'd never be able to forgive himself for not trying harder to make their relationship work.

He murmured, "Where do you want to go?"

"Anywhere, as long as I'm with you. We could go up north to the Bighorn Mountains, the Tetons, or the Black Hills so we can be near Zachary. You said we'd go high in the mountains where nobody could find us." She sniffled and clung to him.

Jesse's body responded to her with a growing erection. Not a surprise since he was pressed up against Silki. She had a way of doing that to him. And it was so good, the best. Yeah, he was hard all right. He nudged his erection against her. "Babe, you think you can help me with this?"

"Hmm?" Silki released the bearhug she had on Jesse and slid one hand down between them. After a slow exploration of his condition which had him breathing harder and faster, she purred against his chest, "Oh, yeah, I've got just the thing to take care of you."

"Let's go in the bedroom so you can show me."

"Do you trust me to take good care of you, Jess?"

A tremor travel through him as he pressed tighter against her. She was asking a lot of him.

His voice faltered. "I'm still trying to get used to it. It's hard to admit but yes, down deep inside, I trust you."

This time was different. When she called him Jess, he knew he was exactly where he was meant to be. Nobody but Silki called him that.

There was nothing left for him to do but confess, "I know it's asking a lot but I need you to love me. Really love me. The forever kind of love. Can you do that?"

"I already do. I thought you knew." She sniffled.

"I'm not sure what I know anymore." He rested his cheek on the top of her head. "I know I should have done a lot of things differently."

"You're a work in progress. You've been getting better from the moment we met." She rubbed her hands over his back.

"You stuck a knife under my nose and threatened to cut my balls off. I didn't have much choice."

"You weren't being very cooperative." She chuckled softly.

"I'm being cooperative now." He swayed from side to side taking her with him. "Tell me what you want and I'll do whatever it takes to make this work for us."

She murmured, "I want everything. I want you to give me all of you."

Jesse pulled back and stared down at her. "Look at me." He waited for her to meet his eyes. "You have to be sure because I'll want all of you in return. I gotta know you're in this with me all the way."

"All the way sounds good." She slipped her fingers around the waistband of his jeans. "I think you need to lie down." She tugged and led him to their bed. "You look like you could stand a little rest after your life altering decision. That kind of thing can be very stressful."

"Whatever you say, babe."

CHAPTER TWENTY-EIGHT

SILKI DROPPED Jesse off at Zach's and headed for the grocery store with her list in hand. The quiet Sunday ride let her daydream about where they would go and how good it would be when they were free to get on with building their life together. She grabbed the ingredients and dropped them in the basket.

She wanted to get home to Jesse and put their dinner on the stove to simmer. She stopped pushing the grocery cart across the parking lot when her phone rang and retrieved it from her back pocket.

She answered, "Hey, Ellie."

"Your Dad's lost his mind!" Ellie hissed. "He called a couple of us in this morning to shred everything in his office. I heard him yelling at Hardcastle on the phone a little while ago. He's loading boxes into his car right now and talking about driving to his place in Mexico."

"Okay. Do whatever he says so you're safe. It's going to be fine and thanks for letting me know. I'll take it from here." She disconnected and called Jesse.

When he picked up she said, "Ellie called and it sounds like my dad is panicking and probably heading for Mexico. Let's be on the safe side in case he stops over there on his way out of town. Close the storm shutters on the Ruins. Once the metal shutters are locked into place the

227

house is bullet proof. The walls and metal roof won't burn so you'll be fairly safe."

"Where are you?" he demanded.

I'm loading the groceries in my truck. I'll be home in about a half-hour." She inhaled. "Jess, tell Zach to open the panels over his closet. Mariah kept her pistols and rifles up there along with the ammunition."

His voice mixed with the sounds of the outdoors came through. "Harvey would be crazy to come here."

"He is crazy in case you haven't noticed. He killed his sister so he could be rich. Now, he's losing everything." She huffed loudly. "Let me get off this phone and get on the road. Tell Zach to call the FBI agent and let him know my dad is making a run for the border."

"I'll wait for you at the gate so you don't have to get out."

"Deal." She disconnected the call and shoved her phone back in her pocket.

It only took a minute to throw the groceries in the truck and climb in behind the wheel. She'd barely turned the key when her phone played the theme from Jaws. "You've got to be kidding me." She pulled it free, laid it on the seat and answered, "What do you want?" She put it on speaker so she could drive and hear Charley the Weasel at the same time.

The weasel demanded. "The money your father promised me when I married you." He exhaled audibly. "I was stuck with your frigid ass for five long miserable years."

"Well, I was stuck with your useless dick. Can I send you a tube of hot-lube?" She broke out laughing. "You got the townhouse and my part of our investment account. That's more than enough."

"It won't cover the losses." He toned it down and wheedled, "I know Mariah left you well off."

Her gaze bounced from one side of the parking lot exit to the other. She did not need to have a wreck. Not that anyone would want to destroy their beautiful shiny car by hitting her calico patchwork truck.

"Daddy told you wrong." She watched for an opening in the traffic. "I have a leaky roof over my head and I'm driving our gardener's old truck. You remember that truck? The one with more rust than paint."

"Harvey told me you're living with Mariah's husband and stepson. They can lend you the money." Charley insisted.

"I don't think they like me all that much. Why don't you get it from your new wife and her family?

"She's leaving me. I'm going to be paying child support." His exaggerated sigh of defeat came over loud and clear. "Look, I'm going broke. It's all falling apart."

Goodie, the weasel was playing the sympathy card. She recognized it. It was a last resort when all else failed. He'd finally hit the end of the line and the money had run out.

She did not try to hide the note of satisfaction in her voice. "Really. Hmm, imagine that. Well, not my problem. Check the boxes the movers took. There was some toilet paper in them. You can use it to flush your life down the crapper." She took a deep breath, pressed on the accelerator, and merged onto the four-lane highway. "You know I've been waiting for this call. That's why I haven't blocked your number. You're finally getting what you deserve. It's your turn to be kicked to the curb. I won't help you. Not sorry."

She disconnected, put her phone beside her hip on the seat and smiled. "I wish Mariah was here to see this. The downfall of the Warfield and Hardcastle empires is happening."

She couldn't wait to get home and tell Zachary and Jesse. The wind blew through the open windows and fluttered her hair. She brushed it back, away from her eyes as she aimed the truck north. Everything was working out the way Mariah had planned. Looking closer had been worth it. Jesse was the worst and the best thing that had ever happened to her. As soon as she got home, she'd kiss him, and hug him, and never let him go.

She turned off onto Bulverde Road and wound her way along the twisting two-lane rural blacktop. Once she crossed Highway 46, she'd be rolling along the lower hay field. Almost home.

She made the turn off the highway and looked out over Mariah's land. It had withstood family feuds for generations. She hoped whoever bought it would find peace in the rugged cedar covered hills and green valleys. It was a good ranch in the great scheme of things.

The loud rapport of a rifle reached her ears a split second before the truck shook and careened off the road. It ran through the barbed wire fence, down the roadside embankment, and into the overgrown weeds and brush. Even with her seatbelt fastened, she was thrown in every direction imaginable. Her hands kept a white-knuckle grip on the steering wheel, until her shoulder strap broke loose and her head collided with the windshield.

$\sim$

Jesse heard the shot, stood up from the tree stump he was sitting on and turned toward the lower fields. Someone shooting a rattlesnake was his first thought. There were small ten-acre lots on the west side of the road and on the other side of the highway. There were plenty of snakes to go around.

At the same time a very bad feeling gripped him. He pulled out his phone and called Silki. It rang and went to voice mail.

He called Zach and opened the ranch gate. "Bring the truck. I think something's happened to Silki, we need to go take a look."

Before Zach had come to a complete stop, Jesse yanked the passenger door open, threw himself into the seat, and said, "Go."

"What happened?" Zach pulled out onto the road.

"I heard a shot from down by the highway, and Silki isn't answering her phone."

They drove toward the lower hay field looking for any sign of trouble.

Jesse leaned across the cab searching for her truck. "There. Stop. I see it." He pointed to a hole in the fence.

Zachary pulled over skidding to a stop and letting Jesse jump out. He ran across the road and scrambled down the embankment dodging around cactus patches. Her truck rested nose down in the overgrown rutted turn row.

He yelled, "Silki, are you all right?"

His hand grabbed the door handle and yanked. She was laying sideways on the seat. Her lap belt was loose but had held good enough to keep her from being flung out the window or onto the floor. His hand grabbed her arm, held his breath and felt her wrist for a pulse.

"Please, babe, don't leave me."

Zach scrambled up behind him and asked, "Is she alive?"

"Yeah, but she's unconscious. We need EMS. Call 911 and get the sheriff, too."

He knew they'd take her truck. She'd be madder than hell if she woke up without her wallet and phone. He knew better than to move her until the EMT's stabilized her neck and back. Finding her things, he handed them to Zach. Their groceries were scattered everywhere and Zach went about picking up what he could find, emptying out the glove box and taking it all to his truck while they waited for help to arrive.

Jesse paced while Zachary sat in the Emergency Department waiting room. He couldn't sit, he needed to move, he needed to see Silki. He'd lied and told the EMT's and nurses he was her husband so he could stay with her until the doctor came in and sent him to the waiting room.

The admissions clerk had shown up then and taken him and Zach to her office to do the paperwork. He continued to lie. Silki would rip him to pieces when she regained consciousness and found out what he'd done.

"Mister High Horse, your wife is awake and asking for you." Jesse spun around and stared at the nurse holding open the door to the trauma rooms.

"Thanks." He moved toward her. "Is she okay?"

"The doctor will explain her condition and we'll give you the discharge instructions before you leave. She wants to go home. We've got a neck support collar on her. It'll help with the soreness." She aimed a thin sympathetic smile at him.

Jesse walked through the door and waited for her to lead him to the room. He wanted to see Silki, and he didn't want to get his ass chewed off.

Silki met his gaze when he stepped into the room. "Harvey shot my truck."

"Same as Mariah." He reached down and took her hand. "When I

231

heard the shot, I was afraid he'd killed you like he did her. I've never been so scared."

"I'm okay, or I will be as soon as you get me out of here." She reached up and curled her fingers around the top edge of the cervical collar. "This thing is choking me." She glared at him. "I need to call the FBI agent. They can compare the bullets. It's going to be Harvey's rifle. He's probably halfway to Mexico by now."

"Zach already took care of that. The sheriff is processing the evidence. As soon as the doctor talks to us, I'm taking you home. Zach's got his truck outside."

They both turned their attention toward the door. Jesse suppressed a grimace. The minute the doctor said boo about him being her husband the shit was going to hit the fan.

Silki acknowledged the middle-aged woman in a white coat who walked in and stopped next to the stretcher. "Doctor, have you met my husband, Jesse High Horse?"

"Yes." She turned to him. "Your wife has insisted that she wants to go home. She has assured me that you'll take good care of her."

Jesse listened to the discharge instructions but he couldn't honestly say he heard them. Silki had gone along with being his wife. He was in so much trouble. He mumbled, "Got it. I'll take care of her. My dad is waiting to drive us home."

Silki waited until they were out of the parking lot to mention, "The nurse called me Missus High Horse. I don't remember getting married. I don't think I hit my head hard enough to make me forget something like that." She pinned Jesse with a stern questioning look. "When did we get married?" She held up her left hand. "And where the hell is my wedding ring?"

Jesse grinned, "Don't worry, babe. I'm going to get you a really nice one."

CHAPTER TWENTY-NINE

AFTER DINNER JESSE guided Silki to the couch and pulled her down next to him. He draped his arm around her shoulders and cuddled her tight to his side while Zach turned on the wide-screen TV.

He leaned in close and spoke softly, "I've waited a long time to do this."

"What?" She ran a hand across his thigh.

"Sit on the couch with my arm around you." His nose nuzzled her hair and he inhaled. "You smell good. It's been tough not having you sleeping next to me every night. From now on we're together like married people, no more sleeping alone."

"You're talking crazy. Are you sure you didn't hit your head somewhere along the way today?" She gave him a side-eye questioning look. "What on earth made you tell the hospital staff you're my husband?"

"I wanted to stay with you and only family was allowed." He stroked the side of her head, pulled her hair back and murmured, "I was hoping you'd go for it. If you didn't like the idea, it wouldn't hurt so bad as being turned down for real."

"Okay, what were you planning to do if I liked the idea?"

"Give you a ring and take you high in the mountains, like I told you." He hugged her a little tighter. "What do you say, will you marry me?"

She looked over at Zach. "Are you hearing this? I want to be sure I'm not having some kind of hallucination."

Zach grinned. "I heard it all right. It sounds like a proposal to me."

"Wow. I'll have to stay up and think about it. Since I have a head injury, I might need to be sure I'm in my right mind before I agree to anything."

He caught the silly grin she aimed at Zach and knew she was baiting him. He offered, "I can stay up with you. I can think of a couple good ways to keep us awake." Jesse watched a soft blush spread across her cheeks.

"You'll be a major distraction, and nobody will get any rest." She squeezed his thigh. "Hush up, so I can watch this movie."

He caught Zach's eye and shrugged his shoulders. He knew better than to argue. "I'm staying up with you. We can play cards." He could go for a game of strip-poker. She might be easier to convince when the lights went down and he could love on her until she accepted.

"No. You'll cheat." She looked down and offered, "We could play Texas Hold 'em." She looked up at him sporting the most innocent expression he'd ever seen.

He knew better. He recognized that look, that sly tone in her voice, he'd end up naked for sure.

"That's okay, we can watch movies." Any way she wanted it; he'd give it to her. That's the way it would be tonight and every night. He's known that from the minute he'd climbed onto her Harley in Martin.

CHAPTER THIRTY

AT THE CRACK OF DAWN, Silki's phone rang with an incoming call from her mother, the final countdown. She sat up from her nest on the couch and blinked at the screen. Amazing. She hadn't heard from the woman since the divorce was filed. This ought to be interesting.

She answered and yawned, "Silki here."

Her mother yelled, "It's your fault. You've ruined everything." She accused, "You did this."

"Did what? I don't know what you're talking about."

Silki got up, stumble-walked over to the counter holding the phone away from her ear, and pressed the button to start the coffee machine. She really needed a cup of java to get her eyes open and the brain cells awake. She ached all over from the accident and they'd stayed up late playing cards. Jesse sure looked good in nothing but his tight black briefs. He'd looked even better out of them.

Her mother screeched, "What do you think? You know exactly what you did. You started this."

Eenie-meenie-miney-mo pick one, she'd done lots of things lately. She'd been divorced by a cheating husband. She'd gone looking for Mariah. She'd kidnapped two men. She'd found Zachary. She'd slept with Jesse. That thought made her smile. She was guilty of all kinds of things.

Silki let her grumpy voice ask, "Did somebody die?"

She'd hadn't killed anyone. Thank goodness she wasn't guilty of murder. Not like some people she could mention.

"You couldn't even manage to stay married. Then you went and found Mariah. But that wasn't enough. No, you had to involve the FBI in our personal business." She stopped to catch her breath. Silki could hear her signature exasperated inhale-exhale. She always made this tired groaning sound before she finished her rant. "Your father came home yesterday and told me we're losing the business and saying we're broke. He spent the night drinking and packing the car."

Silki rolled her eyes. "Are you worried about your bank account or his liver?" She took a mug down from the shelf. "Did he happen to mention he shot my truck?"

"The FBI is here going through the desk and files in his study. He's been arrested thanks to you and your selfish meddling."

"Yes, thank you. It's about time." She rubbed her forehead and winced. Her head was sore and smiling pulled at the injuries. "You should call his lawyers. He can plead insanity."

Zachary walked into the dining room and sat at the table; his eyes trained on her. She met his gaze and shrugged.

Her mother shouted, "You've destroyed our family. I never want to see you again. I'm throwing your boxes out on the curb for the garbage to pick up. Come get them before they disappear."

"Fine, I'll deal with that as soon as I get dressed." She stifled another yawn. "Thanks for calling. Gotta go, Mom." Silki looked across the room at Zachary. "Harvey's been arrested."

"I'm not sorry for him but it must be hard for you. He's your father."

"Not really. I wasn't the son he wanted. Nothing I did was ever good enough, until I married Charley. And we know how that turned out. I've always been a terrible disappointment to my parents."

She carried her coffee mug and one for Zachary to the table. She put them down and held onto the table lowering herself slowly onto a chair.

His voice softened, "Are you okay?"

She aimed a limp smile at him. "I'm a little sore. My truck beat me up yesterday."

"It's in the evidence yard. You won't get it back for a long time, if ever. If they decide it's evidence in Mariah's murder, they have to keep it."

"I liked that old truck after I got used to it. We're both a little damaged but still rolling." She sipped her coffee. "I'll need to get something that can tow a motorcycle trailer."

"We can look for a sturdy four-wheel drive truck or SUV to get you moved up north with Jesse." He sipped his coffee and lowered the mug. "What do you want to do about your things?"

"She's putting the boxes I mailed home out on the curb. I'm going to go get them. I'll take the car." A small smile graced her lips. "I could use some better clothes and there's no point in spending money for stuff I already have." Silki got up from the table. "I'll be back in a couple hours."

Jesse walked up and looked at the coffee pot. "Wherever you're going, I'm coming with you." He asked Zach. "Can we use your truck?"

"Sure, but you'll need to put gas in it." He met Jesse's eyes and sprung a grin. "And bring some lunch back with you. I'd like some fried chicken."

Against his better judgment, Jesse let Silki drive while he tried to relaxed in the passenger seat. She knew her way around town and the quickest route to her parent's house. Even injured she was tougher than a lot of men he knew, but he didn't like her driving with a stiff neck and back. If she got too tired, he'd take over. He eyed the shopping centers and strip malls as the miles rolled by. Where he was going, they didn't have this much to choose from. Would she get bored and want to come back to Texas?

He looked over at her and asked, "Are you gonna miss living here?"

"No, I don't have many good memories. My best times were when

I was old enough to learn to ride my motorcycle and get out on the road with Mariah. I sold mine to get hers running. I'm taking it with me when I leave." She glanced his way. "It brought me to you."

"You kidnapped me on that thing."

"Yeah, I did." A satisfied smile sprang to her lips. "Admit it. You know you loved it. Don't pretend you didn't." She laughed. "It's no use lying. I could feel your hard-on pressing against my butt."

"I've been hard for you since the first night I saw you eating dinner in the diner."

"Is that what all that walking back and forth past my table was about." She chuckled. "I thought you had a stomach ache."

He trained his eyes on her profile. "Something was aching but it wasn't my stomach." His lips curved up in a lopsided grin that quickly disappeared. He turned his face away and his voice faded to barely above a whisper. "I wanted you more than I'd ever wanted anything. I knew my world was going to change and you would be a part of it. I'd never felt anything like that before."

He'd always be that man. No matter how far he went or what he did, that would always be what she remembered about him. That and all the things that came after. He couldn't run from it and he couldn't forget it. He wasn't sure he wanted to look in her eyes and see that man staring back at him. He had to live with his past but that didn't mean she had to.

Before he had time to wander down the road to the wasteland of his regrets, she pulled up in front of a two-story mansion and shut off the truck. He got out, did his best to ignore the house, and walked over to the nearest box. The faster they got loaded and out of there the better. He didn't need to see this. She came from the kind of life he'd never be able to give her. He passed Silki and dropped the box into the bed of the truck and turned back to get the next one.

A movement in the second-story balcony window caught his eye. He stopped and stared. When Silki came up alongside of him, he asked, "Is that your mom?"

Silki looked up. "Sure is." She stepped ahead. "Come on, let's get this stuff and get out of here." She grabbed the nearest box, carried it to the truck and unceremoniously dropped it in the bed. "I haven't lived here in a long time and I'm never coming back."

A couple more rounds and they were loaded up and headed back to the Ruins. Perfect name for the condition his life was in. He'd made it out of Martin and found someone that gave a damn about him and he wasn't so sure he could bring himself to look at her every day and be reminded of the way they'd met.

Her phone rang through the speakers on Zach's dash.

Silki answered, "What now?"

"Is that him?"

"Him who? What are you talking about?" Silki glanced at Jesse.

"One of the men you're sleeping with."

"That is none of your business. I'm driving and I can't talk anymore. Goodbye." She disconnected the call, and looked at Jesse. "I'm sorry you had to hear that. I'll block her number when I get to the house."

"Are you sure you want to keep sleeping with me?" He watched her carefully. The answer was going to make or break him.

"In the movies, this is where I'd slam on the brakes, cause a ten-car pile-up and scream at you. But since this isn't my truck and I don't need to get a second case of whiplash from being crashed into, I'm going to keep driving like a sane person." She frowned at him for a half-second and turned her attention back to the road. "When we get home, we're going to have a serious talk about this."

"We can talk now." He studied her seriously frowning expression from her wrinkled forehead to her downturned lips, and her stranglehold on the padded steering wheel.

"Fine. Here's what's going to happen. We'll eat dinner with Zachary while the chicken is still hot. Then we'll unload the truck. You will go in our house, take off all your clothes and lay on the bed. I'm going to tie your hands to the bedposts, take advantage of your helplessness repeatedly, and not turn you loose until you promise to never say anything like that ever again." She looked at him. "Are we clear?"

Jesse rubbed his straining cock through his jeans. "Damn girl. I think I'm gonna come right here."

"You want to tell Zachary you got off in his truck, or should I?" She smirked at his discomfort.

"We don't have to tell him anything." Jesse kept his hand over his groin and tried to breathe normally. "I always knew you had a mean streak but this is cruel."

"Not as cruel as the things you do to yourself. I'm not stupid. I can tell when your mind goes wandering back to the way things used to be. But that's in the rearview. When we leave here, we're starting over. No Charley, no backseats, no back alley hook-ups." She inhaled deeply. "And we're getting married. Deal?"

He looked out the passenger window so he wouldn't have to see her reaction when he reminded her, "I have a prison record. I can't get away from that."

"It doesn't have to control the rest of your life. We'll figure things out together. It's what you do when you love someone."

He turned in time to see her adjust her hands on the steering wheel. It looked like she was still trying to strangle it.

She stared straight ahead. "Unless this is your way of telling me you don't want to make that much effort and we're through. Do you want to take Zachary and go your own way?"

Her words slammed into him, knocking the air out of his lungs faster and harder than any fist ever could.

"No. We're not through. But I don't want you to wake up one morning in a two-bedroom cabin with a screaming baby to take care of and regret you chose me."

Silki released an unladylike grunt, and said, "I'm pretty sure you're going to have lots of days when you'll wish you'd chosen anybody but me."

"I already tried that and it didn't work. You're the one I want." This was where she should reach over and slap his arm. He raised his shoulder prepared for the hit. When nothing happened, he relaxed and asked, "Aren't you going to smack me?"

"No, not for telling the truth." She glanced quickly in his direction and then back at the traffic ahead. "I shouldn't have hit you, ever. That was wrong and I'm sorry I did that." She inhaled and continued, "I don't want us to have that kind of relationship."

"But you're still going to tie me to your bed, right?" He aimed his sexiest sly grin at her. "Please."

"Damn, can't refuse a man who says 'please' so nicely."

"Great, we have a deal." Jesse relaxed against the seat. "Zach likes the extra-crispy chicken."

She grinned. "I'm going to extra-crispy your ass if you don't hush-up and let me drive in peace. This construction zone is an accident-waiting-to-happen kind of mess."

"Promise?" He cupped both hands over his zipper.

She gave him a quick glance. "Anything you want. Whatever makes you feel good."

Jesse watched Silki like a hawk all through dinner. It was hard to concentrate on the conversation with Zach when his mind continually wandered to the night ahead. Did she mean it? Would she really take the time to please him? He'd always been expected to get it up, get his partner off, and move on. Nobody cared how he felt or if he got off. Not once had anyone asked what excited him, what felt good, what he wanted, or what he needed.

After they cleaned up the dishes and said goodnight to Zach they stepped out into the night. As they walked to the cabin he reached over and wrapped his hand around hers. "I've never walked a girl home holding hands before." He looked at their joined hands. "I like it."

"You're kidding?" She turned her head in his direction.

His eyes met hers. "Not kidding."

"Wow, I'm your first." She tightened her fingers around the edge of his hand. "You have great hands. That's one of the first things I noticed about you."

"You're my first for a lot of things." He stopped, pulled her around to face him and pressed his lips to hers.

An unexpected peace settled over his heart. He pulled back from the kiss, stroked her hair, and murmured next to her ear, "You're the only woman who's ever loved me."

"You didn't make it easy, but sometimes a person has to fight for the best things in life." She angled her head to meet his gaze. "Texans are born fighters but I hadn't found anything worth fighting for until I met you."

He'd come too close to losing her several times. The sad truth was that now he knew exactly what he'd be missing for the rest of his life if he lost her. He needed to know. "How soon can we get married?"

She rested her hand over his heart. "Not here in Texas. Let's get married when we get where we're going."

"It's going to take a while to get things settled and sell the ranch. I'm not sure I can wait that long. Some smooth-talking cowboy might come along and steal you away from me." His intertwined his fingers with hers.

"There only one little problem with that." She tugged on his belt loop with her free hand. "I keep what's mine and I'm not giving you up."

"Promise?"

"Yes, you've got my word on it."

They reached the cabin steps and Jesse stopped, stared at the door and rubbed his wrists. "I don't know if I can take being tied up. Sometimes I can still feel the shackles and chains weighing me down and biting into my skin.

"No problem. There are plenty of other ways to convince you to cooperate." Her hands gripped his shoulders as she pulled herself up to whisper in his ear, "I love you, Jess. More than you'll ever know."

His head turned and their eyes met. "You were awake."

Silki took his hand and guided him up the steps and through the door to their cabin.

CHAPTER THIRTY-ONE

SILKI EXHALED and languidly stretched her legs. Jesse rested beside her with a fine sheen on his skin. She turned, slipped her arm over his chest and hugged him gently.

She said, "It's not much but this place is my ace-in-the-hole. It shouldn't sit here empty and falling apart. I'm going to ask Ellie to check on it when she has time and let her use it when she needs a quiet place."

"I remember Mariah wanted you to own the roof over your head, and I wouldn't want to cross her. She has a way of reaching out from the grave that's kind of creepy." He shrugged around, rolled to his side and looked her in the eyes.

"I've kind of gotten used to this place. It has a certain rustic charm." She chuckled softly. "Maybe we can come back for vacations or a romantic rendezvous when you need to be reminded of how we first got together."

"Babe, we're not coming back." He held on tight.

"What am I supposed to do? I can't let it sit here and rot. Where would I go?"

"Why would you need to go anywhere? We're getting married. We're going to be together somewhere high in the mountains. Right?"

"It's okay, I'll figure it out." She loosened her hold on him.

He pulled her back and rolled closer pinning her halfway underneath him. "There's nothing to figure out. You can sell this place and buy something when we get settled. It'll be in your name and I can sign one of those papers saying it's yours no matter what so you don't have to worry." He reached up and brushed her hair away from her face. "If the day comes when you don't want me anymore, I won't need a house."

Her hand gripped his shoulder and her leg hitched over his hip bringing them in contact skin to skin, body and soul joined together. "I want us to always feel like this. We belong together."

He pulled back and gazed into her eyes. "You kidnapped my ass and stole my heart. You're a dangerous woman Little Red, but I'll love you till my dying day plus some."

"I know. Mariah told me." She ran her fingers through his hair brushing it away from his eyes. "We're going to have a good life together. I'm going to love you through all of it." She pressed her lips to his.

ACKNOWLEDGMENTS

I would like to thank all my readers for their enthusiastic support. I know you have waited a long time for this book. I hope you find the story worth waiting for. I also wish to thank the people of Martin, South Dakota, from the welcoming desk clerks to the friendly waitstaff at the diner. You made my stays enjoyable and productive.

ABOUT THE AUTHOR

Nellie Krauss is an emerging author of Contemporary Romantic Suspense featuring audacious heroines and challenging heroes. This is Nellie's seventh book.

Her cross-cultural stories are inspired by her experiences from traveling foreign countries, living in Texas and spending summers with Native Americans on the Pine Ridge Reservation in South Dakota. The Renaissance Fair is her favorite place to be when she's not in the Black Hills or at the beach. Her biggest thrill is hearing the roar and rumble of her Harley's engine on the open road. In her civilized life she is a Paralegal, a Nationally Certified Investigator, has a purple belt in Karate, is an NRA Pro-Marksman, sky diver, scuba diver, belly dancer, Harley Motorcycle rider, and off road 4-Wheeler. She has travelled the Caribbean, the Bahamas and Western Europe in search of adventure. Her next destinations are the romantic Greek Islands. Opa!

Made in the USA
Columbia, SC
24 August 2022

65721491R10141